The
Granite Coast
Murders

The

Granite Coast
Murders

—❖ **A BRITTANY MYSTERY** ❖—

Jean-Luc Bannalec

Translated by Peter Millar

MINOTAUR BOOKS
NEW YORK

First published in the United States by Minotaur Books, an imprint of St. Martin's Publishing Group

THE GRANITE COAST MURDERS. Copyright © 2017 by Verlag Kiepenheuer & Witsch. Translation copyright © 2020 by Peter Millar. All rights reserved. Printed in the United States of America. For information, address St. Martin's Publishing Group, 120 Broadway, New York, NY 10271.

www.minotaurbooks.com

Designed by Devan Norman

Library of Congress Cataloging-in-Publication Data

Names: Bannalec, Jean-Luc, 1966– author. | Millar, Peter, translator.
Title: The Granite Coast murders / Jean-Luc Bannalec ; translated by Peter Millar.
Other titles: Bretonische Leuchten. English
Description: First U.S. edition. | New York : Minotaur Books, 2021. | Series: A Brittany mystery; 6 |
Identifiers: LCCN 2020047454 | ISBN 9781250753069 (hardcover) | ISBN 9781250753076 (ebook)
Subjects: GSAFD: Mystery fiction
Classification: LCC PT2662.A565 B73713 2021 | DDC 833/.92—dc23
LC record available at https://lccn.loc.gov/2020047454

Our books may be purchased in bulk for promotional, educational, or business use. Please contact your local bookseller or the Macmillan Corporate and Premium Sales Department at 1-800-221-7945, extension 5442, or by email at MacmillanSpecialMarkets@macmillan.com.

First published as *Bretonische Leuchten* in Germany by Verlag Kiepenheuer & Witsch

First U.S. Edition: 2021

10 9 8 7 6 5 4 3 2 1

à L.
à Elisa

Evel-s emañ ar bed
A dreuz hag a-hed

This way and that
Is where the world's at

—BRETON SAYING

The

Granite Coast
Murders

Sunday

The Witch, the Turtle, the Painter's Palette, the Chaos, the Skull. You didn't have to be a Breton with particularly spectacular imagination to recognize them. The same went for the Devil's Castle, the Shark's Fin, the Bottle, the Upturned Boot, Napoleon's Hat, which they had already seen. The Mushroom, the Hare.

All of that on just a single walk yesterday.

Today, by contrast, they were lying on the beach. Commissaire Georges Dupin and his girlfriend, chief cardiologist Claire Lannoy. Looking up from their towel at the fantastic pink granite formations. By late afternoon, and above all at sunset, the rocks would begin to acquire a supernatural glow and glimmer as if they didn't belong to this world. A chaos of mighty, curiously shaped giant rose-colored granite formations, huge lumps of granite, singly or in scattered groups towering above them. All around them: in the sea, rising from the water, on the little island immediately in front of them, but also along the beach, behind them as well, on the solitary Renote peninsula, which was part of the vast strip of sand they were lying on.

All the way along the coast from Trébeurden to Paimpol, the cliffs of the world-famous Côte de Granit Rose were admired. "Rose granite" was the poetic name of the stone that had made this section of coast in northern Brittany famous. It had been used to build prominent national symbols, from the Hôtel de Ville in Paris to the great Charles de Gaulle Monument in Colombey-les-Deux-Églises, and the famed Croix de Lorraine. Even in Los Angeles, Budapest, and Seville there were buildings made from the legendary stone. Even back in Neolithic times they had built impressive structures of this rare plutonic rock that apart from here was visible only in a few places in the world: Ontario, Canada; Corsica; Egypt; and China.

It looked as if the bizarre stones had literally fallen from the heavens. As if there had been a wildly scattered shower of extraordinary meteorites. Miraculous boulders, curious signs and symbols, massive, but at the same time seemingly weightless. As if the next gust of wind might blow them away. A magical background—immediately it became clear why great writers and painters, including many friends of Gauguin, had flocked madly to this little spot of land.

From way back the villages along the Rose Coast had been involved in a ferocious contest: Which of them was home to the most extraordinary piece of rock, the most spectacular shapes and tones of pink?

The beach on which they lay had its sensation: the Grève de Toul Drez was the most northerly of Trégastel's twelve beaches, a "wild beach," shaped like a sickle, framed with rocky tongues of land and comical stone shapes, from the Tête de Mort in the west, an outcrop in the form of a skull, from which you could also see one of the most amusing granite shapes of the region: the Tas de Crêpes, the Pile of Crêpes, which rather detracted from the horror of the skull. The pair of offshore islands—the Île du Grand Gouffre and the Île de Dé—were protected by all too blustery flood tides which at low tide left an enchanting lagoon, like a large natural swimming pool. Even the sand here was pink. Bright pink and fine grained, and only very gradually drifting into the water. Into a sea that was not just clear but completely transparent. A delicate turquoise green initially, it turned into a shining turquoise blue, strangely magnified by the pink seabed. Only far out in the Atlantic did it become a deep blue. Out there where you could see the larger of the Sept-Îles, the focus of legends, five miles from the coast.

Ever since Claire and Dupin had arrived, two days prior, it had been fabulous high-summer weather. All day long the temperature hovered around a standard thirty degrees Celsius, and there was a superb blue sky. No clouds, no haze. The air was crystal clear, thanks to the light breeze from the Atlantic. The dominant colors contrasted exquisitely: the shining blue of the sky, the greeny-blue turquoise of the sea, and the pink of the sand and rocks.

It was breathtakingly beautiful. Surreal even.

"*La douceur de vivre.*" That was the way one felt on carefree, balmy summer days like these, the "gentle sweetness of life." Or as the locals said, *La vie en roz—La vie en rose.*

* * *

For Georges Dupin it was hell.

They were on vacation. A beach vacation. Nothing could be worse.

"Just lying on the beach" was how Claire had envisioned it. No obligations, no meetings, no work. She had insisted on one stipulation, that they would both promise one thing: that for these few days, they would "under no condition" have anything to do with the commissariat in Concarneau or the clinic in Quimper. No matter what.

"Just the heaven of relaxation and doing nothing," she had said and sighed happily.

In fact it was not just for "a few days," but two weeks, a full fourteen days.

It was the longest vacation Dupin had ever taken in his entire career. It had become a subject of conversation in Concarneau. There had even been a short report—wholly gratuitous and satirical—in the local edition of *Ouest-France*: "Georges Dupin in Trégastel; Monsieur le Commissaire on Vacation!"

Claire had been hoping for an "old-fashioned seaside vacation": all arranged, lazy, laid-back. A "charming little hotel," somewhere where you didn't need a car, where you could get everywhere on foot. And most important of all, "a proper vacation rhythm." For her that meant sleeping late—Dupin was an enthusiastic early riser—having a late, relaxed breakfast on the terrace—an extended breakfast was not Dupin's thing—wandering along the beach in airy clothing—Dupin couldn't stand short pants—grabbing a few sandwiches and drinks along the way—on that point there were no objections until it got to the end: making themselves comfortable on a big soft towel and staying there, apart from a few dips in the sea, until late afternoon.

Pure hell.

There was nothing Dupin considered more insufferable than indolence. Nothing got on the commissaire's nerves more than premeditated leisure. Dupin needed to be on his feet, needed to be busy. He was in his element when he was permanently busy; everything else was torture. Obviously Claire was aware of this. After all, she had known him long enough. And she took it seriously. Very seriously. When she had planned her ill-starred vacation she had in no way just been thinking of herself, she insisted, but "quite specifically" of him too. Claire had a theory, which Dupin considered disastrous, that his "dangerous *need* for action" had come about in the first place because he was always busy, because of the overkill in internal and external anxiety in recent years, including, as she preferred to put it, "all these mad criminal cases." And that it had now reached crisis point and he needed a "proper break."

"A radical break, get properly away from things!" The crazy thing was that Dupin's doctor, Docteur Garreg, had exactly the same opinion. He had even recognized "prototype symptoms of pathological tension": his stomach problems, his difficulty sleeping, his coffee addiction . . . to Dupin's mind this was absurd.

It was when Nolwenn, Dupin's irreplaceable assistant, too, had started talking about "absolutely essential time off"—just because Dupin might have of late been occasionally cranky—that he knew he had no hope left. The fact that all three believably insisted they wanted "only the best" for him didn't make things easier. He had given in.

Then everything went ahead quickly. Nolwenn and her husband vacationed last year in Trégastel-Plage, in a "very pretty hotel." They had even become friendly with the pair who owned it. Before Dupin knew what was happening, a room had been booked, "double deluxe" with sea view and balcony.

From then on his misfortune had taken its way, and now here they were lying on the big lilac towel.

Dupin had no doubt that this "recreational break" would have one effect only, and that was to leave him in a dire mental state. But it was Claire he was worried about. Ever since Claire had taken over as head of cardiology in Quimper, she had worked herself nearly to death. She was *genuinely*—unlike him—totally exhausted. In recent months it was not unusual for Claire to have fallen asleep on the sofa before they were both supposed to have supper. She needed a vacation.

And for her, Dupin was regrettably convinced, a beach vacation was just the right thing. Ever since they'd been here she'd seemed more relaxed with every moment.

If being on a towel on the beach was already a nightmare in principle for Georges Dupin, there were other factors in play that made things even worse.

The sun was so strong it was impossible to come out without wearing a cap or a sun hat. Dupin hated both. And in any case didn't have either. So on the way down to the beach yesterday Claire had taken it on herself to buy him a dark blue cap with "I love Brittany" on it, which he glumly pulled on his head. The other thing that was needed at all times was sunscreen. And Dupin couldn't stand sunscreen either. It stuck to him, no matter what it said on the tube. And that meant that the sand stuck to his body, sand that mysteriously always got onto Dupin's side of the towel. There was never a single grain on Claire's side. No matter how Dupin applied the cream, no matter how careful he was, one way or another, sooner or later the cream got into his eye. Both eyes. Which burned like hell, meaning his vision was blurred and he could neither read nor watch the beach life. And apart from reading and watching there was nothing else to do from a towel.

The only relief was the dinner. The hotel restaurant was excellent, and specialized in good-quality local dishes. They had been starving when they arrived the evening before yesterday—Dupin loved it how hungry Claire could get—and within a few minutes they had been sitting out on the terrace with breathtaking views. They had eaten *tartelettes de Saint-Jacques,* scallops from Rade de Brest, definitely the best, after that *cardinal* artichokes with vinaigrette, a local pale lilac artichoke, mild and slightly sweet. Even the wine had been great, a young Pinot Noir from the Loire Valley, drunk chilled, one of Dupin's new preferences for summer days. It had gone perfectly with the marinated salt meadow lamb, and the *cocos de Paimpol*, the tender white beans that Dupin particularly loved.

Amazing as the meal had been—and the second evening in the restaurant had confirmed the phenomenal impression of the first—a vacation day had more to it than just the dinner. There were still a lot more hours of the remaining twelve to get through.

* * *

Dupin had gone swimming six times. And he had even more frequently walked the length of the beach, from one end to the other. And back again.

Before he had gotten down to the beach—Claire had gone on ahead, she hadn't wanted to "waste any time"—he had stopped into the newspaper store in the sedate little center of Trégastel and bought the weekend editions of the daily newspapers, taking his time. By now he had read them all cover to cover. *Ouest-France* had started running its "Summer Special," on the theme "Does someone have to be born a Breton, or is it possible to become one?" One of the most frivolous and at the same time most popular and fiercely disputed local topics. The answer was simple, genial, and yet melodramatic (which comforted Dupin): "To be a Breton, you don't need papers or documents, you just need to have made up your mind to be one!"

At the heart of it, according to the passionate summing up, was behavior, innate attitude toward life, the world, other people, and in particular oneself. Daily over the next four weeks, the paper would bring this to life in an amusing game: *You know you're a Breton if . . .* , followed by a series of unmistakable indicators, undisguisable signs:

You believe apéritif time begins at 11:00 A.M., and from then on anything goes.

If you're intending to commit suicide, you run into a packed bar in Finistère and shout out loud that you're from Paris.

You think the sound of one bagpipe is more tolerable than that of another.

The date 1532 means something to you, and not something good (the year in which Brittany was annexed by France).

Claire had laid the towel in exactly the same place as yesterday. Which indicated that would be their territory for the rest of the vacation.

"I need to rinse my eyes with water," Dupin said, and made a face, "with clean water. In the hotel." He had already stood up.

He didn't have any better idea for how to get up off the towel again for a while. In any case, it was more or less the truth.

"Then bring us back one of those *pains bagnats*."

"Will do."

Dupin had found a little store not far from the hotel whose owner came from Nice and made the traditional southern French flat bread with tuna, tomatoes, olives, and mayonnaise. He had also bought a bottle of rosé wine from Provence that could be taken down to the beach in a portable cooler.

It was half past three.

Claire lay dozing on her stomach. She was wearing a modest black bikini that suited her extremely well. And an outsize straw hat, which Dupin wasn't particularly fond of: it was ancient and had belonged to her grandmother.

"Anything else? I'm happy to go and fetch it."

"No thanks, *chéri*."

Dupin pulled on his washed-out polo shirt. His jeans. He slipped into his battered loafers, which contained an astonishing amount of sand. That was another of his specialties: he always managed to cart around an enormous amount of sand. Into the car, into the hotel room, even—despite showering—into their bed.

The next towel island was about twenty meters away. A family from the hotel. Three little kids, a boy and two girls. Very happy and very friendly. Unfortunately their parents were dreadful. They grumbled noisily all the time. "Sit still!" "Don't drop crumbs from your sandwich!" "We want a bit of peace once in the year." The parents' endless grousing drifted over to them. It was awful. At breakfast that morning their volume had only been outdone by that of another couple: the man in his early fifties, Dupin guessed, the woman in her midthirties, dyed blond—and arguing with each other the whole time.

The joys of hotel life.

"See you shortly, Claire."

"Don't be gone too long." Claire turned over and went back to her book.

Dupin swerved around the family.

It wasn't far to the hotel. Along a narrow path beside the sea, bright gleaming dune grass to the sides, a panoramic view of the Atlantic-granite landscape.

The hotel, L'Île Rose, sat up on a low hill right next to the sea, in between giant pink hunks of granite that protected it on all sides, with huge twisted pines growing among them. The main entrance was at the end of the seafront by the Plage du Coz-Pors. The rough asphalt promenade led to a small public parking lot onto which the hotel's main entrance opened. Also here were the four white-painted wooden huts where you could buy the ferry tickets to the Sept-Îles.

That was something Dupin would have liked to do if it didn't clash uncompromisingly with his dislike of sea trips. It was after all on the Sept-Îles that the "little penguins" lived. The little penguins, Dupin had learned, were not real penguins but rather auks. They looked like penguins and walked like them. Dupin's deep-seated love of penguins generously extended to the little penguins, even if they lived an unreachable distance away on the nearby Sept-Îles.

Dupin had reached L'Île Rose's garden, which Claire had fallen in love with the minute they arrived, particularly on account of the two little clumps of magnificent hydrangea in powerful blue and violet colors. The hotel owners had laid out a little botanical paradise amidst the granite. Beautiful lawns, not overly fastidiously mown, three windblown palms with thick trunks, majestic eucalyptus trees, bushy camellias, rhododendrons, agave, scented lavender, huge bushes of sage, rosemary, thyme, and mint, all grown into one another. The high point was an old overgrown olive tree. Toward the sea the mighty blocks of stone and the sumptuous vegetation opened out onto a magnificent view.

The old house was from the nineteenth century, with a gray white-wash and the obligatory granite to the sides beneath the windows. It was one of the privileged houses to be near the sea, there to be admired singly and loftily all the way along the stretch of coastline. A very desirable villa, restored by hand, tastefully but modestly, in bright colors. The rooms had handsome, simple wooden furniture and pretty materials. And what for Dupin was the decisive feature: a handy espresso machine. The house was a relic—as was the whole center of the town—from the days when the summer vacation had first been invented.

Dupin walked across the garden, heading for the steep stone staircase to the entrance.

"Have you heard, Monsieur le Commissaire?"

Rosmin Bellet, the owner of L'Île Rose—a jovial, rotund character—had popped out from behind the palm trees. He was a genial man, though a bit too much of a chatterbox for Dupin's liking. It was quite clear Bellet liked to look after his guests in his own very individual way.

Dupin stopped reluctantly. His eyes were still burning from the sunscreen. He had no interest in conversation.

"No." Dupin sounded unintentionally surly. "I mean—what is it I should have heard?" Dupin was rubbing his temples.

"The statue of Saint Anne was stolen from the Chapelle Sainte-Anne the day before yesterday. Nobody has any idea yet who it was and how they might have done it."

"I think your gendarmerie will be onto it."

"Alan and Inès." Monsieur Bellet smiled. "Yes, I'm sure they will." The names of the local gendarmes, Dupin assumed.

Two fat bumblebees—the garden was full of all sorts of bees— flew dangerously closely past Dupin's nose, droning loudly.

"The statue is very old." Monsieur Bellet wasn't giving up so easily.

"Even so," Dupin mumbled. He couldn't care less. He wasn't going to get involved. Not with ancient objects that had gone astray, least of all from churches. That was just what he had had to deal with in his last case and it still hung over him, like some dark, mysterious shadow. So much of it had not been solved.

"And on Wednesday last week the Gustave Eiffel House was broken into," Bellet stubbornly added.

Dupin shrugged.

"The Eiffel Tower architect had a house built here in 1903. In Scottish style. It was up for sale. Along with half a hectare of land!"

Bellet sounded as if he had wanted to sell the property himself.

"It has sea on three sides. The house is open to all the winds.

That's why it was called Ker Avel. Right next to Napoleon's Hat. Albert, Eiffel's son, had laid out a labyrinth between the blocks of granite."

"Very nice." Dupin made as if to move on.

"In 1906, Gustave Eiffel had installed a whole row of what were for those days revolutionary devices for measuring the weather. Meteorology owes him a whole series of important discoveries. And beyond that"—Monsieur Bellet raised his voice—"the Eiffel House was locked up!"

"My . . . wife is waiting for her *pain bagnat*!"

Ever since they had arrived the day before yesterday, Monsieur and Madame Bellet had referred to "your wife" and "your husband." At first Dupin and Claire had tried to correct them a couple of times, then simply given up.

Bellet nodded, but continued talking.

"Do you know that Napoleon's Hat played a decisive historical role?"

It was a rhetorical question. "'Is Napoleon's Hat still in Perros-Guirec?' That was the code put out at eighteen hundred hours on April 3, 1943. It was the signal that the fighting was to begin! On the orders of de Gaulle himself!"

There was a dramatic tone to Bellet's voice. And even though Dupin had no interest in continuing the conversation, he found the emotion in the innkeeper's voice fitting. That was really something important.

"Strangely, there seems to be nothing missing from the Eiffel House. In any case it is all but empty. Only a few old sticks of furniture. I have to really wonder, Monsieur le Commissaire, who would break into a house like that?"

Dupin walked up the steps to the half-open entrance door to the hotel.

"Nothing much ever happens here," came the voice from his rear. Dupin hesitated and turned around once again. "But of course, you must know that seven years ago there was a corpse found in one of our quarries. An employee of the quarry company, who worked in the administration. She fell down fifty meters. Every bone in her body broken. Presumably not of her own doing. Even today nobody knows if it was an accident or murder. There was an intensive investigation, but with no result. A sinister puzzle. We call her the pink corpse."

Bellet had theatrically raised his bushy eyebrows, causing deep creases on his forehead. He had an extraordinarily symmetric round head—in perfect harmony with his overall round impression—and very short light gray hair.

"I have to get on, Monsieur Bellet."

"The last murder in Trégastel was thirty-seven years ago," Monsieur Ballet said. He clearly ran a sort of local crimes diary. "That one wasn't cleared up either. A woman that time too. A saleswoman in a bakery. She was strangled after our traditional Fest Noz, the *gouel an hañv*. Just twenty-one years old. We call her the 'pale girl.'"

"I see."

"This year, by the way, we're celebrating the fortieth anniversary of our most boisterous festival. Organized by the ALCT, the Association des Loisirs et Culture de Trégastel. Next Saturday. It's a must. There'll be crêpes with excellent local organic vegetables, local beers and ciders. Lots of wine too, and other stuff. The music will be taken care of by TiTom, Dom Jo, and the Gichen brothers. You absolutely need to come along. Your wife will like it."

Dupin pulled open the door.

"See you later then, Monsieur le Commissaire," Bellet said, and gave him a beaming smile.

Dupin mumbled a final farewell and disappeared in a rush.

It was pleasantly cool in the old house. At the end of the narrow hallway was the staircase on the left of the salon with its three comfortable, thickly upholstered sofas, and a pile of tatty books on an ancient table. In the corner there was a desk with a computer. The salon led into the small restaurant, the end of which opened onto the extraordinary terrace. Immediately on the right was the reception, and beyond that the kitchen.

The steep staircase up to their room was always a bit of a climbing expedition. Dupin entered the room, which was a generous size by French hotel standards. They had the light-colored natural-wood furniture here too. A chaise longue to stretch out on. But the best thing was the balcony. Out there was a little table and two comfortable recliners, one in clubhouse green, the other paprika red. In between them was a large sunshade. Honey yellow. Claire loved the combination of colors.

Dupin went into the bathroom to rinse his eyes. Afterward he made an espresso and sat out on the balcony.

He drank his coffee in tiny sips. The view faded on the dark blue horizon.

All of a sudden a deafening sound broke out. High, penetrating sounds that gradually turned to low dull tones before fading away. Then broke out again as loud as before, this time accompanied by a sonorous motor hum.

Dupin took a moment to pull himself together.

Tractors. Tractor horns. Not one horn, not two; it had to have been a dozen. The sound came from the left, probably from the road just behind the main beach that led to the little parking lot and the hotel entrance.

Dupin stood up and bent out far over the balcony.

He couldn't see the road from there. It was probably a protest by landowners, even if there hadn't been anything about it in the paper. There had been ever more frequent protests of the kind in northern Brittany over the past few years.

Dupin went back into the room and groped in his pants pocket for his cell phone. It was covered in sand too. Even though his phone was an "Outdoor Model," Nolwenn had nonetheless got him a new protective cover, called "Defender" and supposed to be indestructible despite its thinness. Military standard. "Just what you need for the beach," Nolwenn had said.

He pressed the PREVIOUS CALL button.

It rang several times.

"Monsieur le Commissaire!" An extremely severe tone of voice.

"I only wanted to know if everything was okay."

"This is the fifth time you've rung since the day before yesterday, Monsieur le Commissaire! The fifth!"

Nolwenn was clearly peeved.

"And even if something had happened in the meantime," she said in a tone of voice that was even more brutal than the sentence itself, "for the next two weeks under no circumstance would it be any business of yours."

"I just wanted to be sure." A pathetic answer.

"There, see, see the way you are! Be honest, you have gone so far that you actually wish something would happen! A pretty little complicated case. A lovely, extravagant murder. Eventually you'll be so feverish that you won't be able to think the case through!" Nolwenn was not in the least trying to hold back her annoyance. "But that's perfectly normal, that's the way it always is in the first few days." Now she was sounding like a psychotherapist dealing with a routine case. "Docteur Garreg predicted this. Until you get over your 'pathological hyperactivity' there will be recurring withdrawal symptoms. Including physical ones. But Docteur Garreg also said that we had to remain steadfast."

It was totally absurd. This completely idiotic concept of compulsory rest. Obviously he wasn't well, but this had nothing to do with this ludicrous hypothesis of Claire, Nolwenn, and Docteur Garreg. Nobody got worked up about a concert pianist who got nervous and bad-tempered if he wasn't allowed to play. Nobody would take umbrage at that! Quite the contrary! Nobody would talk about "addiction," they would be amazed at his "insurmountable passion"! Dupin had once read about a famous pianist who had his huge piano transported after him at enormous cost, wherever he was. Why should it be different for his profession? Was he not allowed to love it? Was he not allowed to be nervous and bad-tempered when he couldn't give in to it?

"And . . ." Nolwenn's voice yet again made clear how serious she was about this, "that is what we are going to do: keep being hard."

What a wonderful prognosis.

"We want you to get out of this! I'm hanging up now."

With a deep sigh Dupin dumped the cell phone back in his sandy pants pocket.

A moment later he left the hotel.

Monsieur Bellet was still tending to his huge sage bush. Dupin wasn't sure whether or not Bellet noticed him.

He hesitated a second, then went up to him.

"This statue, the one that was stolen, was it valuable?" he asked.

A look of satisfaction crossed Bellet's face.

"Despite its antiquity it had no significant material value." He smiled. "It wasn't made of gold or anything. It was just painted wood. But it had spiritual worth. It's not right that there hasn't been even the slightest word about it in the newspapers. Nor of the break-in at the Eiffel House."

"A spiritual quality also has its worth."

Dupin hadn't a clue what he ought to say.

"Over at reception you'll find a brochure about the church, with a photo in it and . . ."

"Thanks, Monsieur Bellet."

"Do you know what's really curious?"

Dupin stayed silent.

"The Chapelle Sainte-Anne was unimportant compared to the Church of Saint Anne opposite us here." Bellet gave a vague nod of the head. "I mean in terms of art history. The Church of Saint Anne in contrast was built in the twelfth century, in the Roman style, later expanded in the Gothic style. It's sensational. And there's lots inside that's valuable. Unlike in the chapel—"

"I think . . . ," Dupin interrupted him. He took a deep breath in and out. "I think I have to go."

"Don't be afraid if the tractors make a lot of noise again." Monsieur Bellet turned back to his sage bush. "The landowners are gathering on the promenade. They're protesting against the big supermarkets' price dumping." He paused for effect. "And quite right too! This morning they posted 'For Sale' placards outside the private homes of regional councilors. And there's going to be more action over the next few days."

Breton farmers—indeed French farmers in general—were traditionally not ones for kid gloves. Even back in the days of the Revolution they were an extremely powerful body.

Bellet glanced at his sage bush. "Up here in the north, everybody's calling it the 'Crisis Summer.' Milk, meat. There has to be an end to this low-price nonsense!" It sounded as if this was going to be the beginning of a lengthy tirade.

Dupin was not in the mood for it, even though Monsieur Bellet was almost definitely right about everything. But it was his fault, because it had after all been him who had started the conversation.

"The north of Brittany lives on farming. Old volcanic soil with sedge in it, the Gulf Stream," Bellet said, lifting his chin proudly. "For example the famous *cocos de Paimpol:* little white pearls in wonderful marbled shells! Since 1998 they'd even had been awarded *Appelation d'origine contrôlée.* The best beans in France."

Dupin could do nothing but nod in agreement. It wasn't just him, but the whole of Brittany was mad about these beans. Every year people waited longingly for the new harvest.

Bellet chuckled. "The other thing you definitely have to try is the *petits violets,* one of the three types of artichokes we have here, smaller and longer than the flat-nose Camus artichokes. And don't forget the white-blooming cauliflower, or the unique varieties of potato and to-mato, the sand carrots, the spicy leeks, the pink Roscoff onions—and then there's our own breeds of pig, particularly those from Saint-Brieuc that are fed with lentils! The stews, sausages, pâtés."

"We'll try them, Monsieur Bellet. All of them."

That was just what they intended to do. Dupin turned away, de-termined to go.

"Enjoy the rest of your time on the beach." Monsieur Bellet didn't mean it ironically.

Dupin walked past the blue hydrangea and left the garden. Once again he pulled out his cell phone.

For the past few weeks now he had been preoccupied with an is-sue, which it had to be said was a weighty matter. Something that had been going through his head all year. There were one or two things still to clear up. Then he would ask Claire.

Monday

Much as the commissaire loved rituals, he equally hated having a daily routine of things to do. The vacation was a long sequence of them. Today too they got up late. After breakfast they'd strolled "leisurely" down to the beach and had inevitably laid down on their towel on the sand. But they had at least stopped by Dupin's new friend Rachid on the way and stocked up on provisions. Delicious-looking homemade pizza, with chorizo and sardines, along with half a watermelon, all packed into a compact cool bag—the rosé in its own separate cooler—which Rachid had lent them for their whole vacation.

Unfortunately there were no newspapers. The farmers had been petty enough to have cut off all traffic from five in the morning. There were blockades of every access road, and the newspapers hadn't made it to Trégastel. Bellet had only shrugged his shoulders indifferently when Dupin had looked in vain for them on the hotel table where they usually were.

After only fifteen minutes on the beach towel Dupin had gotten up to go for a walk to the offshore stony island of Île du Grand Gouffre. At full ebb tide—especially on these *grandes marées,* when the water retreated extraordinarily far—it was possible to cross on the sand. He had asked Claire if she wanted to come with him, but she had just mumbled that they'd only just got there.

It was a pleasant little walk that cheered up Dupin's mood a bit. Dupin liked ebb tide. It was made for walkers. Every time there were remarkable new views to be seen. Crazy pink scenery as if devised by some fantasy artist; a few of the hunks of granite looked as if they were made of plasticine, kneaded, pulled out, twisted, and squashed. An intoxicating background. Dupin had climbed up to the highest collection of stones and walked around the island. On the landward side in the midst of the rocks there was a little strip of powdery white sand. He would ask Claire if she might not like to lie here for a change. It was more isolated, wilder—even though he still didn't understand why such a pretty island was known as "the bottomless pit." Undoubtedly there was some gruesome story behind it.

Over the course of the long day on the beach Dupin had gone swimming more often than yesterday, every five minutes approximately, and taken more frequent walks along the beach. He had gone up to Rachid twice to fetch cold drinks, water and cola. And once even before they had lunch he had gone back into the hotel. Yet again because of his burning eyes. And yet again he had bumped into Monsieur Bellet, who, amongst other things, had told him about another two crime cases in Trégastel. During the Moules-Frites and Bacon festival the night before, a camera had been stolen, and the local baker had been robbed of three sacks of flour, though that had been two weeks ago. There was clearly some criminal power at work in the apparently peaceful village.

That afternoon Dupin happily thought of something: even if there were no newspapers, a trip to the newspaper store was a good excuse for leaving the beach. Dupin would buy himself a book. A book would keep him busy. Claire had, weeks before, thought about which books she wanted to read on vacation. An adventurous collection. Something about "*hidden realities and parallel universes.*" Two thick volumes of Proust, and an even thicker tome on "international heart catheter technology," the latest novel by Anna Gavalda, a cookbook of Éric Fréchon's bistro recipes. Dupin had only packed the morning they set off. And hadn't brought a single book.

He spent a wonderful hour in the newspaper store. And finally, having had dozens of books in his hands, bought a thin volume of walking routes in the area: *Les Incontournables—Balades à Pied: Trégor—Côte de Granit Rose.* Extremely welcome suggestions. Straightaway there were four suggested walks in the immediate vicinity. "*La couronne du roi Gradlon*": a walk to the most curious stone formations and finest beaches. Île Renote: a discovery of the peninsula behind their beach, La Vallée de Traouïéro: an apparently spectacular valley, GR34: a celebrated hiking route along the pink granite coast between Trégastel and Perros-Guirec. It all sounded very interesting, and every expedition meant one thing above all else: not having to lie on the beach.

Out of habit Dupin had almost bought himself a little red Clairefontaine notebook and a couple of Bic pens to go with it, his classic equipment for all his cases. He hadn't just been using the notebooks since—like his father before him—he began working for the police in Paris, but since his childhood. What nobody knew was that it had been his father who had bought him his first Clairefontaine. Dupin had used it to imagine whole crime cases. Fantasies that for him took the shape of reality and captured his attention for weeks at a time. Right now it was only at the last minute that he put the red notebook back on the shelf and bought an inconspicuous blue one. Claire of course knew that red notebooks meant work.

Maybe he could make up some imaginary crime cases while lying on the beach, just like in the old days, to keep himself busy.

There was another thing the notebook could be used for, in any case: he could make a list of excuses for needing to get up from the towel over the next eleven days. He would vary them cleverly. He'd already thought up a couple yesterday—for example the need to go to the barber, something he never managed to do in Concarneau, and the vacation would be an excellent opportunity.

Chatting with the friendly, rather hefty woman at the cash register in the newspaper store, Dupin found himself asking about the incident in the chapel. The stolen statue. Not that he had intended to ask about it. The woman, who as it turned out during the conversation was the store owner, already had several ideas. The "most probable" was a "mysterious art collector" from London who worked for an auction house but came from Paimpol. She had bought a house in Trégastel at the beginning of the year, as a second home. But beyond that the story didn't go very far. "Or maybe it wasn't her? Who knows? In any case she preferred to buy her newspapers elsewhere."

As for the Eiffel House break-in, she had an explanation: "Well-organized international gangs." Then to put things in context: "A bunch of stupid kids." Whatever the case, the store owner was able to say that the two local gendarmes—she too referred to them as Alan and Inès—had officially taken charge of things.

The Chapelle Sainte-Anne was almost directly opposite the newspaper store. Dupin noticed it straightaway and took a stroll around the light gray granite building with its wonderful roof of natural slate. He took the chance to christen his new—blue—Clairefontaine. There were three entrances to the chapel and annex but unfortunately they were "closed to the public" for a choir practice.

Up until now Claire hadn't said a word when Dupin set off on one of his little excursions, hardly taking notice and just giving a nod or an indifferent "Aha." Dupin thought it was perfectly possible that her relaxed attitude was part of a therapeutic strategy: to ignore his restlessness at first, only to intervene as gently as possible.

"This morning," Claire had announced earlier, completely out of the blue, "the clinic called; Pierre has the flu." Pierre was her first chief doctor in the cardiological surgery in Quimper. "He won't be able to work for a couple of days. They asked me if I could come in for two days. It was Monsieur Lepic, the director, *personally*." She'd taken her time over the word and followed it with a dramatic pause. "Of course, I told them no.

"Now they're trying to get somebody from Rennes. You see, they can do without me." Claire had smirked. Dupin gave a low sigh. After the strict telling-off yesterday Dupin hadn't tried calling Nolwenn again. He'd tried Riwal several times instead. And strangely only got through to him once. His inspector was unusually open. He was quite clear; Nolwenn had given him "instructions." An off-the-cuff test proved that. Dupin had asked Riwal about the business with the resistance and the wartime code: "Is Napoleon's hat still in . . ." which normally would have led to a lengthy lecture on Breton history. Not today. That was a definite indication. Dupin found it hard even to get "Interesting" out of Riwal, followed immediately by a reference to some pile of papers that he needed to deal with urgently. Dupin didn't even try his second inspector, Kadeg, who would follow Nolwenn's instructions even more enthusiastically than Riwal.

Kadeg would be busy dealing with a multitude of e-mails from the prefect, who at the beginning of last week—it sounded like a completely unbelievable joke but was true—had broken his jaw while eating a ham sandwich. He had just barely avoided needing surgery, and had been strictly ordered not to speak for three weeks. Since then he had been sending e-mails every minute. Dupin hadn't bothered looking at even one of them. And over the next two weeks he wouldn't get annoyed by them either, because Nolwenn had redirected his e-mails to her account for the length of the vacation. In principle a period without any contact with the prefect would have been pure joy if vacation weren't so disagreeable.

* * *

Eight o'clock. Dinner was served.

The event Dupin had been waiting for all day.

From the raised terrace the view was out across the garden, to the bizarre stone formations in the water and on land shining with a pink magic, a dreamland in the evening light, a pair of windblown black-green pines, the now deep dark blue Atlantic, and the Sept-Îles, rising proudly from the sea. On the side of the terrace facing away from the sea, a small staircase led down to the garden.

There were fourteen tables on the terrace. Dupin had counted them. And the same number in the restaurant. Those not reserved for hotel guests were extremely sought-after. There were serious waiting lists. The head chef with whom Claire and Dupin had chatted on their first evening—gray-white stubble beard, passionately sparkling eyes— turned out to be a real artist. His wife, Natalie, who had a warm smile and a sunny disposition, looked after the service energetically, with two young, friendly waitresses by her side. The chef produced a new, inspired menu every day. Four courses. Always a brilliant combination. Natalie announced it every day between 10:00 and 11:00 on a large slate hung in the hallway near the door. If they were lucky they could already read it before heading down to the beach, and look forward to it all day. For Dupin that was an important motivation.

The Bellets had given them one of the most privileged tables on their very first evening—the one with the most beautiful view—right by the balustrade facing the sea, "in the first row." Dupin sat with his back to the stone wall of the house.

At the table next to them was a wholly pleasant family with a daughter, called Elisa, sixteen by Dupin's reckoning. At the last table in the first row of the terrace sat the couple who argued all the time. At the table next to the couple, fittingly, were the family with the horrible parents and nice children. To the side of Claire and Dupin sat a smart but somehow bored young couple who drove an expensive red convertible. Out of the rest of the hotel guests one stood out, a permanently frowning man, probably in his late thirties, sitting alone at a tiny table at the farthest right corner of the terrace.

"Isn't this a dream?" Claire interrupted his thoughts.

She sat opposite him across a generous table for two, wearing a dark blue dress that looked both light and elegant at the same time. She had done up her shoulder-length dark blond hair loosely. She had a glass of cold Sancerre in her right hand, as did Dupin. The heat of the day had faded, leaving behind a balmy dream of a summer evening.

Claire gazed at the bay. "Perfect. The hotel, the room, the restaurant, the sea, the fine sand. Our place on the beach. The weather—summer vacation days don't get any better. Don't you think?"

"I was thinking," Dupin said, "that maybe I ought to go to the barber. When it's as hot as this, it's much more comfortable to have short hair. And in Concarneau I never get around to it."

Claire didn't seem to have heard him. Natalie had arrived with the first course.

Millefeuille de tomates saveurs d'antan, yellow, green, and red tomatoes. Heritage varieties, a real sensation. "Fresh from our hotel garden. Right around now the *coeur de boeuf* are at peak flavor." With this proud statement she set the plates down in front of Claire and Dupin. And immediately vanished. No time for chitchat this evening.

Claire already had her fork in her hand, as did Dupin.

"I'll go by the little hairdresser's tomorrow," Dupin said casually.

"Wonderful," Claire said. She was eating slowly and thoughtfully. "Yes, do that. And the hairdresser's is—"

Claire was rudely interrupted by a furious deep voice: "I've had enough," followed by a high-pitched, aggressive "No! I'm the one that's had enough! You idiot!"

The couple who fought all the time. Their exchange was heard across the whole terrace. Up until now they had been unusually calm. At least Dupin hadn't heard them.

Claire quickly pulled herself together.

"The hairdresser's isn't far from the chapel, is it?" Was there a certain undertone to her question? "Where somebody stole the statue of Saint Anne?"

The undertone had gotten stronger. How had Claire heard about this incident? Probably also from Monsieur Bellet. It had sounded a bit like a warning, but maybe Dupin was just imagining it.

"Nothing of importance, if you ask me."

"Too curious, this thing." Claire dipped a slice of tomato in the olive oil and ate it with the baguette.

Her gaze turned again out toward the bay. "A walrus, no doubt about it!"

Dupin immediately spotted the rock formation she meant.

On their first day when they had gone out for a walk, they had agreed on a little competition for the rest of their vacation: apart from the "officially" named formations and figures, they would make up new figures, animals and things out of the granite. In fact the game invented itself: the curiosity of the shapes automatically focused the imagination of those who saw them. Enforced by the permanent change of perspective during the walk and even more so the changing position of the sun and the shadows that changed with it, there were ever more shapes to be seen. All of a sudden there would be a duck, a nostril, a mushroom, a pan, a toaster, a carp, a dwarf's hat, and of course it would be Dupin who spotted it: a penguin!

"A point for you—today I had the mussel, the giant's nose, and the dinosaur." Dupin was being serious.

"I want to see them all." Claire laughed. "You don't get the points until then."

"That's that!" came the harsh scream across the tables. The same aggressive female voice as before. Accompanied by a loud clattering noise.

Every head—including those of the "Dupins"—reluctantly turned to the couple.

The bottle blonde had sprung to her feet, letting her chair fall.

She reached for her handbag, stood there for a second, and then stormed off. Past the tables of the perplexed spectators, toward the steps, then down into the garden. Without once turning to look back she took the steps and vanished the next second. A dramatic departure.

Her husband had remained seated and seemed not so much embarrassed as resigned. He shrugged and then—equally demonstratively—got on with his meal. As everybody awkwardly turned their faces away he let out a quiet growl: "She'll be back."

Slowly the conversation at the table resumed, and became jovial again before long.

Claire said: "Monsieur Bellet has told us all about the summer tourist events taking place in Trégastel this week and next. Including the traditional Fest-Noz on Saturday. We might find one or the other interesting."

Dupin wasn't really keen on tourist event programs. But maybe one of them took place during the day. At beach time.

"Tomorrow there's a *salon des vins* in the Centre de Congrès, lasting until Sunday," Claire said.

That didn't sound bad.

One of the young waitresses brought the second course: lobster with Kari Gosse, a Breton style of curry.

"He gave me this little brochure." Claire pulled it out of her handbag. "Twenty star prize-winning winemakers from all across France are going to present their wines. Including a couple from the Loire."

It sounded even better.

"Along with that there will be stands with *terrine de foie gras,* cheese, salami, and chocolate. One stand with only regional pâtés, as large as laundry baskets, mushrooms, seaweed, bacon. Wonderful products, Monsieur Bellet said."

Now it was sounding perfect. This vacation, it was now clear, would also be something else: a food fest.

"We can go there in the evenings or we can bring provisions down to the beach."

"I . . . it's so nice here in the evenings. I wouldn't want to miss one of their dinners."

"We have to try at least one other restaurant, according to Nolwenn."

Dupin's face showed signs of deep distress.

"In Ploumanac'h. La Table de Mon Père, right on the beach. It's supposed to be one of the prettiest bays on the pink coast. And Ploumanac'h was chosen as one of the prettiest places in France. On the TV show."

Clearly Dupin knew it. *Village Préféré des Français.* Every year one town or village was chosen from a ready-made selection. Millions voted. Obviously—how could it be otherwise—ever since the beginning of the show, Brittany had been amongst the overall leaders.

"Maybe for lunch one day," Dupin said. Under those circumstances, the restaurant would definitely be tempting.

Claire noted the suggestion with a dismissive look.

"But Ploumanac'h . . ."—it was the ideal moment to bring up the point—"you're quite right, we need to go there."

Dupin had put the little book from the newspaper store deliberately in his pocket and now took it out and laid it on the table. "I found this great book with tips for walks in the area. There are spectacular things to see."

Claire lifted it with a clearly skeptical look. "Not during our beach time, though," she said in a conciliatory tone. "At any other time, gladly. But first of all we should concentrate on Trégastel itself, there's already a lot to experience here."

What was "any other time" supposed to mean? Tomorrow instead of breakfast?

"On Thursday," Claire continued, "the locals collect sharks' eggs, on the beaches early in the morning. Afterward we could go to the aquarium to learn all about sharks. Wouldn't that be something?"

Nolwenn too had enthusiastically recommended a visit to the "unusual" aquarium. It had been built directly into the pink granite itself just behind Plage du Coz-Pors. It had originally been used as a chapel, during the Second World War for ammunition storage, after the war as an information library, and then finally as a museum of history. There were examples of all the local maritime flora and fauna. A particular feature was the multiple phenomena of the tides.

"Shark eggs? From here?"

"Blue sharks, cat sharks, mackerel sharks, and dogfish, they're all types of shark. And others too, according to Monsieur Bellet."

The expression on Dupin's face led Claire to add: "All more or less harmless."

"Little sharks."

Dupin was in the sea most days and often enjoyed swimming far out beyond the bay.

"A blue shark can grow up to three meters fifty," Claire said.

"Not small then."

"The blue shark is most commonly found in the Atlantic. But it rarely comes in at the shore. I did some research, and we're not on his menu." Claire laughed.

Dupin thought of the old joke: *Has anyone told the shark?*

"Are there no recorded instances of blue sharks attacking people?" he asked.

"They're very rare. And mostly false."

"What other things are there going on?" Dupin tried to change the topic.

"The Breizh Tattoo Studio is offering small tattoos free every evening this week."

Dupin didn't react.

"The owners of the restaurant Les Triagoz"—Claire had laid out her brochure on top of Dupin's little book and was reading aloud— "are turning their restaurant into a boutique to sell the greatest Breton brands: Amor Lux, Saint James, Guy Cotten, Hoalen. You can eat and shop in between courses."

Dupin wondered if this was a serious suggestion. Just to be careful he wouldn't inquire.

"Then on Saturday evening there's a long-distance race along the beach. To Perros-Guirec and back, along the famed coastal path. But that's probably not something to do on vacation." Dupin took a breath of relief.

"The community also has organized a series of lectures. On classical Chinese medicine, for example. In the big communal hall with three hundred seats, not bad." She sounded genuinely impressed. "On the geology of the pink granite. On the Église Sainte-Anne or the neogothic fairy castle on the little island, and the Gustav Eiffel House too."

"Maybe we should go and see the Eiffel House on our own? As I said, one of the walks leads there. I'd like to see that, and the castle too," Dupin said.

"Wasn't there a break-in at the Eiffel House recently?"

Dupin had feared as he ended the previous sentence that it had been a mistake to make his interest in the Eiffel House so evident. Claire was astonishingly well informed. But he might have known it, she always knew about everything.

He ignored the question.

"I'd like to do a few excursions too." Dupin tried again. "For example, the rebuilding of the world-famous little Gallic village in Pleumeur-Bodou."

Riwal had only recently told him about it. He had been there with his little son, who had just learned to walk. A little early for an excursion like that, Dupin had felt, but Riwal had rejected the idea: "It's never too early to get to know his Celtic roots."

Claire smiled at him. "I'd definitely like to see one of the quarries where they mine the pink stone. Thousands of millions of years old, and it was exposed on the surface of the earth three hundred thousand years ago."

Claire, the inquisitive scientist. Who loved clothing stores at the same time. And everything to do with food.

"I think," Claire continued, "we should start right in the middle of the village, which we can do in a couple of small excursions. Between breakfast and the beach. And between the beach and dinner. And then we can see." Her concession sounded like tactical mildness. "We haven't even seen all the beaches of Trégastel yet. We absolutely have to go to the famed Grève Rose and Grève Blanche. And see all the curious stones. There's a tour here intended to do just that. One way or another"—she smirked—"there are some of these stones that remind me of you."

It was clearly meant in a nice way, but Dupin was irritated nonetheless.

"I mean that you—"

The sudden sound of sirens interrupted Claire. A police car and an ambulance, coming ever closer. From the direction of Plage du Coz-Pors.

All of a sudden the sirens stopped.

The table conversations abruptly fell away. Concerned glances wandered around.

Dupin's muscles instinctively flexed.

Obviously Claire had noticed, and shot him a serious glance.

The next minute, Madame Bellet appeared on the terrace. In a loud voice that contrasted with her petite form, she announced: "Somebody has thrown a stone through Deputy Rabier's window. Madame Rabier was sitting directly behind it, at her desk. She was seriously injured by the shards of glass. And she's such a wonderful person." She took a deep breath, then looked all around the room and said, "For you there is no reason to be afraid. The deputy's house is on the street, for sure, but nearly a hundred meters away."

The anxiety on the faces of the guests caused her to add:

"I'm certain it's to do with the farmers' protests. But no matter how much I agree with them, this is unacceptable." Her eyes moved from one guest to the next as if she wanted to see if one of them might be the villain.

"But please get on with enjoying your meal," she said abruptly. "The main course will be served in a second."

With those words, Natalie and two waitresses entered, skillfully balancing big plates of roast pork in cider.

It was a view that let the atmosphere on the terrace turn jovial again. Only seconds later the seductive aroma also reached Claire and Dupin.

"That's dreadful." Claire tried to put sympathy in her voice, though it wasn't easy when looking at the roast pork. "An unfortunate accident. Or was it possibly deliberate?"

"Deliberate? What makes you think that?"

"Politicians have enemies. You know that more than anyone. But the gendarmes will sort it out as usual. There's a lot going on here, for a quiet little seaside resort."

Dupin wondered if he ought to say something, then let it go.

He too tucked back into his roast pork.

In the meantime the sun had lowered to reveal the glowing pink that in places had become a glaring violet coloring the sea as well. The pine trees, the sky, the whole world seemed rose-colored. Nature wasn't afraid of kitsch.

Tuesday

On this glowing hot afternoon on the beach towel Dupin was already on his fourth cold drink. A cola. Breizh cola, of course. Even Claire wasn't averse. She never drank cola normally. The high-tech digital display outside the Tabac-Presse had shown a hard-to-believe thirty-four degrees at eleven o'clock already.

In the newspapers—happily the supply had been resumed or else Dupin would have personally thumped the farmers—there was nothing yet about the smashed window. On the other hand, Monsieur and Madame Bellet had already brought Dupin up to speed on his first *café* on the terrace while Claire was still asleep. The deputy had sustained two serious cuts, one on her left wrist, the other on the left shoulder. And lost a lot of blood. A hypovolemic shock. It had been a close call: one of the shards had seriously injured the artery on her wrist. Whether injuring her had or had not been the intention, the stone throwing had been a de facto attack on a deputy to the Breton regional parliament. "Halfway to murder, right in our neighborhood," Madame Bellet had repeated several times with a look of horror on her face.

It was unsurprising that nobody had owned up to the attack. The farmers who had explicitly made the deputy's chambers the target of their protest, who had posted the "For Sale" sign outside and had two tractors standing there day and night as a blockade, had specifically distanced themselves from this incident. According to the Bellets, they were suggesting a conspiracy to put their protest in a bad light. There were no eyewitnesses. Already early that morning there had been a crime scene team working on the spot to determine where the stone thrower had stood. But so far no footprints had been found on the dry gravel. Of course, the commissaire from Lannion had taken on the case personally. "A blasé ape," was Monsieur Bellet's opinion.

The previous night the missile had been secured: a piece of granite around nine centimeters long and four wide. Gray, not pink. A color also found in the region, if not so often. The stone was uneven with tiny bits of dry earth in little holes. On the even part the forensic people had found a blurred partial print. Nothing else. Dupin knew they couldn't do much with that. And even if they could, any kid could have touched the stone. They were hardly going to take fingerprints of everybody in the village and all the tourists. The stone had been taken that morning to Rennes, where they would be able to carry out a more exact examination.

"Amazonite."

Claire had just pronounced the word with no obvious connection. Without moving her head, she had lain for hours in more or less the same position on her stomach.

"What do you mean?"

"The color of the sea, just there, where it's so still. It's like amazonite. A hard-to-define greenish blue. My necklace, the new one that the saleswoman insisted would help with vertebral disc complaints, neck problems, osteoporosis, bruising, sprains, and ganglions."

Dupin remembered now. They had bought it in Concarneau. "Ah yes, and heart problems too."

"Also for excessive nervousness, mental unrest, sleeping problems, mood swings, and hyperactivity, a stone for you actually." After a few moments Claire added in a similarly neutral tone: "Amazonite protects the aura and stabilizes the ethereal body."

Claire was unquestionably a woman of science, but now and then she had disturbingly irrational moments. Dupin—usually—found them wonderful.

"What do *you* make of this attack on the deputy?" Claire's change of subject was abrupt.

Dupin was taken aback; he wasn't certain what the purpose of Claire's question was. He would do his best to answer reservedly.

"Maybe it was just an accident. Maybe someone had deliberately wanted to break the window but not known that the deputy was sitting behind it."

"But surely he would have seen her." Claire's voice was strange. Was she trying to test him? "I've just read an interview with one of the protesting farmers, about their recent actions. Very reflective, very analytical. He was right on every point," Claire said, deliberately stressing her words. "The world is going to pot, in big things and small things." She didn't sound so much resigned as quite the opposite, aggressive. "We have to put up resistance!" She was sounding like Nolwenn now.

"Smashing windows," Dupin intervened, "is still an act of violence."

"Hm," Claire said.

"By the way, there's an envelope for you down at reception." Monsieur Bellet had drawn Dupin's attention to it, but he had forgotten it.

"Thank you, I got it," Claire said, a very businesslike tone to her voice. "Have you noticed"—all of a sudden Claire sounded gentle, reconciled—"that pink is to be found here in every shade and nuance? Sweet pink, deep pink, coral pink, rose pink, orange pink, magenta, anthracite pink. Depending on whether the rock is wet or dry, smooth or rough."

She let her words echo.

"Oh, another thing, your mother just rang. Your phone was busy." On his way to pick up drinks he had spoken—very briefly—with Nolwenn. And he had tried Riwal, who didn't pick up. Nor had he replied to Dupin's text message, ordering him to call back. On his way back from buying drinks, Dupin had made two more phone calls regarding Claire and himself. Things looked good on that front. He hadn't noticed until now that Claire had been taking her phone to the beach.

"My landlord," Dupin said. He couldn't think of anything better. "You know the hot water boiler sometimes goes on strike. I thought I'd get it repaired while we were on vacation."

"I never noticed that."

"It's been two or three weeks now."

"Whatever, your mother has arrived in Kingston, I was to let you know."

Dupin sighed audibly. The story was absurd. Unimaginable, frankly, if you knew his mother. That was why he tried as hard as possible not to think about it. His mother, the nose-in-the-air Parisian *grande bourgeoise* in Jamaica, the island of hippies and Rastafarians. Of all possible times it had been during the celebration for her seventy-fifth birthday that she had gotten to know a gentleman just turned seventy, in a dump near Cognac, the most extreme opposite to the capital, who after long years in the cognac trade had now successfully got into the rum business, and five years previously moved back home to Jamaica. Rum! He was a friend of her closest friend, who had brought him along to her birthday, right at the last minute, which initially hadn't pleased Anna Dupin at all. But in next to no time there was an official liaison established. Following that, Monsieur Jacques came very frequently to Paris, and at some stage had suggested to her that she spend "a few months" with him in his "Caribbean paradise." She had agreed there and then. All in all a completely unbelievable story—but at the same time one of those stories that made life life. Almost overnight everything in Anna Dupin's life had been turned on its head, and she was happy.

"Should I call her back?"

"No. And you're not to worry if you don't hear from her in the next few weeks."

Dupin scratched the back of his head.

"I'm a bit tired." With that Claire indicated that the conversation had come to an end.

Dupin tried to make himself comfortable on the sand. Even though it was soft sand he could never really get comfortable. He flicked mechanically through the newspaper.

The questions in the *Ouest-France* "Are You a Breton?" quiz of the day were:

You know you're a Breton if . . .
You know not to talk about the "Breton dialect" but the "Breton language," which is fifteen hundred years older and wiser than French.
You've had rubber boots since birth.

You only need water to wash potatoes.

It's only at apéritif time that you can't decide between Hénaff
(the ancient Breton name for a pâté made from expensive
Breton pigs) *and foie gras.*

Dupin realized he was also a bit tired. Maybe he should take a
little nap. And then go swimming.

* * *

Monsieur Bellet came hurrying up to them with two uniformed gendarmes trailing behind him.

Dupin sat up suddenly. He had fallen into a deep sleep and only
just now woken up. He quickly pulled his polo shirt on, just in time to
find them standing next to the towel.

Claire and he had been lying back to back.

"What is it, Georges?" Claire turned round. "Oh!" She sat up and
reached for her beach dress.

"Monsieur le Commissaire." Bellet was obviously worked up.
"Our two gendarmes want to talk to you."

Dupin stood up, and felt ridiculous in his swimming shorts.

The two gendarmes—a man of about thirty and a woman somewhat older—had positioned themselves to the left and right of Monsieur Bellet.

"Commissaire Dupin!" It was meant as a greeting. The female
gendarme seemed to set the tone for the team. "My name is Inès
Marchesi, and this," she nodded toward her colleague, "is Alan Lambert. From the Gendarmerie de Trégastel. Please excuse us disturbing
you on vacation"—it sounded like a token gesture of politeness—"but
we need you."

Dupin glanced at the gendarme in puzzlement.

"As a witness."

"As a witness?"

"Yes, as a witness."

"To what—I mean, in relation to what."

"A guest at the Île Rose hotel, where you are staying, has been reported missing this morning. Alizée Durand, the wife of Gilbert Durand. A married couple from Paris."

The gendarme left a pause. Dupin still didn't know what she was talking about.

"Monsieur and Madame Durand are spending their vacation in the same hotel as you. They sit just two tables from you in the evenings. Last evening they had a serious argument, during which Alizée Durand left the terrace suddenly and hasn't been seen since. Neither here in Trégastel, nor at their apartment in Paris."

"She hasn't turned up since?"

Dupin had assumed that the woman had come back at some stage during the night. Fit and well to start the argument again. There were couples who just fought continuously and tirelessly, a sort of ritual, you might say.

"No, and that's something that's never happened before in their marriage, according to Monsieur Durand. He got more worried as the night went on, and turned up at the gendarmerie this morning at eleven o'clock. At first he wanted to know if anything had happened in the neighborhood. Then later to officially report her as a missing person."

"And you want to know whether, sitting at a close table, we overheard much of the argument?"

"That too." The female gendarme looked at him calmly. "But above all we want to know whether Monsieur Durand left the table immediately after the event. How long he continued to sit on the terrace afterward. The three family members at the table between you and them left relatively early."

"Do you have a particular suspicion?" Nothing had occurred to Dupin, nor could he remember anything specific.

The younger policeman, who hadn't said a word so far, continued to stare seriously at the sand.

"Just going through the routine. You know how it is."

Dupin couldn't tell whether or not she was being ironic.

"Monsieur Durand, we didn't know what he was called until now." Claire joined the conversation, having put on her beach dress, and now stood next to Dupin, having been listening with a resolute look on her face. "He didn't leave the table until the dinner was finished. After the scene with his wife he remained sitting there and swore that she'd 'come back soon anyhow.' He sat there until about eleven o'clock. Their argument happened at about twenty past eight, I think." Claire swept her hair from her face. "He even had a coffee and a *digéstif* after the dessert." She dictated her words as she might a medical procedure. "He seemed at that moment in time to be completely untroubled, not upset, or even embarrassed, as we surely would have been. We hadn't exchanged a single word with the couple, and nor did we get any idea what the argument was about. I certainly didn't. And nor did my husband."

Claire had said, "My husband."

"Or did you hear something, Georges?"

"No, I didn't catch anything," Dupin said reluctantly.

"As a matter of principle, we don't listen," Claire concluded. It was a sentence which, formulated the way it was, sounded odd. "I mean we aren't the sort of people who eavesdrop on others' conversations."

"Did you see whether Madame Durand took her handbag with

her? Monsieur Durand claimed she did," the female gendarme asked.

Claire answered without hesitation. "Yes, she did. I saw her do so."

"And for the rest of the evening Monsieur Durand didn't leave the table once? Not one single time?"

"No."

"Are you sure?"

"We are."

Dupin was impressed by the certainty with which Claire answered. He would have had to think a bit and even then not been able to answer for sure. But it was bound to be true.

"Completely sure?"

"Completely."

The gendarme took a step back and looked at Claire.

"Very well, Monsieur le Commissaire," she said to Dupin, not Claire, even though he had hardly had the chance to get a word in. "That's it, then. We're done."

Monsieur Bellet had kept surprisingly silent, perhaps out of respect, despite the beach and the swimming shorts, for the official character of a police interrogation. But he could no longer keep his comments to himself.

"I told you, Inès. The commissaire would have noticed if anything . . . unusual had happened in his sight."

"Even a commissaire doesn't have supernatural powers, Rosmin."

The female gendarme turned back to Dupin and Claire and said her farewells. "Thank you very much, Monsieur le Commissaire, madame." And with that she turned away.

"Au revoir, messieurs, madame." These were the first words—spoken

in a hoarse whisper—the young policeman had uttered. Dupin hoped for his sake that he was usually more loquacious.

"I'll be right with you, Inès, just give me a moment," Monsieur Bellet added.

He came over to Dupin and spoke as quietly as he could. "She can be a bit harsh sometimes. But it doesn't mean anything. Inès is a charming person, really."

"Have the two of them already spoken to other guests?"

"Up until now just with my wife, Natalie, the waitresses, and me. But they are going to talk to the other guests too. Inès wanted to see you first."

It sounded as if it was an award.

"Was this the first time the Durands had spent their vacation with you?"

"The first time."

"What about Monsieur Durand? What will he do now? Will he stay here?"

"At least for now, he said. Understandably he's a bit confused at the moment. My wife is certain that Madame will turn up again soon. That she just wanted to get one over on her husband. That's what I think too. She's almost certainly just moved hotels. Maybe not in Trégastel, but somewhere nearby. Inès and Alan will check up with all the hotels and B and B places. Inès has already checked all the hospitals in the region and none have admitted a new patient who fits the description."

"That's how it'll go." Claire intervened, her voice as resolute as ever. "I agree with Madame Bellet. Now we can relax again."

She gave Monsieur Bellet a challenging look.

"And obviously I need to go," Monsieur Bellet said, and turned away.

Claire lay back down on the towel and rummaged in her red-and-white-striped linen bag.

"Just one more thing, Monsieur Bellet," Dupin said. He took a step after him and continued, as softly as he could: "Do you know if Madame Durand went up to her room after the scene? To pick up a few things before she disappeared? She would have had to go through the garden to get to the main entrance, and from there unseen . . ."

"Georges!" Claire stared in their direction, frowning.

"No," Bellet said just as quietly. "Inès and Alan checked that out. They haven't been able to prove anything's missing. Monsieur Durand also checked that during the night. As far as he could say, all their luggage is still there. The room too looked just as it had before they went to dinner. All her lotions in the bathroom were also still there. And she wouldn't go anywhere without her lotions."

Bellet had increased his walking speed. Dupin kept up with him.

"Has the commissaire from Lannion also taken charge of this case?" Dupin tried not to sound too derogatory.

"No, it would appear it's too banal for him. There's no sign of any crime, he said. So he's given it over to the gendarmerie."

"Did he say that, that—?"

"Monsieur Dupin is on vacation." All of a sudden Claire had appeared on the other side of Monsieur Bellet.

"He is not on duty, monsieur. Vacation and nothing else."

She smiled. A smile that made clear she was serious about this.

"But of course, madame."

Monsieur Bellet hadn't seen Claire's comment as an instruction.

"Madame, monsieur. I'll see you this evening at the latest. Monsieur, perhaps before, if he comes to rinse his eyes." He gave Dupin a conspiratorial glance, which Claire noticed, which hardly helped. Then he upped his pace and headed off.

Claire and Dupin turned around.

"This is nothing more than a trivial marriage spat, Georges." The first sentence sounded neutral. The follow-up didn't: "You know the rules for this vacation. Our rules. No work, under any condition. Not even the most rudimentary."

Dupin nearly blurted out that their agreement was strictly limited to Concarneau and the commissariat, including anything that had to do with them. But he knew that was splitting hairs.

"And I am following them to the letter," Dupin said, trying hard not to appear to be trying hard.

They were back at the towel. Claire leaned over Dupin and kissed him.

Obviously Dupin knew that it would be wise right now to spend some time lying on the towel next to Claire. He just wondered how long. And decided that an hour would be a good, if generous, time. Somehow he had by chance got his blue Clairefontaine with him, and began taking notes.

If you thought about them, they were curious incidents. All four of them.

Including that which was the current topic: the disappearance of Madame Durand. For one reason above all: if the Durands were typical of couples who argue all the time, then her disappearance didn't fit the mold. According to Monsieur Durand, nothing of the sort had ever happened before. It was a breach of the basic ritual. On the other hand, it was quite possible that they really had gone too far and the situation was abnormal. It was unfortunate that Dupin had heard nothing of the conversation between the pair. Whatever the case, it was a fact that Durand had sat on the terrace until the end of the evening. Dupin had immediately understood what was behind the policewoman's question. Purely statistically, it wasn't rare in cases where someone disappeared—if there really was a crime—for whoever reported the person missing to be the one responsible.

The incident with the deputy, too, was strange. It was possible that one of the farmers' protests had gotten out of control. Whoever had thrown the stone had simply not seen that the deputy was sitting directly on the other side of the window. Perhaps because the glass was very reflective. Or someone had just taken advantage of the protests. Someone who wasn't a farmer at all. Taken advantage to commit the attack for other, perhaps personal or political, reasons. Quite deliberately. Even though in his little spell of Internet research that morning Dupin had only found good things about Madame Rabier, she could still have enemies.

Dupin had found that his rummaging around in these crumbs of criminality had substantially improved his mood. Not just because they provided distraction, but because they were part of his being, he couldn't help himself.

On to the next incident. The theft of the wooden statue of Saint Anne from the chapel in Trégastel. Approximately one meter long. He had taken a close look at photos he found online. It dated from the seventeenth century. Nonetheless it was unlikely that anyone looking to make quick money would steal a statue like that. You would have to be thinking of someone with "special interests," whatever they might be. For example, this art collector that the owner of the *Tabac-Presse* had mentioned. The possibility that she was a suspect was out of the question. Dupin had casually asked the Bellets about her this morning. Of course they knew her and also knew that she was in New York for two weeks.

Monsieur Bellet also knew—also in response to a "casual" query from Dupin—more details about the theft. The chapel had been locked at 7:00 P.M., as it was every night, by one of the commune employees. She hadn't noticed anything that evening, though she hadn't been inside the chapel. The next morning she had immediately noticed that the statue was missing. Given that there were no traces of a break-in, none that either the gendarmes or the specially requested crime scene team could find, and that there were only three keys, one of each with three people who were above suspicion, the nearest assumption was that it had to have happened the previous day. Sometime during late afternoon. A nurse lit a candle for her sick cousin at a quarter past four, and was—at the moment at least—the last person to have seen the figure. There was no doubt that it was a very strange incident.

Then there was the fourth factor: the break-in at the empty Eiffel House, during which nothing was stolen. Dupin had discovered that it had been locked, but there was no additional security.

Dupin let go of his pencil and closed the notebook.

He plucked his ear. The little moment of euphoria had gone, and he didn't know why.

Perhaps he was exaggerating. Had he begun to fantasize? Just to have something to do? Maybe he was seeing ghosts everywhere.

"Are we going swimming, Georges?"

Claire had gotten to her feet. She seemed already to have forgotten the gendarmes' visit.

"Come on, let's go!"

Dupin had nothing against the idea. Quite the contrary. It would be refreshingly welcome. And a distraction.

Wednesday

The previous evening had been particularly long: Dupin and Claire had been very late to leave the terrace. A dream of an evening. It had gotten cooler by the hour, but stayed mild enough that they were able to sit outside. They had drunk two bottles of a famous rosé from Saint-Tropez. Around half past twelve they had tried a Breton whiskey from Lannion and found it very good. They'd had another on the balcony of their room.

They had talked, laughed, stared out into the night, amazed by the phenomenal starry sky. Stars and above all else spectacular shooting stars. Dozens of them. There had been reports in the media for days now: this year, as every year, the sky was going to "cry." The tail of a comet on its way around the sun crossed the path of the Earth, and over several days myriads of stone showers would burn up in the Earth's atmosphere.

They had breathed in the wonderful fresh air coming in from the sea, and tasting just a little of salt. For a time they just sat there to-gether, happy in the silence. It was three before they got to bed.

Nonetheless Dupin still felt fresh when he woke up next morn-ing at half past eight and quietly left the room a quarter of an hour later. He had first gone into the salon, to the computer, which had an amazingly fast Internet connection, much faster than his cell phone, the tiny screen of which he hated, and then to pass the time before breakfast on the terrace with Breton newspapers that were laid out by the hotel. Dupin had a brief chat with Monsieur Bellet, who was very busy: a major delivery of wine had just arrived, a day early. Monsieur Bellet managed to tell him that the forensic laboratory had also been unable to reconstruct any fingerprints on the stone and that they con-sidered the half-smudged print unusable.

Dupin paid close attention to what there was on the Internet and in the papers about how things stood. Deputy Rabier's health was still unstable: her shoulder wound had become seriously infected and they were having to treat it with high doses of antibiotics. The missing wife was mentioned for the first time in *Ouest-France* and *Le Télégramme*, but only as a brief notice. There was still no mention either of the break-in at the Eiffel House or the disappearance of the Saint Anne statue.

His subsequent—critically short—calls to Nolwenn and Riwal were both in vain. Dupin had tried, very casually he thought, to make the injured deputy into a topic, but both avoided talking about it. The same went for the case of the missing housewife. Dupin had only wanted to know if a nationwide missing persons report had been sent out, but neither Nolwenn nor Riwal wanted to get involved.

Today's installment in the daily "Are You a Breton?" quiz in *Ouest-France* was:

You know you're a Breton if you turn up late and used one of the
        following excuses:
I came on the tractor.
I was attacked by seagulls.
I injured both hands on a sardine can.
My favorite pig died.

Simple but precise.

Claire came down just before ten and after breakfast together they went straight from the terrace to the beach.

Dupin had headed off to the newspaper store. After the brisk morning business and before the lunchtime rush it was very quiet. The air smelled of freshly printed paper.

Dupin greeted Madame Riou with a nod. He had known the *Tabac-Presse* owner's name since yesterday. Élodie Riou. Short, curly brown hair, a compact figure with a pretty, very relaxed face. She could go from being friendly to forceful from one moment to the next.

Madame Riou seemed clearly pleased to see him, and rushed over to him.

"It just dawned on me last night. You're that famous Parisian commissaire from Concarneau," she said.

"Georges Dupin. Yes. I'm here on vacation."

"I saw you on the television last year. That story about the vanished cross."

She had put it relatively neutrally.

"As you're here, will you be helping out in the attempted murder of Viviane Rabier? You're an expert on murders."

"Absolutely not, Madame Riou. Like I said, I'm on vacation.

Nothing more than vacation. It's wonderful." He sounded like Claire. "In any case, there is no evidence to point toward a deliberate attack."

"You're really going to leave the case to this lame Desespringalle? A commissaire from Lannion?"

It seemed the commissaire from Lannion wasn't exactly loved around here.

"Yes indeed, Madame Riou. Absolutely. It is his business and his alone. I have nothing in the slightest to do with it. And purely formally nothing at all. I would get into serious trouble if I were to investigate here." It was true, and he wasn't just thinking of the prefect. "The case will be in good hands with him, I've no doubt." Dupin noticed that he was rhetorically exaggerating a little.

"This stone throwing"—Madame Riou shook her head in disgust—"had nothing to do with the farmers' protests. I'd put money on it. Somebody has a score to settle with the deputy."

Dupin had begun to go along the shelves working down the list Claire had given him. Riou stuck by his side.

"What makes you say that?"

It had been a reflex to ask. Nonetheless it was compatible with his own, purely speculative, thoughts.

"Her decisive way of doing business in recent years hasn't just made her friends, even though she's been absolutely right in all she's done."

"Are you thinking of anyone in particular?"

"Oh, yes. Jérôme Chastagner. A real rogue." Madame Rabier didn't exactly hold back in her judgments. "Stinking rich. He inherited a quarry, the Carrière Rose. But he doesn't lift a finger. Leaves all the work to his clever business manager. On top of that he runs a large factory for making agricultural machinery. Very specialized. Exports them all around the world. Just like the granite. A confirmed bachelor and womanizer."

Madame Riou had the amusing habit of throwing clipped sentences together one after the other.

"Always a new woman. None of them more than a couple of weeks. He lives here in Trégastel. In that fairy-tale castle on the island between Trégastel and Ploumanac'h. You must have seen it already, one of our major attractions. Chastagner wanted to buy the old post office in Trégastel. Just a few months ago. To turn it into an ultramodern headquarters for his two companies. So that he wouldn't have to drive so far!" Madame Riou was getting ever more angry. "Just for that. And Viviane Rabier was against it. Fought for the mayor and the council to get involved. An excellent mayor. Things got tough, I can tell you that."

"I understand."

Mechanically, Dupin pulled his blue Clairefontaine out of the back pocket of his jeans. There was a mixture of amazement and delight on Madame Riou's face.

"Just notes, not an investigation, right?" she said.

"Monsieur Chastagner, got it." Dupin made a note of the name.

"Jérôme Chastagner, precisely. Normally he spends Monday until late Thursday evening in Saint-Brieuc. He comes in here around ten o'clock on Saturday mornings. Regularly. You can wait to see him here. He buys magazines. About cars, fishing, computers, property, swimming pools, but first and foremost, boats."

"I won't be waiting for Monsieur Chastagner."

Dupin put his notebook away and turned to the register. He had everything he needed.

"Fine. Now, to the vanished blondie. How are your investigations on that one?"

Dupin was about to protest, but didn't.

"This Durand is a property shark from Paris." Madame Riou

seemed to know everything. "He's made a lot of money in recent years. They own a smart apartment in the fifteenth arrondissement and drive a big Mercedes. This is their first time here. His wife is rather ordinary, a naïve little girl, not yet thirty-five. He's twenty years older."

Dupin had by chance run into Monsieur Durand in the hotel lobby. Dupin had given him a friendly hello. A tall man with a large head, bald, striking cheekbones, in blue cotton trousers and a lilac Lacoste polo shirt. He seemed absorbed, deeply worried. Dupin had tried to start a friendly conversation. "We're terribly sorry about what's happened, monsieur," he said, but Durand had just mumbled, "Yes, yes," and moved on. Understandable. But as difficult as the situation had to be for him, and as sorry as Dupin might be for his situation, he still came across as unlikable.

"And where do you get all this information, Madame Riou?"

"From Raphaël, our hairdresser. Madame was there twice in the days before she disappeared."

Perfect. Another reason to go to the hairdresser's. Hairdressers were natural communicators, psychologists, therapists, confessors, all in one.

"What else did the hairdresser say?"

He had his notebook in his hand again, standing next to the till, with Élodie Riou behind it, scanning the magazines as she spoke.

"She had repeatedly cursed her husband like a fury, saying he was a 'dreadful idiot' sometimes. An 'unbelievable egoist.'"

"She said that? 'Sometimes'?"

"I—"

Madame Riou was interrupted by the sound of Dupin's phone.

"Excuse me." Dupin had seen the number; he had to answer. Without waiting for a reaction he walked out the door only to come back within less than a minute with a smile on his lips.

Madame Riou had packed his newspapers into a bright red bag. Next to it lay his change.

"We were at the 'sometimes' point," he said, returning to their conversation.

"All I can tell you is what Raphaël said. They had apparently had a big fight the morning before her second visit to the hairdresser's."

Everything that Dupin had heard fitted the pattern of a couple for whom major arguments were part of their relationship. And not necessarily fights about the state of that relationship. It was their means of being unhappy together—but nonetheless together—and who knows: maybe in a perverse way they were happy like that.

"Did Madame Durand say anything about a particular incident or event? Something that made it a particularly serious argument?"

"Not that I know. But go and see Raphaël for yourself. I'm sure he has an appointment open."

"I actually do need to go to the hairdresser's."

Élodie looked skeptically at Dupin's short hair. "As you will, Monsieur le Commissaire. As you will." She shrugged her shoulders indifferently.

"Unfortunately I can't tell you anything more about the break-in at the Eiffel House. I've heard nothing more about it. Maybe it really was just a couple of stupid kids. I really think you should be working with the gendarmerie, it would certainly help them. And speed up your investigations."

"Conversations, Madame Riou. I'm just having a few conversations." It was a very clumsy comment, Dupin knew that. "It is in no way an investigation. Pure curiosity. Just a professional habit. The curse of the job."

"I understand." Her tone of voice made clear she didn't believe a single word he said.

"Well then, Madame Riou. Have a nice day." Dupin tried to sound as much in vacation mood as possible. "See you tomorrow."

He turned toward the door, his bag held tight under his arm.

"See you tomorrow, Monsieur le Commissaire, see you tomorrow." Madame Riou was speaking overly loud, Dupin thought. Two elderly ladies standing by a rack of greeting cards turned their eyes nosily toward him when they heard the word "commissaire."

"Oh, one more thing." Madame Riou left the counter and came over to him.

"I don't know why I didn't think of it earlier," she said, finally dropping her voice. "There's one of the farmers who under the circumstances might be particularly suspicious."

Dupin made a dismissive gesture but Madame Riou continued nevertheless: "Madame Guichard. Maïwenn Guichard, she grows vegetables. All organic. She also breeds a few pigs, Breton woolly pigs. And chickens. Coucou de Rennes, the perfect chicken for a Sunday meal, juicy and tender, with a slightly nutty flavor." She beamed at the thought. "She has an issue with the deputy, a personal thing." Madame Riou was whispering now. "Allegedly Madame Rabier had an affair with Maïwenn's husband. Last year, although Maïwenn herself is a highly attractive woman!" She faltered. "Strictly speaking they are all just rumors. But there are a lot of them. If you're looking for information from Raphaël, ask him about that too."

"I shall definitely not be doing that, Madame Riou."

"And there's another suspicious connection." She took a deep breath. "Madame Guichard also knows the mysterious art collector I told you about. Madame Guichard sold her the house she's living in. At one of the seven approaches to Traouïéro Valley. Maïwenn lives just a few hundred meters away."

A connection that sounded absolutely random, but one that Madame Riou had loaded with dark significance.

"The art collector has been in New York for more than a week. She can't have had anything to do with the disappearance of the statue."

"She might have had helpers. Do you know the valley?"

Dupin shook his head.

"It's a magical valley. Particularly crazy granite rocks. Like on the Île Renote. A thick, dark forest. Meter-high ferns. Things aren't quite right there. A whispering stream runs through it. The valley even has its own microclimate. It's always warm, always damp. There are elves, fairies, and gnomes, once upon a time even smugglers, pirates, and bandits. That's where she lives. Are you going to interrogate her too?"

"No. Definitely not. Like I said, there is no question of her being the culprit. And even if there were, what connection do you see?"

He really shouldn't have asked.

"Well, the art collector is a suspect for the Saint Anne theft, and Maïwenn Guichard a suspect for the attack on the deputy. And one of them sold a house to the other. That can't be coincidence. And that's what your investigation is about: revealing hidden connections." She didn't let the helpless expression on Dupin's face bother her. "Even if at first glance it does seem unclear and puzzling."

It was on the tip of Dupin's tongue to say that using her method and speculation would open the doors for even the most far-fetched ideas. There was a sea of unlimited possibilities to drown in.

"Thank you, Madame Riou. I really have to go now. My wife—"

"Yes, a bit of a break is necessary too. That will certainly do you good. You already look relaxed. The lady farmer comes in here every morning around half past eight to buy her newspapers."

With that Élodie Riou moved back to the register, where the two elderly ladies were standing, each with a card in her hand.

Dupin left the newspaper store quickly.

It had been a longer visit than intended, but informative and somewhat strange.

He had to hurry now to drop in at Rachid's. Claire had decided to have *pains bagnats* again today, and he would drink a *petit café* while he was there. In addition to the rosé, he would pick up a big bottle of water and two Breizh colas.

And book the appointment with the hairdresser for tomorrow morning. Half an hour later, Dupin was back at the lilac-colored towel. He had just popped into the chapel and made a few notes. He had seen the spot where the statue must have stood, but didn't notice anything unusual.

There were beads of sweat on his forehead by the time he got to Claire. There wasn't a breath of air.

"You took your time." Claire was lying on her back, engrossed in her book. She only glanced up briefly at Dupin.

He knelt down on the towel and opened up the bright red paper bag. "Voilà."

Philosophie, Beaux Arts, Journal de la Science, Saveur—one of Claire's favorite culinary magazines—*Côté Ouest*. Claire's choices, an eclectic selection. On top of that the obligatory *Le Monde* and *L'Observateur*.

"And *pains bagnats*." He set the chiller bag on the towel. "On top of that, wine, water, and cola. All cold."

"Wonderful." She beamed at him. "Have you finally found a book for yourself? Did it take that long because you read each and every one to check them out thoroughly?" Claire grinned.

"Yes, I found one."

"And?"

"A Sherlock Holmes case, *The Sign of Four.*"

"So where is it?"

"I'll buy it tomorrow." He only hoped Élodie Riou had the book. "But I got all the magazines you wanted," he said, and nodded at the pile. "And made the appointment with the hairdresser. I had a hard time getting a connection."

"There's excellent reception from here on the beach."

"I always forget that."

"Georges." Claire paused for effect and looked Dupin directly in the eye. "No secretive investigations?"

"What is there for me to investigate?"

He thought he sounded convincing. It was important for a policeman to sound in charge, especially if things were on edge.

"Exactly. There's nothing to investigate."

As calm as could be, Claire turned to lie on her front.

* * *

Dupin made himself comfortable on one of the brightly colored loungers in the middle of the green oasis.

From now on he was going to begin the evening with a pre-apéritif in L'Île Rose's garden, before the main apéritif with Claire, who in the meantime would be getting ready for the evening meal. He had three-quarters of an hour all to himself.

He had barely sat down for a minute when his cell phone rang. A number he didn't know.

"Yes? Hello?"

"Commissaire Desespringalle, Commissariat de Police de Lannion."

"Good evening."

"I believe you've undertaken certain investigations. In two grotesque cases, which aren't actually two cases, but one, and one which *I* am handling. The escalation of violent protest against Deputy Viviane Rabier. I don't have to remind you that this is my district. My personal responsibility. You are in a separate *département* and another prefecture. Apart from all that, you are not on duty!"

The commissaire from Lannion spoke in a tone that was sharp and cutting, sarcastic but not quite furious.

"In no way have I begun any investigation, Monsieur . . . my dear colleague." Despite Dupin's advanced "Bretonization," this sort of local name always turned into a disaster for him. "There must be a misunderstanding."

"No misunderstanding," snapped Desespringalle. "I have every confidence in my sources."

"Sources?"

What could he mean? Dupin wrote off the Bellets, and Madame Riou as well. She had quite unmistakably made clear what she thought of the commissaire. But of course she hadn't been the only one in the newspaper store when they were talking. There had been a number of people. He had perhaps simply not been careful enough.

"It has also come to my attention that you intend to carry out another interrogation early tomorrow morning."

"You mean my appointment with the hairdresser? A haircut, nothing more. Of course, unless you have some police objections."

One of the friendly waitresses had arrived with the Americano Dupin had ordered: red vermouth, Campari, and gin, much loved in Brittany. Dupin covered the microphone with his hand.

"Many thanks, and a few chips, please." *Brets,* Breton chips, made with Breton potatoes, with salt from Guérande.

"Hallo, are you still there, Dupin?"

"Of course."

"You're making yourself guilty of several transgressions"—again there was that low-level irritation in Desespringalle's voice—"that could get you into enormous trouble."

Dupin gave a deep and audible sigh. "I'm on vacation, monsieur, nothing more. And everybody in this country is free to talk to whomever they like. About whatever they like whenever they like." Dupin wasn't going to let this puffed-up character corner him.

The chips arrived.

"I have—" Desespringalle was interrupted by the quite audible sound of Dupin munching. "I have my eye on you, Dupin. I'm watching every step: what you're doing, what you're saying. And if you mention a subject relating to my investigations even once in a conversation, then I will immediately contact the supervisory authority and my prefecture."

That could be a problem. Dupin had been subject to a series of supervisory complaints over the last seven years. To the extreme anger of the insufferable supervisory chief, Dupin had only got off lightly because most of these complaints had been related to cases which in the end he had famously solved.

"And they will immediately pass the matter on to your prefecture."

And that could promise to be awkward.

Locmariaquer had not been at all happy about Dupin's vacation plans—despite it being agreed weeks before. Given the "extreme circumstances in the whole of Finistère"; particularly now that he, the chief of chiefs for security and public order, was "seriously injured," everyone else "should work overtime for once."

Dupin pressed his ear to his phone. The commissaire from Lannion had hung up.

Dupin lifted his Americano and leaned back.

A completely ridiculous call. Even if it might be wise to consider just how and whether he should continue his "private investigations."

Dupin took a very large sip.

He would order another apéritif. As he was looking around for the waitress, his phone rang again.

A hidden number. "Just a moment," he said into the phone, turning with a smile to the young woman. "One more please," he said, nodding at his empty glass.

"I'm listening," he said roughly.

"*Bonsoir*, Monsieur le Commissaire," said a woman's soft voice. "This is Viviane Rabier."

Dupin sat up straight: the injured deputy.

"Excuse me for disturbing you." The woman's voice betrayed the effort she was making to speak.

"I'm having my apéritif, madame." Dupin was still puzzled.

"I need your advice."

"My advice?"

"This afternoon I received an anonymous letter at the hospital." She was speaking more slowly now. "A threat. This stone-throwing wasn't an accident, Monsieur Dupin." Her voice was shaking.

"A threat?" Dupin had to watch out that he didn't speak too loudly. "What did it say exactly?"

"I'll read it to you. '*Deputy Rabier, be careful. I know everything. Don't get involved. And don't go to the police.*'"

It was clear, but at the same time completely vague.

"The letter wasn't handwritten, I assume."

"No."

"Did it come in the mail?"

"It was put into a general mailbox at the main entrance to the hospital."

"What does this threat relate to? What are you supposed to not get involved in?"

"I have no idea."

"Do you have any idea who might have sent it?"

She hesitated. "My job involves conflicts. But I honestly don't think any of those who oppose me would be capable of this."

"Do you have enemies, madame? Real enemies?"

"That's a big word."

There was a pause.

Dupin had to be careful. And sensible.

"Why did you call *me*?"

"I don't know what to do. I'm afraid to go to the police officially. My sister lives in Concarneau. She's told me only good things about you."

"And where did you get my telephone number?"

"Your prefecture. I have my sources."

"Madame Rabier, it is simply impossible for me to undertake an investigation in your case, or to get involved in any way. I am on vacation."

It was going to be the phrase he would say most often in these fourteen days.

"I know, but what do you think I should do?"

"In your place, despite the threat, I would go to the police. Right now."

"Do you think?"

"Definitely. The police know how to deal with situations like this."

"Really?" She sounded skeptical. "Won't the police just immediately start investigations that the anonymous sender will sooner or later find out about?"

"They will act inconspicuously. Nobody will find out anything."

She was silent.

"I assure you."

Dupin hoped he was right. Even the police made mistakes. It all depended on the commissaire.

"If you say so. I'll take your advice." She didn't seem totally convinced.

"That way you're doing the right thing. Just one question, Madame Rabier. Who are these other parties you refer to? Who is it you're in dispute with?"

"I've been thinking about it. I'll tell you who occurred to me: a deputy of the other main party. Hugues Ellec. He's also in the Breton regional parliament. We've been fighting each other for ages now."

Telling the story was obviously sapping her strength. She kept pausing. "Particularly right now, because of a few impending important decisions. An unscrupulous man, one Jérôme Chastagner." Dupin pricked up his ears. Chastagner, the owner of the quarry and machinery builder the newspaper store owner had told him about. "He owns the biggest quarry in the region. He's expanding it illegally, and hoping to get permission retroactively. My office has just started to document the whole business . . . then—" She broke off. "No, that's it."

"You were about to name someone else."

"No, no."

Dupin didn't believe her, but it was hardly fitting to press her.

"Thank you very much, Monsieur Dupin. Visitors have just arrived."

"I understand. Just one thing, madame. You mustn't mention this conversation to anyone."

"I would ask the same of you."

"Above all not the commissaire from Lannion."

It sounded strange, but that was the way it was.

"Perhaps I might call you again sometime, if that's all right."

"Of course."

"*Au revoir*, Monsieur Dupin."

She hung up before Dupin could say the same or wish her "get well soon."

He leaned back and picked up his second Americano, which the waitress had discreetly set on the little table beside him. Once again he took a large sip, and ran his other hand through his hair.

"I was as quick as I could be."

Dupin started. Claire had appeared as if from nowhere and made herself comfortable on the lounger. "The apéritif in the garden is a great idea. I've ordered myself a Kir Breton."

Her hair was still wet from the shower.

Dupin tried to give the impression of being relaxed, and not let it show that he had just had two interesting phone calls.

Claire settled back comfortably. "Wonderful, what a fabulous place. We'll have to come here again, Georges."

Before Dupin could reply, the waitress brought the Kir Breton: cider with cassis.

"The courier was just here, Madame Lannoy. It's on the way."

"Thank you."

Claire lifted her glass, ignoring Dupin's querying look.

"*Yec'hed mat*, Georges. Here's to an undisturbed vacation!"

"*Yec'hed mat.*" Dupin raised his glass automatically. The ice cubes clinked against one another.

This was a *real* case. He wasn't imagining it.

* * *

Twenty minutes later they were sitting at their table on the terrace.

There was still a high summer sun, flooding the pink world with light. Everything seemed over-illuminated. The blue of the sky and that of the sea were like a wholly flat surface, not bright blue but almost white, and had merged with each other. It was only by following the pale line of the horizon that you could see the nuance that separated them. Even the pink had a white tinge. There were evenings like this when the sun almost wiped out the colors rather than exaggerating them or lighting them up. The larger bits of quartz in the granite giants shimmered like ethereal sources of light.

Dupin's thoughts revolved around his chat with Madame Rabier.

Why had the threatening letter arrived just today? Maybe because the sender wanted to make sure that the deputy would be up to reading it herself. There were a lot of open questions.

Dupin noticed that he was feeling unwarrantedly exhilarated. There was at least one case here, and that really gave him something to do. On the other hand, the situation was a lot more complicated. Suddenly things were serious. Wasn't he now at least slightly personally obliged to the deputy? Because she had, to an extent, taken him into her confidence, and he had given her a decisive piece of advice, that she should, despite her own doubts, "officially" go to the police? That meant he had a certain responsibility. Which meant he had to speed up the tempo and urgency of his investigations.

Dupin forced himself back to the here and now.

It was unbelievable how relaxed and wound down Claire seemed already. A few strands of her hair had been turned light blond by the sun, her face, arms, and shoulders browned; she was wearing a black linen dress.

They had ordered the obligatory white wine, a fresh Saumur today. The menu promised to be fabulous. Yet again the *cocos de Paimpol,* this time with oysters gratin, quiche with caramelized Roscoff onions and lilac artichokes, a main course of lobster à l'Armoricaine. And to finish, a strawberry sorbet made from the sweet aromatic *fraises de Plougastel,* a tiny village famed for having "the best strawberries in the world." And Dupin totally agreed.

This was looking like a good evening for Dupin's little project. What could go wrong? The last matters had been cleared up in two phone calls in a row.

Then he remembered what it was he had intended to ask Claire in the garden.

"What was the courier for?"

"There was something I absolutely had to send Lydia."

One of her friends she had met swimming at Beg-Meil.

"Apparently something urgent?"

"She needed a prescription. Her doctor is on vacation."

It had been a very large envelope for a prescription.

Claire took another sip, then beamed at him. "I just can't have enough days on the beach. But maybe it is time we took a few excursions. What do you think, Georges?"

He ought not to sound too euphoric, but try to direct the discussion in the right direction.

"Why not? I'd love to. We ought to take a look at this enchanting valley everybody raves about. That would be a nice excursion. From the entrance to the valley to the sea, strolling along the wild, romantic path."

"Or to the Roi Gradlon. There's an exquisite view there over the whole district and we would be directly next to the aquarium. Then end up crossing the Île Renote to the fairy-tale castle. Tomorrow afternoon?"

Just the afternoon. All the same, a much shorter day on the beach.

"The Eiffel House is nearby too."

Following the phone call from the deputy, the investigation priorities were now quite different, but Dupin would be well advised not to let the seemingly irrelevant incidents out of sight. And you never knew, there might be connections.

"We won't get that far tomorrow. But we really must get to Ploumanac'h. For the restaurant."

Claire downed her last drop of the Saumur, with obvious pleasure.

"Claire," Dupin said. This was the right moment. "I wanted to discuss something with you." A much too prosaic introduction. Maybe he should have thought about this a while; it was, after all, a huge decision. "I wanted to say something to you, to ask you something." That was a bit better.

"Monsieur Dupin." Monsieur Bellet had popped up on Dupin's right, clearly distraught. He gasped for breath and tried to conjure up a halfway understandable sentence. "You have to come with me. Immediately." Despite his state of excitement, Bellet managed to keep his voice low.

"What's happened?" Dupin got quickly to his feet. Claire did the same.

"Come!"

Bellet disappeared into the house, with Claire and Dupin on his heels, and hurried with quick steps to the reception, closing the door behind them.

"They've found a body." Bellet's voice shook. "A dead woman. In the quarry. The Carrière Rose. The biggest of the three still working. Where the other body was found seven years ago—the pink corpse." He'd gone pale as chalk. "Back then they—"

"Who is it?" Dupin interrupted.

"The body," Bellet stammered, "is in a pretty . . . ugly state. The drop-off is fifty meters there." He stared rigidly ahead. "Just like seven years ago."

"Could it be Madame Durand?" Claire's calm but direct question was the most urgent in the room.

"The police from Lannion have taken Monsieur Durand with them to possibly identify the body. They're on their way. It's only a stone's throw. They warned him that it would be a terrible sight. But he insisted. Inès and Alan are on their way too."

"When did it happen?" Dupin would more than anything have loved to go with them.

"They don't know yet. Quarry workers came across the body by chance, in an area not being worked at the moment. She might have been lying there a while. On first glance it didn't look like it had just happened."

"Madame Durand disappeared on Monday evening. The timing would fit." Claire was speaking matter-of-factly, quite the experienced doctor.

"A gendarme from Perros-Guirec who's already at the scene thinks he recognized her as Madame Durand. He had seen the police missing-persons photo," Bellet said.

"Wouldn't it be a curious coincidence? If it wasn't her, I mean?" Claire asked.

"Did they say anything about the cause of death?" Dupin broke back into the conversation.

Monsieur Bellet raised his eyebrows questioningly. "She fell fifty meters."

"She might already have been dead before the fall."

It was clear from the expression on Bellet's face that he hadn't thought of that. "They didn't say anything about that. The pathologist has just arrived."

For a time nobody spoke.

"What a mess," Dupin muttered. He went to the window of the little room. Monsieur Bellet's eyes followed him.

It couldn't be true. A horrific turn of events. Now, it seemed, there were two cases. Two serious cases. Dupin's thoughts were racing. If it really was Madame Durand, they were probably dealing with murder. An accident seemed unlikely. And there was nothing so far to suggest suicide.

"Is it the quarry that this machinery constructor inherited?"

"Chastagner," Bellet said, and nodded. "Yes."

Chastagner yet again. Dupin pulled out his phone, and immediately dialed Nolwenn's number.

"What are you doing?"

Dupin hadn't noticed Claire come up next to him. She was giving him a penetrating stare.

"I thought I . . ." He canceled the call. "It was just reflex."

"It's not your case, Georges." Claire wasn't speaking particularly strictly, more understandingly. "Even if it is Madame Durand, it's not your case."

She was right.

"You have nothing, but nothing to do with this. However dramatic it all might be."

Dupin turned to Monsieur Bellet. "Is the commissaire from Lannion already there?"

"By now, definitely."

"There you are, Georges, they're onto it. The case is in good hands." She gave him a searching look again. "And we're going to continue our meal," she added determinedly. She went to the door and pulled it open forcefully.

Bellet used the opportunity to come close to Dupin.

He whispered so quietly that Dupin could hardly hear him. "You should continue to investigate. I mean, properly. And not leave the business to Lannion, or such an average character as Desespringalle. We're counting on our gendarmes here in Trégastel. And on you. Nolwenn said you're the best, and you're playing on our team!" There was something desperate in his voice.

Of course, Dupin should have thought of it: Trégastel versus Lannion. It was the Breton local identity thing. Neighboring villages felt themselves farther away from each other than places really were. The real strangers were their closest neighbors. On top of that, and Bellet didn't try to conceal it, came the lust for sensationalism, to experience a criminal case close up.

Claire was standing in the doorway frowning. Dupin got away from Bellet.

A minute later they were back at their table again.

The mood on the terrace was convivial. Nobody seemed to have noticed their abrupt disappearance. Only the dreadful parents with the nice children turned around and whispered to one another.

"You attract crimes like moths to a flame, Georges," Claire said as she was dealing with the last oyster gratin. "Wherever you turn up, something happens."

At that moment it was hard to deny.

"What was it you wanted to say to me before we were interrupted?"

"I'll tell you another time."

Claire didn't insist.

"Poor Monsieur Durand. This must be awful for him." Claire was as preoccupied as Dupin by the terrible turn of events. It was easy to see her emotions.

"Two days ago she was sitting here on the terrace enjoying her meal." She let her gaze sweep out to sea. "I'm no longer very tempted by an excursion to the quarry."

Claire could make statements like that without sounding macabre. Dupin had been silenced.

He was still trying to connect the events. Even though it was a waste of time. He knew too little. What was essentially bothering him was: Were the two crimes independent of each other? It would be a crazy coincidence. But that meant nothing. Thanks to his job, Dupin had an intimate relationship with chance. The totally unpredictable lay at the heart of his existence, in every way. There was no rule, no method to be guided by. At best a sort of intuition.

"We should—" His phone interrupted him.

He checked the number.

"Nolwenn. I'll take it briefly." With that he stood up and disappeared.

Claire seemed at the moment too absorbed to say anything to the contrary.

Dupin walked to the steps leading down to the garden. "Yes?"

"I've just heard about the body found in the quarry. Even if it does turn out to be Madame Durand, you are not to investigate this case, Monsieur le Commissaire. I've once again given out serious instructions here, and neither Riwal nor Kadeg will tell you anything. You'd be in hot water, you know that."

"I know."

"That's all good, then." And with that she hung up.

Dupin was standing on the bottom step. He turned around and a second later was back at the table with Claire.

"Everything okay?"

"Everything okay."

Unusually, Claire asked no more.

How could Nolwenn have known so quickly? At this time of the day? She surely couldn't still be in the commissariat.

"This onion quiche, you really must try—"

"Monsieur le Commissaire." It was Bellet again, once more standing to the right of the table, and once more he was extremely agitated. "I need you again."

Dupin and Claire tried to make their getting up from the table more discreet this time. They followed Monsieur Bellet, who had hurried on ahead of them.

"The hairdresser called, Raphaël Julien." Bellet was building up his emotions for the next revelation. "It's not her. *It's not Madame Durand*. Definitely not. Monsieur Durand said so categorically."

Just as last time, they had gone into the reception, but Bellet only went as far as the doorway before he came out with the news.

"They're getting two of Madame Durand's dental x-rays sent from Paris, but only for form's sake. Isn't that wonderful?"

This latest news had every bit as much effect as the previous.

"Yes, that's wonderful." Claire's expression showed she was hugely relieved.

"Wonderful" wasn't exactly the word that would have struck Dupin. There was still a dead woman who had undergone a terrible fate. Dupin was pleased, too, he had to admit. Nonetheless the confusion was now even greater than it had been.

"So who is it?"

"They don't know that yet, Raphaël said. They estimate her to be in her mid- to late thirties. One meter seventy. Long dark hair, even though it's hard to tell because of the blood. Madame Durand is very blond." Bellet sounded happy to have this additional proof. "Her face is relatively unmarked. Armani jeans, a Ralph Lauren T-shirt, both fairly inconspicuous."

Dupin hadn't much of an idea what "inconspicuous" meant in these circumstances.

"No purse, identity card, or cell phone, I assume."

"Correct."

For some reason Claire let him carry on with his investigative questions, probably because she was asking herself the same questions and was curious.

"Nothing to identify her?"

"No, but the pathologist's first statement is that she had not been dead for just a few hours. He reckoned at least a day. Or two. But not any longer."

"Do they know anything about cause of death?"

"No, and the pathologist says that could take a while."

"They'll be taking the body to the laboratory," Dupin said absently. It felt strange. He was so near and yet so far. He knew every step, every sequence of events in the police process that could now be going on—it was all being acted out almost in front of his nose—but he had no part in it.

"A real crime case." There was an unconcealed smile of happiness playing on Bellet's lips. "We haven't had anything like that here for ages."

It was as if he were welcoming a new tourist attraction.

"Will Monsieur Durand come straight back to the hotel?"

"I assume so."

"I'd like to have a word with him. We did sit practically at the next table, after all."

Claire took a long look at Dupin. She seemed about to intervene, but then in the end decided otherwise.

"A bit of human contact will do him good," she said.

Bellet glanced automatically toward the window. "Like I said, it's only a couple of minutes' drive to the quarry."

He went over to the desk and sat down at his computer. He gave the impression of being almost elated; all that was missing was for him to start whistling. When he noticed Dupin's look, Bellet hastened to say: "I'm so relieved that it's not Madame Durand. Can you imagine what that would have meant for our hotel?" Dupin understood him. More or less. "I'll have a look if there's anything on the Internet about the incident in the quarry. We should maybe inform our guests. If only to preempt any possible concern."

"It's really turned out rather well." Claire had positioned herself next to Bellet and was looking at the screen.

Dupin had to butt in: "Madame Durand is still missing. For two days. As if swallowed up by the earth. And another woman has found things not turning out at all well."

It seemed as if neither Claire nor Monsieur Bellet had heard him.

"Nothing," Bellet said, with some disappointment. "But," and he seemed to cheer up a bit, "that's probably just because we have exclusive information."

"Our onion quiche is still sitting on the table, Georges. Let's sit down and finish our meal. Monsieur Bellet will let us know if there should be any more important information."

Dupin turned around.

"There, they are coming now." Monsieur Bellet had sprung to his feet and was pointing out the window that overlooked part of the parking lot.

They could see the front half of a police car. Shortly after, they could hear doors opening, then slamming shut.

"It will be best if we meet Monsieur Durand by the door."

Claire and Dupin nodded in agreement and followed Bellet.

They had just reached the entrance door when it was flung open. Monsieur Durand stormed into the hallway.

Dupin hadn't noticed what penetrating brown eyes Monsieur Durand had, a piercing look that made him seem strong despite the deep rings around his eyes.

"We wanted to tell you personally, Monsieur Durand, how relieved we are. It must have been hard for you." As always, it was Claire who found the right words.

Monsieur Durand was standing unsteadily.

"I'm sorry, we've taken you by surprise," Claire said.

"Thank you," Durand said, looking at Claire, Bellet, and Dupin in turn. "For your sympathy. It's very kind of you. Excuse me if I'm not in the mood for conversation. I have to get my thoughts in order."

Claire, Bellet, and Dupin stood aside. Monsieur Durand walked past them toward the stairs. Despite his situation, Dupin didn't find him any friendlier.

"We understand that absolutely, monsieur. But perhaps it might do you good to talk a little," Claire said. Dupin knew this tone of voice. It was part of her renowned ability to be persevering without being offensive.

Durand turned around and smiled politely. "As I said, that is very kind of you, but right now I need rest."

"Will you continue to wait for your wife here in Trégastel?" Dupin had tried to make the question as friendly as possible.

Durand sighed. "For the moment, yes, I think so." He turned around and reached the staircase in a moment.

"Monsieur Durand, I'm a doctor, and you can turn to me at any time if need be," Claire offered.

"Many thanks," Durand said without turning.

Bellet, Claire, and Dupin went through the restaurant, toward the terrace.

"In situations like this, everyone reacts differently." Claire's voice was filled with empathy. After a short pause, she added in an almost jovial tone: "And Georges, the most important thing is that you have nothing to do with either the body in the quarry or the disappearance of Madame Durand."

Thursday

T he only appointment the Salon Raphaël could offer with Raphaël Julien himself was at nine in the morning. Dupin was the first customer of the day.

Dupin had slept little, even though they had been in bed by midnight, earlier than any other evening on the vacation. Claire had fallen asleep right away. Dupin had too many thoughts going through his head to be able to rest. He had gotten up again at a quarter to two and sat on the balcony for a while.

Despite how little sleep he had had, Dupin felt wide awake and rested the next morning. In top form and ready for action, both physically and mentally. It was still too early for a *café* in the hotel at 6:30 A.M., so he had gone directly into the village, found a place at one of the upright tables in a very good *boulangerie* just obliquely across from the chapel and the *Tabac-Presse*, and had his first two *cafés* there. He'd pulled out his blue Clairefontaine, made notes of the events of the previous evening as systematically as possible, and the most important thing: a plan of action going forward. His current list linked the deputy with the machinery manufacturer, the lady farmer, and the deputy from the other party. The case of Madame Durand's disappearance remained unchanged. The horrific turn of events with the dead woman in the quarry—almost certainly a murder—appeared at first glance to have no relation to the stone-throwing attack, the threatening letter, or any other incident. Only the place where the body was found had a connection—possibly—and that primarily to an unsolved incident seven years ago that might have been an accident. The only thing that was clear was that it was Chastagner's quarry.

What disturbed Dupin's good mood was that he couldn't be in the hairdresser's and the newspaper store at the same time. He would probably only get the chance to meet the lady farmer early in the morning, Chastagner whenever he wanted, on Saturday at least; unfortunately he couldn't just get the two of them somewhere at the same time. But as he couldn't carry out any proper investigative conversations with them he would have to get his information about them however he could.

From the *boulangerie* Dupin walked past a couple of houses to the Office de Tourisme, which opened at 7:30 A.M. Dupin picked up a tourist map of the village and the surrounding district: Trégastel, Ploumanac'h, Perros-Guirec. Everything was clearly marked on the map: the castle, the valley and the quarries, the Eiffel House, the chapel and the church of Saint Anne, and obviously the famous pink stone formations. Dupin would make a note of everything that was relevant. Including the homes of people who might be involved in the events.

Then he strolled back leisurely, still—there was no other way to put it—in the best of moods.

It was a beautiful morning, the air still fresh and clear. There were just a few locals out and about. On the way back, Dupin took a longer look at the House of Deputies.

It was eight now, and Dupin was sitting on the terrace at L'Île Rose.

None of the other guests were out yet, even though breakfast was to be had from eight every morning. Madame Bellet and Natalie took care of it lovingly. Excellent croissants, exceptionally good baguettes—crisp on the outside, soft inside—breakfast cake, a bit like the *quatre-quarts* in the Amiral, a creamy *miel toutes fleurs,* homemade jellies: blackberry, mirabelle, and golden quince. In addition there were Dupin's favorite cheeses, all from the north, just a few kilometers from here: Darley; a mild Val-Doré; the Grand-Nadeuc, with its flowery aroma; and the Tomme-du-Vaumadeuc. Paradise.

Natalie had brought him a perfectly mixed café au lait.

He was sitting at "his" seat, with his back to the house wall. Claire would still be asleep. He looked out at the wild garden and the rocks still showing pale pink in the morning sun, at the sea, majestic and calm, without the slightest movement on its silver surface.

"Still no news about the identity of the corpse, Monsieur le Commissaire!" Bellet had just appeared from nowhere next to Dupin's table. His tone of voice was affable, complicit, almost conspiratorial. "She still hasn't turned up in any of the police missing persons files."

It was astonishing how much Bellet knew. But Dupin was familiar with that; the smaller the village, the faster news spread. So fast that even the Internet lagged behind.

"Desespringalle," Bellet continued, "has moved heaven and earth to find out something about the deceased. So far in vain, according to Raphaël."

"What does the hairdresser always have to do with everything? Where does he get his information from?"

"Inès."

"The policewoman?"

"Yes."

"And?" Dupin had no idea what the connection might be.

"Hasn't anybody told you that Inès is Raphaël's niece? Inès Marchesi, daughter of his favorite sister."

"The woman gendarme is the niece of the hairdresser? And that's how he gets all his information from the police?"

"Probably not everything, but yes, that's the way it is."

That explained some things, and made the visit to the hairdresser all the more attractive. If he had known that, Dupin would have gone to have his hair cut sooner. It was too strange. And why hadn't the Bellets said so straightaway? Or Madame Riou? Whatever. One way or another an information net had grown up and he was profiting from it.

"It works the other way around too. Raphaël has regularly given her clues about complicated local cases."

"Any news yet on the cause of death?"

"No. I specifically asked Raphaël about that." Bellet formulated the phrase as if it were praise. "He said Inès had told him that it would take a while. However, the pathologist has estimated the time of death to be ten thirty P.M. on Tuesday, give or take an hour."

Dupin was deep in thought.

"How are your investigations going, Monsieur le Commissaire?"

"You know that I—"

"I know, I know." Bellet laughed mischievously. "You aren't investigating, you're on vacation. I keep strictly to that expression in everything I say. You can rely on me. And on my wife."

Dupin felt uncomfortable, but what could he do? In fact an accomplice was exactly what he needed. It would make things easier.

Then he realized with horror that Nolwenn knew the Bellets.

"What about Nolwenn, she—"

"Nolwenn is a friend, Monsieur le Commissaire, but we see this situation differently. And, my wife and I can keep secrets. It is a basic part of our job. If you had any idea how many secrets we know."

"Good." Dupin made it sound as binding as possible.

"Okay, so how are you going to proceed?" Bellet asked.

"Monsieur le Commissaire!" Madame Bellet was hurrying toward them frantically, a phone in her hand, which she held up directly to Dupin's face. "It's for you. Madame Riou."

"It's bad timing, I'm—"

"Very urgent!"

Dupin took the phone hesitantly. "Yes?"

"The woman that disappeared, the blonde. Guess who she was seen with the evening before she disappeared? In Paimpol? In a bar? Les Valseuses." The Tabac-Presse owner's typical short, factual sentences came across this time as thrilling for her. "With Monsieur Chastagner."

"Madame Durand from our hotel?" Suddenly Dupin sat up straight as a broom.

There was a short, puzzled pause. "Who else could I mean?"

"With the machine manufacturer?"

"And owner of the quarry! Where they found the dead woman! Precisely!"

"Madame Durand was in a bar in Paimpol on Sunday evening?"

"Sunday *night*. She came in just after midnight."

This was a spectacular piece of news, even if Dupin did not yet know what it meant. In all events it meant one thing: that Chastagner was a key figure in two cases.

"Madame Durand had been drinking. Eventually Chastagner and she left together. Around half past one."

Monsieur and Madame Bellet stood there with tension written on their faces and making no attempt to conceal it.

"How do you know this, Madame Riou?"

"Today there was a photo of Madame Durand in the local editions of *Ouest-France* and *Le Télégramme*, with a request for anyone who had seen her to report it."

The newspapers were lying next to Dupin but he hadn't opened them yet.

"One of my regular customers was just here. He has friends in Paimpol and goes to this bar with them. They were there on Sunday and he saw her there. She is, how would you say it, a conspicuous person. He recognized her. And Chastagner sticks out like a sore thumb."

"And your customer is quite certain?"

"Absolutely."

"Has he already reported it to the police?"

"I'm obviously about to call Inès but I wanted to tell you first."

"Madame Riou, do me a favor. Get your customer to tell you everything once again in as much detail as he can. Whether or not he heard what the two of them were talking about. How they behaved. And if you could tell him the information is just for you. Tell him you are very curious."

A brief silence.

"No problem. But wouldn't you rather speak to him yourself? Inès wouldn't have anything against it."

"He should go to the police immediately. They know that I'm on vacation and not investigating anything." The situation was too ludicrous. Dupin quickly added: "Not officially."

"Then talk to him completely unofficially."

"If you want to help, Madame Riou, then see to it that the police know everything as soon as possible. I'm afraid I have to go now."

"I understand. A question of priorities. Then you can talk to my customer later. I'll—"

"I'll see you soon, Madame Riou."

Dupin ended the conversation.

Official investigation or not, it was always the same. You had to get to know people: the bakery saleswoman, the butcher, the harbormaster, the hairdresser, the doctor, the concierge, the owner of the *Tabac-Presse* store. You had to talk to them to get an opinion of them, to understand them, in the most natural way possible. Without them, police work would be unimaginable. That was the heart of the business. And would remain so, no matter what technological methods they devised. In this respect Dupin was doggedly old-fashioned.

Monsieur and Madame Bellet had overheard everything. They had come so close to him that they had probably heard every word Madame Riou said.

There was a mixture of excitement, curiosity, and sorrow on Madame Bellet's face. Monsieur Bellet's showed consternation.

"Well, that makes the disappearance of Madame Durand into a real case! Even if it wasn't her body they found in the quarry. The woman has been caught out with somebody else! That is a fact!" Madame Bellet was now totally excited.

"If this is confirmed, Madame Bellet," Dupin said, ostentatiously levelheaded, trying to nip the excitement in the bud, "if it really was Madame Durand sitting there with Monsieur Chastagner in the bar, that does not necessarily mean she was 'caught out' with him. And, even if that were true, and right now that's just wild speculation, it wouldn't be a matter for the police. It would be a purely private issue for the Durands."

The hotel owner appeared deeply disappointed.

Monsieur Bellet was unusually silent.

Dupin stood up. He turned to the Bellets and asked, "Have you seen Monsieur Durand this morning?"

"Yes. He's already left the hotel," Monsieur Bellet replied. "He had to go to the gendarmerie, to deal with some documents. He confirmed that he'll be staying here for a while. He still assumes that his wife will be coming back soon. Today he was looking particularly distressed."

"What does he actually do all day?"

"He goes to see Inès every day, looking for more information. He takes walks. And he works, he says, to distract himself, that works best. In a situation like this he can't be on vacation. On Friday when the weather was good they rented a boat for the entire week. He's a passionate angler. After the disappearance of his wife, he returned the boat. Most of the time he's in his room. They rented our only suite. He has breakfast there now, and dinner too. On his own. He's not one for company." Bellet sounded very sympathetic.

Dupin had taken out his blue Clairefontaine, and written down a few things.

"It's always reported that you use a red notebook," Bellet said.

"And the Durands' big Mercedes, is it here all the time?"

Madame Bellet wrinkled her brow. "Of course. In the hotel parking lot, between the rocks."

"Did you see whether Madame Durand ever left the hotel in the late evening or at night? If she ever took the car out alone?"

"No. But that doesn't mean anything. We're busy until half past one every night and don't notice much. And the suite has a little spiral staircase outside leading down directly into the garden. She could have used it any time."

"That means Madame Durand's chances of getting out of the hotel unnoticed at night weren't bad."

"Absolutely. But Monsieur would have been bound to notice."

Dupin made a move to go. "I need to hurry. My hairdresser's appointment."

It was only now that the pair retreated a bit from the table.

"I wish you success, Monsieur le Commissaire."

Dupin hurried off.

* * *

The hairdresser's was near the baker's and a cozy-looking village bar called Ty Breizh on the little square with the chapel. A pretty stone building with two floors and a steep dark-tiled roof.

As soon as Dupin entered the salon, he was greeted by a portly man with thick hair with an elegant touch of gray, in a wide black shirt and dark blue jeans. "Ah, Monsieur le Commissaire. Élodie just called me. It's an honor for me to give you what help I can in your investigations," he said. It didn't sound remotely ironic.

"I'm not investigating."

"I know." Raphaël Julien gave Dupin a knowing wink. His whole face, from his pronounced cheeks to his chin and neck, showed that he enjoyed his food and a good glass of wine with it.

"Inès has ears everywhere." Deep, thoughtful lines had appeared on his forehead. "She's a good kid, that one. You see, it's never boring in Trégastel. On the subject, has Monsieur Quilcuff been in touch with you?"

"No, who's that?"

"Word's got around in the village that you're here. You don't want to take the old guy too seriously; he's a bit confused, but good-natured, ninety-four years old. He's noticed over the years that Monsieur Nolff's baguettes have been getting smaller while the prices have risen. Monsieur Nolff disputes it strongly. The *boulangerie* near the fire station. Monsieur Quilcuff will drop in and see you at the hotel."

Dupin didn't want to go into that.

"Whatever . . . now, about your hair." Julien walked around, taking a look at Dupin. "There's nothing really to be done. But of course you needed an official reason to come and see me, the Bellets explained." Another wink. "So, first of all we'll give your hair a good wash, and then give it an excellent conditioning treatment. To protect it from the extreme UV rays and sea salt. A few days' vacation by the sea is enough to completely ruin your hair. And after that, my colleague"—he nodded toward a young woman standing by the register—"will give you a relaxing head massage."

Dupin had never in his life had a hair-conditioning treatment; he honestly didn't really know what it was. And he knew even less about a head massage.

"Just a cut, please. No conditioning, no massage. Nothing." He was quick to add, "In these temperatures, I'm glad for every centimeter less."

Monsieur Julien raised his eyebrows. "Seriously?" He was silent for a moment and then smiled understandingly. Then his eyes lit up. "Fine. The camouflage must be good."

Dupin didn't reply.

"You do realize that—how shall I put it—that it will be *very* short?"

"No problem."

"Well then, let's get started," he said, and pulled out a thin black cape. He draped it expertly around Dupin and pulled out scissors and comb. "Lean back and relax."

It was one of those old, deeply upholstered hairdresser's chairs, well used, faded brown leather. Dupin was glad of it. The chair was comfortable.

"Now, to business, what is it you want to know? You've already heard about Madame Durand and Chastagner in the bar. There's no more news about the body found in the quarry. But there's one very recent piece of information that you probably don't know about." The hairdresser made a dramatic pause. "One of the two tractors that on the day of the protest blocked the entrance to the deputy's house belonged to a lady farmer from Trégastel. Maïwenn Guichard. An extremely good-looking woman."

Dupin suddenly reached for his notebook in his pants pocket and pulled it out from under the cape.

"It's also certain that her husband is having an affair with the deputy. Madame Rabier is single. And also very attractive."

"I've heard the rumor."

"I can tell you it's more than a rumor."

"How do you know?"

"I just know it. And my assumption is that it's ongoing."

Dupin had also been thinking about it the night before. If the story about the affair was true, then Madame Guichard had a motive for the attack.

"And how certain is that?"

"Reasonably."

The hairdresser didn't seem perturbed by the vagueness of his answer.

"The business with Madame Guichard's tractor, does the commissaire from Lannion know that?"

"Only since yesterday. One of the hoteliers at the front on Plage du Coz-Pors noticed it, but only reported it yesterday. Pierrick Desespringalle has made an appointment to see Maïwenn Guichard this morning." Monsieur Julien shook his head sorrowfully.

"The police are still not sure if it was an attack or just a tragic accident. Commissaire Desespringalle was back on the spot with the crime scene people last night. They were checking if it was possible to see if there was somebody in the room, directly on the other side of the glass."

"And? What was the result?" Dupin interrupted impatiently. That in itself was new. Monsieur Bellet hadn't mentioned it, which most probably meant he didn't know either.

"A woman dressed like Madame Rabier turned out to be hard to see. They reconstructed everything as close as possible. Which seems to suggest an accident."

Dupin didn't believe it.

"But the conclusion wasn't absolute," the hairdresser said.

Dupin would have liked to know when the deputy had called the commissaire in Lannion. Probably only that morning. Otherwise Desespringalle would have had no reason to carry out his test.

"Has anyone in the village any serious suspicion who might have thrown the stone?"

"Most people think it was a mistake. That one of the farmers threw a stone, but didn't aim to hit Madame Rabier."

The hairdresser was now working on the back of Dupin's head. Dupin saw a surprising amount of hair had fallen to the floor.

"Have there been other confrontations between the lady farmer and the deputy?"

"Dozens, for ages now. Agriculture is a hot topic in Breton politics. It's escalating all the time. The farmers will be stirring up a new revolution if it keeps on like this. They're fighting for their survival. You've experienced the protests. In reality the regional politicians are the wrong target. Today they're blocking the parking lots at the big supermarkets."

"What does that really mean? What is it actually about?"

"It's about the amount of milk, and prices. On a European level. Ask Monsieur Bellet, he knows more about it. In any case, Madame

Guichard is the spokeswoman for the protesters. And she's never at a loss for words."

"Do you think she would be up to doing something like that? Purely hypothetically. To target the deputy on purpose?"

"One thing is certain, she can be quite ruthless. She runs her farm with just two employees. Vegetables, pigs, chickens, that's a lot of work. Her husband works for the firm that's studying the planned gigantic offshore wind farm in the bay of Saint-Brieuc. He's their chief scientist. That means that apart from private matters, he deals on a professional level too with Madame Rabier, who's active on behalf of the wind farm. Maïwenn Guichard, on the other hand, is strictly against the wind farm, even though her husband is extremely involved with it. She opposes the disastrous consequences for the underwater world. Monsieur Guichard is regularly in Rennes, where his firm has its headquarters."

Dupin was making extensive notes, his notebook covered in tiny hairs. "And do you think she's responsible for the attack?"

"No." A decisive no. "I have the impression"—the hairdresser took a step back and looked Dupin over—"that in your eyes the throwing of the stone was not an accident. You believe it was an attack, right?"

"I don't believe anything, I'm just trying to make sense of it all."

The hairdresser stepped closer to Dupin again and started working on the side.

"This Chastagner. What disagreements with the deputy is he involved in?"

"Lots. The business with the pink granite is complicated. China sells it at a fifth of the price, with free delivery. Anywhere. Chastagner needs to expand his production to stay profitable. But expansion clashes with environmental production, the eternal dilemma." Raphaël Julien sounded neutral. "But it's a question of their livelihood for the quarry owners. Madame Rabier has spoken out against expansion. She said in an interview that if everybody is allowed to expand, within a few years we'll have used up the entire planet. Over the last few months the row has got dramatically worse."

"Have there been threats?"

"I don't know of any threats. But very serious arguments. Insults, derogatory comments. Chastagner plays hard. But then Madame Rabier isn't too sensitive either."

"Some people say Chastagner has already expanded the quarry illegally?"

"Everybody knows that. But so far nobody has proved it or challenged him legally."

"Have the authorities been onto it?"

"Not that I know. The other current argument between Chastagner and Rabier is over the headquarters site for his firm."

"I've heard that."

"Then you already know the two hot topics of the past few months."

"And that too's an issue?"

"Oh yes, Chastagner gave an interview, and laid into Madame Rabier publicly. As far as he's concerned, it's a very emotional business, he takes it personally."

"Did Madame Rabier hit back?"

"She has other methods."

"What do you mean?"

"The more aggressive Chastagner gets, the more determined she's been to make sure all his efforts are in vain."

Monsieur Julien stood in front of Dupin, adjusted his head, then walked around him silently.

"Just a few tweaks," he said.

"Is the deputy also a customer of yours, Monsieur Julien?"

The hairdresser gave him a surprised look. "But of course."

"And Madame Guichard, the lady farmer?"

"Yes."

"Monsieur Chastagner too?"

"He would never set foot in such a simple 'salon.'"

"What sort of a guy is this Chastagner?"

"He's one of those who wants to run with the big boys, no matter the cost. Not one to be underestimated. He's been extremely successful with his firm making agricultural machinery, particularly combine harvesters and fertilizer spreaders. He also exports them to lots of countries. He has his ways. Over dead bodies, if need be. Even if most of the time he'd like to come across as an affable guy, a pal or a patron."

"In other words, you wouldn't put an attack on the deputy past him?"

Monsieur Julien took his time answering, as if he wanted to put the question seriously to himself once again.

"I guess not. But the other person you definitely have to have your eye on is the deputy from the other party, Hugues Ellec."

Madame Rabier had mentioned him briefly the day before.

"He too has had fights over the years with Madame Rabier. They oppose one another in virtually everything. They always have contradictory opinions, and not just because they belong to different parties. Even though I'm always on Madame Rabier's side, in a few things their opinions are very similar. That's politicians for you. Extremely calculating when it comes down to it. Except that Ellec lacks the popular feel." A brusque conclusion. "If you want to meet him, Élodie will tell you what time he usually comes in to pick up his newspapers."

"What are the concrete points of conflict between Madame Rabier and this Ellec?"

It wouldn't be a bad idea to put all the topics that could be involved on the table at once. Sometimes being methodical did the trick.

"The main thing is how to find a basic solution to the agricultural crisis. Whether through targeted European and national regulations or totally free play of supply and demand. To put it straight: political means. Or the subsidies issues. Or the wind farm: she's for, he's against. Or last year's big project in Lannion Bay. Where, despite massive protests and warnings from scientists, permission was given to remove an ecologically irreplaceable underwater sandbank. He was in favor and she was decisively against."

Dupin put things together. That was the project Nolwenn had vehemently protested against. For months it had been *the* subject in the commissariat. During the most recent big and stressful cases, Nolwenn had been taking part in various demonstrations. Even still the topic was a red flag to a bull as far as she was concerned. It had been a bitter defeat, and Nolwenn had taken it personally.

"And Ellec was in favor?"

"Yes, he'd put everything he could into it. And made himself very popular in Paris. Madame Rabier suggested he'd been bought. Like I said, it's a war with a lot of injuries."

"Who did she suggest bought him?"

"Various firms owned by powerful people, people in government in Paris. Not just a question of money but 'reciprocal deals' and favors. Including very advantageous deals for him. You know what I mean."

"For example?"

"Last year he suddenly submitted a claim for an exceptional permission to build a house on a piece of land directly by the sea. In Ploumanac'h, right up at the top, even though it was forbidden by the strict coastal regulations and nobody had been given permission for ten years. The piece of land had belonged to his family for generations, and all of a sudden it seemed that several years ago a special permit had been issued by the highest authorities and up until now the family simply hadn't taken advantage of it."

"I get it."

"Obviously Rabier and Ellec fought over the extension of Chastagner's quarry."

Dupin's methodical approach had the disadvantage that it threw up lots of topics, but that couldn't be helped. He continued to take notes.

"I—"

The woman from the desk came over to him with the phone in her hand. "Monsieur Julien, for you, personally," she said.

"Just a moment, Monsieur le Commissaire, I'll be right back."

He vanished behind a hanging curtain at the end of the room.

Dupin had gotten a lot of very interesting information. He was very pleased with his visit to the hairdresser's. There were just a couple more questions.

Dupin wiped the beads of sweat from his forehead. The sun was streaming unhindered through the salon's large windowpanes. There obviously wasn't any air-conditioning. At midday the conditions here would be almost unbearable: sweltering heat and high humidity mixed with the smell of hairspray and shampoo.

"My niece," Julien said when he got back. "The case of Madame Durand's disappearance is back exclusively in her hands. Desespringalle has dropped it. He sees no possible connection with the body found in the quarry."

Dupin was about to make a biting comment but restrained himself. He would have done his best not to exclude any connections at this point, but the dead body in the quarry was the more important issue.

"Have you any idea what happened there? With the dead woman in the quarry?"

"Not the slightest, to be honest. The phone didn't stop ringing last night and this morning, but nobody knows anything. Even Inès says they've no leads of any sort. Desespringalle is fumbling in the dark. He's come up with the most abstruse ideas. For example, that this crime has something to do with the unexplained death of one of Chastagner's employees seven years ago. The pink corpse."

"You think any connection between the two cases is a fallacy?"

"If you ask me, it's completely ridiculous. The investigation went on for two years and nothing indicated anything other than an accident. Which was a big disappointment for most people, as they would have preferred an exciting murder case. In fact it was quite banal: the woman worked in administration and on that particular day was intending to pick up her husband from work, that is vouched for. He was one of the quarry workers; they had gotten to know each other at a work party and got married six months before the incident. It was assumed that he had been showing her around the quarry—against regulations—and that's how the tragic accident happened. He had to seriously dispute that, as otherwise he would have been punished for dangerous driving. Whatever the case, everybody had them down as a happy couple. In the end no accusations were made, and the husband moved away."

The fact was, there had been no proof, a conclusion that Dupin usually considered particularly skeptically. But he had to admit it could have happened like that.

"Whatever," the hairdresser resumed. "What could any sort of connection look like? And if there was one, it would have to be particularly sinister."

"Such as?"

He was letting Monsieur Julien use his imagination.

"Purely speculatively, maybe the 'accident' allowed Chastagner to deal with an employee who had somehow found out something about his 'deals.' And the woman found yesterday fitted into this scenario somehow. Maybe she had found something out. Maybe the old case itself? Maybe she knew it was murder?"

"But in that case, surely the woman would be known hereabouts?"

"Quite. I find the whole idea absurd."

Now it was Dupin's phone that interrupted them. He hesitated, then awkwardly pulled it out.

"Madame Riou," he told Julien.

Julien nodded understandingly and disappeared behind the curtain again.

Dupin took the call.

"Monsieur le Commissaire, I know that you're in an important conversation." Dupin squeezed the phone tight against his right ear. "As agreed, I had another chat with my customer. He could only make out snatches of the conversation, but he was of the impression they were seriously flirting, Chastagner and Madame Durand. Her in particular. He's going to tell Inès right away."

"Seriously flirting?"

"Yes, and not very subtly, if you know what I mean. She wanted to 'just pick him up'; that's a quote."

"That was his impression?"

"Exactly that. And that was it. I've got a delivery coming in. New Clairefontaine notebooks. I have to hang up."

The conversation ended.

A little later Monsieur Julien returned, in a good mood.

"I've finished, actually, but I can make it look like I'm snipping here and there so we can continue to talk. What did Élodie have to say?" Dupin gave a brief synopsis of the conversation. He didn't really want to get involved in a communal investigation. But the hairdresser would find it all out from his niece anyway.

"Madame Durand came to see you twice?" Dupin hadn't the faintest idea why someone would come to see a hairdresser so frequently.

"Indeed, but only for a wash, condition, and style."

"Tell me about her."

"She comes from simple origins and considers herself to have made a good match. Rather naïve, if you ask me. She tries to make herself look chic. At times she can be quite vulgar, without noticing it. But I think despite doing silly things, her heart's in the right place." Monsieur Julien had said the last sentence with rather touching sympathy. A double-edged verdict.

"These arguments she told you about, did she explain exactly what it was they were fighting over?"

"Money. At least one of the fights. Her husband had threatened to have her credit cards blocked. She got furiously upset." Monsieur Julien had taken the scissors behind Dupin's ears. "There was some serious cursing. I'll spare you that. At the end she said he won't really do it, he's threatened a thousand times."

"Was that during her first visit?"

"The second. The first appointment was Thursday morning, the day after their arrival, the second on Saturday morning. I specifically checked the calendar." He nodded vaguely in the direction of the register. "She was very worried about her hair, because of the salt and the sun and so forth."

"What else did she tell you? Was there a particular incident?"

"Not really, she just said their arguments were as insufferable on vacation as they were at home. Not least about the tiny rooms, by which she meant the suite. And she couldn't stand fishing. Late on Friday afternoon, when after two days of bad weather the sun finally came out again, her husband and she went out in a rented boat, she was afraid every day would be given over to fishing."

Dupin thought to ask Bellet if they had separate beds in the suite.

"If it was up to her, she said, they could leave immediately. For her this wasn't a vacation. 'With this idiot.' But it seemed more as I said—out of anger, I mean. Rather than a serious plan to go."

Whether he wanted to or not, Dupin felt he had something in common with Madame Durand. Which certainly included a spontaneous dislike for Monsieur Durand.

"You don't think it's likely that she just took off on her own?"

"Not really, no. But who knows, maybe she's gone to her best friend's. She mentioned a best friend."

"Did quarrels like that seem unusual for the pair of them?"

"To be honest, no. I couldn't stand it, but I know a few couples who need to be like that."

Monsieur Julien seemed to have a good grasp of human relations.

"What about affairs? Do you think that's a possibility?"

"I can't say. That's something you never know. Sometimes those who seem most permissive are the most restraining, while those who go on about the importance of morality are the worst of all. I've seen it all. Only Madame Durand herself knows the truth. On the other hand"—he shook his head—"she would appear to hang around in bars with other men. With Chastagner at least. There again . . ." He hesitated.

"Yes?"

"Somehow it just doesn't feel right."

That was Dupin's feeling too, but in reality it was as the hairdresser had said. People regularly did things that others would say weren't really what you'd expect, based on their personality.

"Whatever," Monsieur Julien said, and plucked a bit at the hair above Dupin's left temple. "Chastagner loves women. He's always ready for an adventure. He's unscrupulous in that respect."

"The name of her best friend, did she ever mention that? Or where she lived?"

"No."

"Hm." Dupin ran his hand through his hair. It felt very different.

"Inès was as disappointed as you. By the way, she thinks you're very nice."

"Me? Nice?" That wasn't the impression Dupin had from their conversation on the beach. But then again it could be to his advantage.

He winced involuntarily. Now there were at least four people in the know: the Bellets, Madame Riou, Monsieur Julien—and the policewoman as well. Things were threatening to get out of hand. Claire, Nolwenn, the commissaire from Lannion, the police supervisory board, his prefect—Dupin had no idea which would be the worst, if his clandestine investigation were to come to light.

"Inès can't stand Desespringalle. She finds him self-important and arrogant. And obviously she regards Trégastel as her bailiwick. Which is quite correct. We ought to see to it that we can clear things up here by ourselves, a Lannionais has nothing to do with it. I've recommended seriously to Inès that she work together with you. The Bellets like Nolwenn, and you too. You may not belong here, but you're sort of part of the family."

Perfect Breton logic. With Nolwenn thrown in!

"And like I said, my niece likes you a lot. As does Madame Riou."

"I think you and Madame Riou are good friends."

"We went to school together. Here in Trégastel."

"And the Bellets too?"

"We were in the same class."

How could it be otherwise?

Raphaël Julien stood in front of Dupin, holding up a mirror. "So, now you can take a look at the back and sides. And here as well, a lot shorter, so you can see the difference. Just as you said."

Dupin was shocked to the bone. He had been so taken up by the conversation that up until now he hadn't properly looked in the mirror.

His hair was now really short. A close, almost military cut. It was horrible.

The hairdresser put his head on one side and looked at Dupin from that perspective. "It looks dynamic. A short cut is always a bold decision."

He walked around Dupin once again. Dupin had to be fair. He was the one who had gone for a cut instead of a head massage.

"I suggest you use gel, that way you won't be quite so conspicuous from the front."

Dupin had never used gel and had no intention to start now.

Monsieur Julien hadn't been waiting for an answer; he already had gel on his fingertips.

"Take a look, you'll see that looks much better."

Dupin could see no more than the minimum of difference.

"I recommend you take a tube with you." Monsieur Julien used a broad brush to wipe Dupin around the neck, and then removed the cape.

Dupin got up. And then his phone rang again. He pulled it out. Claire.

He took a few steps to the side and picked up.

"Georges, where are you?"

"I'm just paying the hairdresser."

"You're still at the hairdresser's. What's he doing? Giving you highlights?"

"He's given my hair the treatment. And put gel on it. You'll see shortly."

"Treatment? Gel?" She didn't sound very amused.

Speaking as softly as he could, he added: "It's only a light treatment, and the gel is only up front."

"I got up a bit earlier today, and have already had breakfast. I want to go down to the beach now. Have you got our picnic supplies?"

"I have. I'm on my way now, Claire."

Dupin had almost forgotten the beach in the past happy hours. Their agreement was the following: lie on the beach until 2:30, and then go on their little "excursion."

He would have to hurry. He hadn't picked up the newspapers yet. Nor had he any water, rosé, or sandwiches. Absolutely nothing.

"I'll see you down by the towel, Claire."

"Fine, Georges. See you soon." She sounded at ease again.

"I need to go, Monsieur Julien. Many thanks. For everything."

"Have you got the most important information? Do you know what you want to know?"

"I think so."

"If something occurs to you, come back to me. I'll tell my assistant to give you an appointment at any time. Officially then I'll give you another trim."

He saw Dupin's look of horror.

"I can always pretend. And I'll give you Inès's telephone number; you might want to talk something over with her directly."

That was a good idea.

The hairdresser walked toward the register. "That will be twenty euros for the haircut and ten for the gel. An extremely high-quality hair treatment gel. Your wife will recognize it."

Dupin pulled out his wallet. Monsieur Julien set a business card down by the till.

"And the disappearance of the Saint Anne statue from the chapel? You've decided not to investigate this business anymore, Monsieur le Commissaire?" The hairdresser had lowered his voice.

"No, no. It just got sidelined. I was talking about it with Monsieur Bellet yesterday."

"Unfortunately there have been no new developments. Apart from a second statement from the nurse who'd lit a candle there."

"Yes?"

"Leaving the chapel yesterday it occurred to her that she'd seen an elderly man, about seventy, she guessed, but still with dark hair, who'd gone up to the statue. He hadn't looked as if he wanted to look around the chapel. Unfortunately she couldn't say any more. She couldn't describe him any better. Her report didn't help Inès much. But maybe it might help you."

Dupin had yet again taken out his Clairefontaine. And immediately found what he'd noted about the incident before.

"That would have been around a quarter past four."

"Exactly. Oh yes"—something else had occurred to Monsieur Julien—"Élodie spoke to a famous art dealer in Rennes. To get a more exact valuation of the material worth of the Saint Anne statue. He said you might get seven hundred or eight hundred euros for it, but no more. But that there was an old story that the legendary ruby Côte de Bretagne was hidden in one of the statues in the chapel. A precious stone shaped like a dragon, a part of the golden fleece, once owned by Anne de Bretagnes, long ago vanished without a trace."

Dupin wouldn't bother himself with stories of that kind.

"And what you also need to know: there were two more reports of thefts in the region yesterday and the day before."

"More precisely?"

"The ninety-six-year-old widow of the former harbormaster is missing a golden candlestick which she swears always stood on her dinner table," Monsieur Julien said seriously. "And a sleazy insurance dealer reckons he's lost his ancient scooter. Both events in Perros-Guirec."

Dupin was familiar with the phenomenon. After one theft became widely known, over the next weeks all sorts of things started to "disappear."

He had his notebook and pen still in his hand. "And what about the Eiffel House break-in? Any more news there?"

"Hasn't anybody told you? I told the Bellets and Élodie yesterday afternoon."

"*What* did you tell them?" Dupin was wide awake.

"The mayor got a letter yesterday. From four walkers from the Pyrenees!"

"And?"

"They apologized and sent a check."

Dupin gave the hairdresser a puzzled look.

"A week ago last Wednesday there was a dreadful storm here with a drop of ten degrees in temperature, and lightning everywhere. The storm hit us really fast and unexpectedly, and settled in for two days."

"Yes, yes," Dupin said impatiently.

"They were on the GR34, the legendary walking route that goes all the way around Brittany, and were taken by surprise by the storm. They used a credit card to force open the lock on the door, to seek shelter. People from the south don't see abrupt changes in the weather. When they set out again a few hours later, when it had cleared up a bit, they had to hurry to reach their planned target for the day. And they didn't even manage to leave a note. But when they got home they immediately wrote to the mayor. Even so."

"That's it? That's the solution to the Eiffel House break-in?"

Dupin rubbed his temples. That's how it was. That was the solution. This case was purely imaginary. The hairdresser gave no sign of adding anything more. Dupin put the Clairefontaine back in his pants pocket.

"Then I'll be off." Dupin grabbed the door handle.

"Enjoy the rest of your vacation, Monsieur le Commissaire," the hairdresser called merrily after him.

Unfortunately, by the time Dupin got to Rachid, the *pains bag-nats* were all gone. And so were the mini pizzas. He had to improvise.

The newspaper store was empty. Dupin was pleased that Élodie Riou wasn't there; he really had no time. A pale young man was at the counter.

Even though he hurried, it was still a while before Dupin got to the beach.

"Here I am."

He was panting audibly.

Claire was lying facedown with her eyes closed, her head toward the sea. She didn't move. Perhaps she was asleep. It wouldn't be easy after the morning to start leisurely lying on the towel again, to be on vacation. For the last few hours he had actually felt totally normal again. A case. An investigation.

"Where have you been?"

She wasn't sleeping, then. But she still hadn't moved.

"Just in the newspaper store." That was the only thing he hadn't claimed already to have done. "It was chaos there. No idea why. It's normally empty at this time of day."

He couldn't dismiss the possibility that Claire might come with him at this time of day.

"What time did you actually get up?"

"I'm not absolutely certain. The air was wonderful; I went for a walk and then had breakfast."

Claire didn't reply.

But she did turn around and sit up.

"What's happened to your hair?"

Dupin had already almost forgotten about it. Suppressed the memory.

"It's better in this heat. More comfortable, believe me." He tried hard to sound convincing, which wasn't easy.

On the way from the hairdresser's to the beach he had already painfully noticed that with hair this short he had little protection against the sweltering sun. He was going to have to wear the cap he hated once again.

"It's short. Very short." Claire's tone of voice made quite clear what she thought of his new hairstyle.

She had in the meantime arranged herself into a cross-legged position on the towel. Something Dupin couldn't conceive of.

Claire was still staring in horror at Dupin's head.

"I bought the Sherlock Holmes case today." He'd been in luck; Riou's store was well stocked. "And two more. And I brought you a special edition of *Journal de la Science,* just out. With the headline: 'What If the Laws of Gravity Aren't Universal?'" As a layman, Dupin found the question unsettling. The other headline story in the magazine unleashed an even greater unquiet in him: "Memory, a Sensation: Ten Times the Capacity Than Previously Assumed!" An explosive discovery. It was Dupin's impression he could only remember at maximum a tenth of what other people did.

"And *Bretagne Cuisine,* the latest edition—cult products. A new interpretation of Brittany."

Claire took time to react. Then she smiled, without saying a word, then suddenly beamed at him.

Dupin suddenly felt unwell. He quickly threw open the newspaper. The best thing would be not to speak for a while.

The page he opened was dominated by the "Are You a Breton" quiz of the day.

> *You know you're a Breton if you basically don't get on with the English.*
> *You don't think that andouillette sausage smells like your butt.*
> *You drink exclusively dry cider and leave the sweet stuff to the Normans.*
> *Even in your sleep you can recite how much more rain there is in the southern parts of France than in Brittany: for example Biarritz 1450 millimeters per year, Nice 769, and in Rennes by contrast just 694.*

* * *

It really was spectacular how the aquarium was built into and around the mass of pink granite blocks. A bold idea. Even if it was nature that had created the scene, it gave the impression of being the imposing work of some daredevil architect or artist. Meandering pathways, steps, corridors that led unmistakably to individual chambers with pools. A perfect labyrinth. New perspectives at every turn: the white houses of the village, rooftops, the sea, but only ever just parts of them, so that you felt as if you were in a cubist painting. From the highest rocks you could see over the entire region. Trégastel, the coast, the Atlantic, the Sept-Îles. The shallow pools were positioned outside, between the pink giants, the larger ones built into the granite caves.

Dupin loved aquariums.

The Océanopolis near Brest of course—that was where his favorite penguins lived—but all others too. Whenever he was traveling, and had the time and there was an aquarium in the neighborhood, he went to visit it. Often he went to the one in Concarneau, directly opposite his apartment. He could never get enough of the sheer unending funny, often hilarious shapes and colors that nature had given the inhabitants of the sea. Monsters small and large that went well beyond the imagination of science fiction and fantasy films; by comparison aliens were pathetic creations. You only had to look at a full-grown lumpfish—which existed in different colors—the legendary melon butterfly fish, the moon jellyfish, or the snake starfish. Wonderful, but at the same time threatening, weird, frightening. Above all, totally wild.

"That's fantastic." Claire was beside herself. "Born in 1624 and still alive! He's been swimming the oceans for nearly four hundred years! When Europe was in the midst of the slaughter of the Thirty Years' War. He's lived through everything, Louis Quatorze, the Revolution, Napoleon . . . the species itself is over a hundred million years old, they think."

The exhibition was entitled "Ice Sharks—the Superlative Sea Predators." Next to a lot of charts there was a depiction of "Ice Shark 28," also known as "Mandy." Five meters long. Torpedo-shaped body. Gray-brown to olive green.

Dupin was standing right in front of it, Claire on the other side, next to the charts with the explanations. They were the only ones in the room; in this weather the aquarium was as good as empty, with people enjoying the high summer weather out on the beaches.

"*Somniosus microcephalus!* No other vertebrate was as large or lived so long. Much older than turtles. When they weren't eating, they just glided slowly through the seas. They were also known as sleeper sharks. But there was no mistake, they were nimble hunters with a menu not very different from that of their fellow family member, the white shark." Claire was standing in front of the display panel. "Their stomachs have been found to contain boned fish of all types, and every possible marine mammal, including seals, dolphins, and even penguins."

That didn't make the ice shark particularly pleasant in Dupin's eyes.

"And they live in Arctic waters?"

"Not only; their habitat ranges from Cape Cod in the West Atlantic to the north coast of Portugal in the east, and one was even seen off the coast of South Carolina."

The name "ice shark," Dupin reckoned, was a bit of a misnomer. South Carolina was a good way farther south than Brittany.

"But I imagine they live a long way out to sea."

Happily Dupin had forgotten the talk they'd had about sharks the day before yesterday, before they went swimming.

"That too is variable. Some of them play around in fresh water." Claire's eyes were still fixed on the board. "But by far the most, as far as current knowledge goes, live way out in the North Atlantic."

Just one of them reaching the Breton shallows would be enough, Dupin thought. He should consider cutting down on the swimming.

"Let's begin the tour, Claire; after all, we still want to take a walk to the castle."

They had set out as planned but it would be dinnertime before too long.

"I'd like to look at the other charts, but go on ahead."

Even though Dupin did want to go to the castle, Claire's desire was a lucky coincidence; he needed to make a few more telephone calls. There was a lot still to do.

"Then let's meet up in one of the caves."

Dupin got his bearings. A conspicuous notice showed the way to the aquarium tour.

A little later he was standing in front of one of the first pools, laid out grandly. The aquarium's rooms were grottos in the bare granite. It was dark except for the pools, which were lit by a greenish-yellow light. That in turn gave the pink of the granite unearthly violet tones.

Dupin had his nose nearly up against the glass. In front of him were baby seahorses, ever-changing transparent strings of water, already taking the typical seahorse shape. He had never seen anything like it, like unearthly visions.

It was enough for him to carry on a conversation with Claire about the aquarium. Dupin looked for an exit. He went over to one of the giant rocks and had already lost sight of the pools.

Dupin pulled his phone out of his rear pants pocket.

He had what he hoped was a good idea. It had occurred to him earlier that morning.

They didn't see one another often, but even so maybe once or twice a year. They had liked each other since they were together at the police academy. It was only by chance that they had not become closer friends. Jean Odinot, who despite his nonconformist character—unlike Dupin—had flown high in the Police Nationale in Paris, as far as the rank of inspecteur général. They had handled several dangerous cases together, and that had brought them close.

"*Salut*, Jean."

"*Salut*—Georges, is that you?"

He had sounded just the slightest bit testy, and there was loud, lively chatter in the background.

"It's not the best of times. I'm sitting in the Brasserie Dauphine—there's hare braised in mustard sauce on the menu." That had also been one of Dupin's favorite brasseries. "It's a madhouse here and I've only got a quarter of an hour."

Jean was approximately the same height as Dupin but was annoyingly thin.

"I'll be quick. I need you to research somebody. Just a few bits of information."

"Unofficially, you mean?" He laughed. He knew Dupin.

"Exactly."

"You're doing an investigation on your own? In a case that isn't even yours?" Jean didn't seem in the slightest surprised. He knew about the numerous comments in Dupin's file.

"I really shouldn't help you, you know that." He took a breath. "All right then, give me the name." He was, as always, curious.

"Gilbert Durand, big-time property speculator in Paris. Married to Alizée Durand. If you can find anything about them, then—"

"Then you'd like to know too. Understood. Now, my hare is calling."

"Just get in touch via phone, or leave a message if you want. There are times I can't pick up."

"I understand. You haven't let your famous assistant in on it then."

"Thanks, Jean."

"I'll be in touch." With the last syllable he had put down the phone.

Excellent. Dupin was happy. And it had been quick. That left him time for the next operation, even if it was going to be a lot more difficult.

Dupin already had his phone at his ear. It took a while before Nolwenn answered.

"Monsieur le Commissaire, weren't you supposed to be at the aquarium this afternoon?"

Dupin had turned off location services for the duration of their vacation. Which meant: Nolwenn could only have known that from Claire or the Bellets, both of which were disquieting scenarios. But there were more important things. And in any case, Nolwenn never revealed her sources.

"I was at the hairdresser's this morning." On the way back from Monsieur Julien, Dupin had gotten this spectacular idea; a treacherous idea, he had to admit. "A proper beach vacation hairdresser. The hairdresser's niece is the village policewoman and—"

"You know you are going against all the rules and—"

"It would appear that Deputy . . ."—Dupin had taken out his notebook—"Hugues Ellec has been influencing political decisions in favor of generous donors, in return for personal advantage. As far as bribery. And do you know what matter that includes, amongst others?"

There was a brief silence. Nolwenn seemed uncertain as to how she should behave: a rare situation.

"Including giving permission for removing the underwater dunes in Lannion Bay."

A long silence, then: "Is that true?" A sort of hiss. "Was *he* involved in it?"

Dupin could almost feel her anger coming down the line.

"It would appear so."

"Disgraceful."

She was beside herself. Perfect. The first part of his plan was working.

"And has the Trégastel gendarmerie got viable evidence? Justified suspicion? That Ellec had his finger in the pie?"

"I don't know how viable it really is. But that's what I've been given to understand."

A lengthy silence.

"You know," he continued calmly, "that there is no way in which we should investigate. But obviously you could do some research in the background."

The reply came in a split second: "Monsieur le Commissaire! It must be perfectly clear to you"—Nolwenn's voice was suddenly calm, collected, and unyielding—"that that is out of the question."

Dupin couldn't believe his ears. "You're not going to look into the matter?"

He had considered his plan totally infallible.

"Of course not. Our colleagues are already looking into it. So, enjoy the rest of your vacation, Monsieur le Commissaire. *Va-ca-tion.*"

The conversation was over.

It was unbelievable.

He heard echoing steps coming rapidly toward him.

He quickly turned back to the tour route, which was now leading toward the grotto with the next pool.

But it was a false alarm: instead of Claire, he came across a pale woman in a colorful summer dress, who shot him an indignant glance.

Claire studied exhibitions with such concentration. Dupin remembered long visits to the Louvre, the Musée d'Orsay, or the Centre Pompidou. She'd probably only got to the seahorses by now.

Dupin went into the second cave, stopped for a while in front of a pool, then turned left again. If he carried on like this he would be well ahead of Claire, and would have no problem making his other two calls. Out of the corner of his eye he had glimpsed a greater weaver fish in the sandy floor of the pool. It was one of his worst enemies; the previous year, he had stepped on one of these malignant fish with poisonous spines on Plage Tahiti, his favorite beach. Rarely in his life had he experienced such pain. Luckily his experienced friend Henri had treated him straightaway. He had burnt out the spot with a cigarette. Dupin hadn't complained, had just wanted the pain to stop.

Once again he detoured from the set route, and walked off between two particularly long, large rocks.

Quickly he groped for his phone, and had just got it in his hand when it rang. Far too loud. An anonymous number. He took the call.

"Monsieur Dupin. I hope I'm not disturbing you." He recognized the voice. It was the deputy, Madame Rabier.

"No. Not at all."

"I've heard about the body found in the quarry. Terrible." A brief silence. "Do you think that there could be something bigger going on here?" Her voice still sounded weak.

"At the moment we're still stumbling in the dark. Do you have any reason to connect this incident with the attack on you?"

"I wouldn't know what connection there could be."

"Have you spoken to the commissaire from Lannion?"

"Yes, this morning around eight. I didn't manage it yesterday. He's very upset that at the moment it looks like an attack. Like you said, he promised me the highest sensitivity in dealings with the police: that for the moment he would keep it to himself. But that there would be a plainclothes police officer sent here."

"Did he offer any suggestions?"

She hesitated before answering with an uncertain voice. "He considers a local lady farmer suspicious. *Very suspicious,* he confided to me. Maïwenn Guichard. He went to see her this morning. For an official interview. Thanks to his intensive investigation, he found out that one of the two tractors parked in front of my house on the day of the protests belonged to Madame Guichard."

A dubious procedure, Dupin thought: to present the victim with totally fanciful speculation. And in any case, the commissaire from Lannion was decking himself in false feathers.

"What do you think about it?"

"I . . ." She paused, seeming to collect her thoughts. "You already know. Am I right?"

"Yes."

"The relationship is still going on. Her husband has told her he's going to leave her." Madame Rabier sounded sad, even though she might turn out to be the victor in the story.

"In order to be with you?"

"I don't know. And I don't know whether he himself knows. He's going to remain in Rennes for now, that's the seat of his company which is doing the research for the big wind farm in the sea. It's clearly the right thing for him to do. The distance will do him good." She sounded rather dejected.

"You had thought it might work out differently?"

"Yes, a lot differently."

"And Madame Guichard is blaming you for everything, not her husband?"

"Yes. I've been—how shall I put it?—rather restrained, at least at first." It was clear from her tone of voice that she was glad to talk about it. "He said the marriage had been long over by the time I first met him."

"Has Madame Guichard ever threatened you?"

"No. Never. But she'll have cursed me a thousand times. We see each other now and then, out of necessity, it's hard to avoid. She gives me dirty looks. Sometimes we argue in public over agricultural questions, as just two weeks ago at a big event about the building in the Trégor."

"What did she say?"

"That I am destroying her and all the other farmers. *Destroying.* She's adamant on that." Madame Rabier sounded totally exhausted. "Yet we both have the same ideas."

"Have you ever . . . talked about the matter together?"

"No. Never." Her voice was ever more sluggish. "I would have liked to, just to tell her that it's not just my fault. I . . . I need to lie down again, Monsieur Dupin."

"You told me that you had already started taking notes on the illegal extension of Monsieur Chastagner's quarry."

"Yes, my assistant and I."

"Do you think I would be able to take a look?"

"Have things changed—are you actually investigating?" There was a hint of hope in her question.

"Not at all, Madame Rabier. I have nothing to do with any of it."

It was important for him to say that, despite how absurd it sounded.

"I understand. But yes, of course. Go see my assistant, Aiméric Janvier. Bellet has his number."

Dupin took a note of the name.

"These 'deals' that Deputy Ellec clinches to his own advantage, can you tell me anything about them? The one involving the building site, for example?"

It took a while for her to answer. "You're well informed. We've also done a bit of research on that, Janvier and I."

"All the better," Dupin said in a totally unsuitable jovial tone of voice. "Many thanks, Madame Rabier. Go back to resting."

"I'll try, *au revoir*, Monsieur Dupin."

She hung up.

Dupin should have asked her for her telephone number. But he would be able to talk with her assistant.

It had been an unexpectedly fruitful conversation.

Dupin had almost forgotten where he was. During the conversation he had, without noticing it, wandered ever farther into the labyrinth of granite blocks. Somehow the pink blocks suddenly all looked the same. Strangely he could no longer hear any noise. It was as still as a tomb. The stones absorbed any noise.

He turned right, then left, then right again, then left again. All of a sudden he was standing in front of a massive pink wall. He spotted a narrow crack. With a bit of effort he could push himself through. On the other side was a long corridor with high walls on both sides.

"This can't be true." Dupin swore.

How much ground did the aquarium take up? Surely somewhere he had to come upon the path again.

He walked to the end of the corridor. Another narrow crack. He turned sharply to the right and found himself in a sort of cave. On top of several strangely smooth stones, like overlarge perfectly polished pebbles, there was a single flat stone stretching for maybe ten meters. Like a roof. Obviously the stones didn't completely close off the cave, there were bright blue spots to be seen, strangely two-dimensional, depthless; you wouldn't have imagined they were the sky if it weren't for the fact that that was what it had to be. Dupin searched the rest of the cave. It was a dead end.

He had lost his sense of orientation.

An unpleasant, sinister feeling came over him.

The best thing for him to do was to retrace his steps the way he came.

Dupin turned around and after a few seconds found himself back in the long corridor, except that this time the only crack, the one he thought he had come through, was on the left rather than straight ahead. Was the labyrinth somehow or other confusing his perception? He forced himself through. And found himself in a sort of square about ten meters by ten. How could there suddenly be so much open space?

He pulled out his cell phone. It was ridiculous, but he would zoom in on the map of where he was and immediately get his orientation back.

No reception, not the tiniest of bars. Nothing.

Suddenly he heard something. Softly spoken single words. Whispered.

A woman's voice.

". . . definitely, I would say . . . yes . . ."

Dupin recognized Claire's voice immediately. It was her speaking, probably on the phone, and she couldn't be far away. Probably beyond the side wall. How come she had reception?

". . . the left aorta, there . . . but be very careful . . . and a stent, yes, there's no other way . . . no more time, I'm afraid . . . I have to get going."

There was no doubt. Claire was on the phone to her clinic.

And then the penny dropped. The envelope and the courier. The phone calls. The cell phone on the towel. She'd received documents from the clinic. And now she was carrying out an operation remotely.

". . . today around six . . . yes, as soon as possible . . . I'll try to be punctual . . . Bye."

It was unbelievable. He would be fascinated to hear her explanation.

Even so, it meant he hadn't got lost in the labyrinth.

A minute later—he must have taken two sharp bends to the right and found himself back on the official tour—Dupin was in the last cave. Strangely, there had been no sight of Claire on the path.

Dupin was still stunned. Just in the past minute dozens of possibilities had gone through his head as to how he would tackle the matter with Claire.

He was standing next to one of the pools on the "shallow coastal zone," a large pool with almost everything he liked swimming in it.

He found his mouth watering automatically: bass, red mullet, and down at the bottom, turbot and brill and a big lobster.

"We ate one of those recently in the Amiral," Claire said from behind him. She was nodding enthusiastically at the brill, *barbue*, the one the Bretons refer to as the "little cousin" of the turbot, which had an even finer taste.

Claire seemed to be in the best of moods.

"Did you know all the things scallops can do? They're amongst the most useful scientific tools. You can use them to track climate change year by year, month by month, extremely accurately. Using petrified leaves, or air bubbles frozen in ice, you can track the changes, but only on the scale of thousands of years. Scallops are vastly more accurate."

"From behind one of the rocks"—Dupin had decided to tackle the matter directly—"I heard . . ."

Claire seemed perplexed. "What did you hear?"

"Oh, nothing."

He had a bright thought. He would say nothing. Not a single word. Not even hint at the fact that he had overheard her. That he knew about her "activity." He would let her go on. For lots of reasons. If Claire kept on with her work she would be wanting free time to herself regularly. And then he wouldn't have to have a bad conscience anymore if he carried on with his investigation. And then if it all went wrong, at least he had a rabbit up his sleeve.

"But you have—" She was interrupted by the soft, relatively quiet sound of her phone. She pulled it out of her handbag.

"Some number from around here." She sounded relieved.

She took a few steps aside. "Hello?"

Dupin stood still. Indecisively.

For a moment or two, Claire just listened. Then she waved him over.

"You want to speak to my husband?"

Dupin gave her an inquisitive look.

"No . . . yes of course, he's with me. I'll hand you over to him."
She handed the phone to Dupin, obviously reluctantly.

"Yes?"

Bellet sounded out of breath. "The dead woman had been staying
in the Hôtel Castel Beau Site. In Ploumanac'h. Almost next door.
Raphaël Julien just called me. He'd tried you a few minutes ago, but
didn't get through. Nor did I . . ."

"Who was it?"

"Her name is Virginie Inard."

"And where does she come from?

"She had an address in Bordeaux."

"Bordeaux?"

"Indeed."

"Was she on her own?"

"Yes, she booked a room for one week three months ago."

"What else about her is known?"

Claire had by now come much closer to him.

"Nothing else so far. They've told the police in Bordeaux. And
Desespringalle is in the hotel, asking questions."

"Does anyone know when she was last seen? What time she left
the hotel? What she intended? What—"

"I'm afraid I have to go shopping now, Monsieur le Commissaire.
So far all I know is what I've just told you. And that Virginie Inard
didn't come back to her hotel Tuesday evening. I'll let you know if
there's anything new. Or Raphaël himself will."

"Then talk to you later."

Claire gave Dupin a penetrating look, putting her phone away again. "It's not your corpse. You are not to get involved with anything that happens."

Dupin had to restrain himself from saying anything in return, but her sentences were interestingly a little more mechanical than earlier.

"The poor woman." Claire shook her head. "Nasty business."

The way she said that sounded somehow strange.

"But now," she said, more cheerfully, "let's devote ourselves again to this brilliant exhibition."

"I need to disappear for a moment, Claire, I'll be right back."

Dupin smiled to himself. It felt great no longer having to have a bad conscience.

"Okay, then let's meet up outside in front of the aquarium."

Dupin knew what was going on. She was going to finish off the conversation she had just been having. His plan was working. His strategy was functional. However hard it had been for him not to say anything, it was worth it.

He left the cave and headed back to the entrance, precisely to the signposted path. From the coffee machine he had taken notice of when they were coming in, he got a double espresso and found a position on the other side of the road where he would be able to see Claire right away when she came out.

He knocked back the *café* in two large gulps and already had his phone to his ear.

The policewoman replied immediately.

"Hello?"

"Georges Dupin here."

"Got it."

"I've just heard about the identification of the deceased."

"I can't tell you any more at the moment. The case isn't ours."

Dupin couldn't really detect any sign that she found him nice, as her uncle had claimed.

"Do you think perhaps we could meet up? I could come around to the gendarmerie."

"I'm okay with that. My uncle is very keen that I should work with you." That sounded relatively neutral.

"I'll try to come around today. Late afternoon. Or else tomorrow morning."

Despite the "new state of affairs," finding times for an appointment was still difficult.

"Fine. There is one bit of news. About the woman who disappeared."

A genuinely cooperative gesture.

"Which is?"

"I've spoken to Chastagner. He readily admitted meeting Madame Durand in the bar in Paimpol on Saturday night. Also that he drove off with her. But he wouldn't say anything more than that."

"How and when did he get to know her?"

"On Sunday, about half past two, in a café on Plage du Coz-Pors. Madame Durand was sitting at the next table and they got talking."

"Just like that?"

"How else? And they agreed to meet up late that evening."

"So, just like that, after they've only just met over a coffee? And despite the fact she's on vacation with her husband? Late evening?"

That was not, however, so much to do with Chastagner as with Madame Durand. "She makes a date with a strange man in a bar, and then afterward drives off with him?"

"Chastagner says they were together in the café for about three-quarters of an hour."

Dupin hadn't really listened. There was something not quite right here. Objectively it was all reasonable enough; things like that happened all the time, the world was full of stories like that. But it didn't fit in with the picture he had of Madame Durand; something in him resisted it. But then, he didn't know her.

"Did Madame Durand say anything to Monsieur Chastagner that could explain her disappearance?"

"Not in the slightest, according to him."

"Did she mention a particularly severe argument with her husband? An incident of some sort?"

"No, she just mentioned that she was married, but that it was 'okay' for them to sit like that."

"She said it 'was okay'?"

"Just like that, according to Chastagner."

"That makes Chastagner the last man—apart from her husband—that she spoke to before she disappeared."

"She spoke to Monsieur Bellet on Monday before dinner. For about ten minutes, he said, at the bar in the restaurant."

Bellet hadn't mentioned this conversation.

"But just about the weather, the beach; trivia, according to Bellet. Nothing that could be in any way connected to her disappearance."

Nonetheless he would speak to Bellet about this. Why had he not mentioned it to Dupin?

"Have you spoken to Monsieur Durand about his wife's little trip to Paimpol, asked if he knew about it?"

"He just said that she did things like that sometimes. She liked nightlife, he didn't. She's twenty years younger than he is. He seemed quite cool."

"Really?"

"Yes."

"Oh well. I'll come by later."

"Yes, do that." There was total indifference in her voice.

"Just one more question. The documentation about the death of the woman seven years go—I assume it's with the commissariat in Lannion?"

"I had a copy made, through contacts of mine."

"Why?"

"I don't know. It all seemed a bit strange to me. But maybe it was pure chance. Seven years ago I hadn't even started working for the gendarmerie."

It wasn't her case at all, but she had the same idea that Dupin did.

"And did you discover anything unusual?"

"No."

"The story of the accident, did it sound plausible to you?"

"At the time, yes, but that means nothing."

She was right.

"I'd like to take a look at the paperwork."

"No problem."

It was all going much more easily than he had expected. Somehow it seemed she had taken him into "Team Trégastel," even though it could cause her proper trouble if it came out, but she didn't seem to be the worrying type.

"And then"—Dupin figured he ought to make the most of the good atmosphere and the opportunity—"I'd like to talk to you about Madame Guichard, the lady farmer, and Deputy Hugues Ellec."

"Fine."

Astonishing. Her uncle really had done great work.

The policewoman hung up.

Dupin had wandered up and down during the conversation without losing his view of the big windows of the entrance hall and museum shop. There was still no sign of Claire. She would be hidden some-where in the labyrinth, talking on the phone to the clinic.

Dupin was extremely satisfied.

He pulled out his notebook, and was pleased to see that he had set in motion most of his initiatives and errands. The nets he was spinning were getting ever larger and at the same time more stable. Not that he should be overconfident.

The indirect investigation was hard work basically, and there were a lot of blind spots.

He made a few notes about the conversation.

Suddenly he spotted Claire. She was flicking through a book in the museum shop. Then she headed for the exit. Right at that moment Dupin's phone rang. Obviously he shouldn't really answer, but then of course it might be something urgent.

Dupin answered quickly and began walking slowly across the street in a way that meant he didn't lose sight of Claire. She hadn't noticed him yet.

"Yes?"

"Commissaire Desespringalle here. I warned you. I am now notifying my prefect, your prefect, and the service supervisory authority."

"What for?" Dupin interrupted the commissaire from Lannion, even if he could imagine the answer.

"I'm just informing you."

Claire had spotted him now.

"Good."

"Is that all you have to say?" Desespringalle seemed just about to lose it.

Claire was heading rapidly toward Dupin.

"Great. Then everything is working fine. Thank you very much."
Dupin hung up.

Claire was already standing in front of him.

"The hot water boiler has been fixed." He tried to give a smile of
relief. The potential of that excuse had finally been exhausted.

"A magnificent aquarium, isn't it? It was a lot of fun." Claire beamed
at Dupin. "So, are you still interested in walking to the castle?"

"Absolutely." The message from the commissaire from Lannion
was worrying him more than it should. On the other side, maybe
he was bluffing. It would be hard for Desespringalle to prove he was
really investigating, and Dupin would strenuously deny everything.

* * *

The tide was at its lowest and they could walk across the seabed of the
Baie de Sainte-Anne to the Île Renote, shoes in their hands, toward
the fairy castle, hidden behind tall trees so that only part of the roof
was visible. Claire wanted to make a quick stop at their hotel, which
was on the way. Dupin waited outside.

Despite all the thoughts going through his head, the landscape still cast its spell on him. It was intoxicating. An enchanting
landscape of pink rock—hundreds, thousands, tens of thousands of
stones. A sea of rock stretching to the horizon. Even the seabed was
pink granite sand. And on top of it neon green, almost fluffy carpets
of seaweed, with dark, almost black seaweed on top of that. Tiny
silvery pale blue patches of water, here and there sparkling white
buoys, and sometimes even large shallows. Then once again wide
areas of calm water made to shine an almost unearthly metallic color
by the sunlight. In places where the sand had dried, it shimmered
bright pink. Boats were visible, generously spread out, as if placed deliberately, lying sleepily on their sides, sailing boats for the most part,

but fishing boats too. And above it all, the brilliant bright blue sky. A bitter, spicy smell of seaweed, algae, salt, and iodine.

Dupin loved walking over the seabed at low tide.

"The mouse ear, over there!" Claire had discovered it first. One point for her.

"The sad lizard's head." Dupin was pointing at a rock formation in front of them.

"Only with a lot of imagination," Claire admitted generously. "You always see more than is actually there."

After a long curve around a shallow arm of the sea, they approached the castle from the front now.

Basically the island was nothing more than a particularly large collection of rocks piled together; except for the small, dense pine wood growing as if out of the granite exactly in the middle of the island. And in its turn—or so the castle's creator must have seen it—out of the wood rose the castle itself. A cleverly thought-out composition. It was in full view from here.

"Fairy castle" was precisely the right description, as if it were conjured up, a strange, wildly romantic fantasy, obviously made completely from the pink miracle stone. Two high, round towers with conical slate roofs and lots of windows, a lordly main building with curved windows, highlighted by brighter stone. The castle itself looked as if it were something of a labyrinth. The entrance to the castle territory was via a small stone tower with a round arch. The entire island was enclosed by stone walls, which made the castle look something like a little fortress. A small road winding out of the muddy seabed ran up to the castle, past it, and disappeared behind the walls.

"'Costaérès Castle, or in Breton, Kastell Kostaerez, is a neo-Gothic castle,'" Claire read from the little book she had brought along in her handbag, which contained an unimaginably large quantity of things that seemed to have nothing to do with physical space. They were heading toward the little road.

"'This imposing building was erected in the neo-Gothic historic mode in the style of medieval fortresses between the years 1892 and 1896 as the home for the Polish-Lithuanian mathematician, electrical engineer, and inventor Bruno Abdank-Abakanowicz. The castle was a meeting point for many Polish emigrants, including the Polish Nobel Prize for Literature winner Henryk Sienkiewicz. His 1896 novel *Quo Vadis* was written on Costaérès.'" She turned to Dupin, then continued: "'In 1988 it became the second home of a very famous German actor, who restored it lovingly and true to the original, before it was acquired by Jérôme Chastagner in 2008'—not bad, eh?"

Dupin actually preferred getting to know new places and landscapes by simply experiencing them.

"Fascinating."

"We could—"

The noise of a car engine interrupted her. They turned around automatically. A car was coming toward them with unnecessary speed. It was a fat SUV, pearly white, splattered with mud, its windows tinted.

Claire had left the road and climbed onto a rock. "What a jerk."

Dupin kept on walking leisurely. At the last minute the driver stepped on the brakes, and blared the horn deafeningly.

The car came to a halt barely half a meter from Dupin. Only then did Dupin turn around. Slowly.

The driver's side window rolled down to reveal a brown, tanned face with long, straw-blond hair. A casual smile. Dupin had been expecting a bright red choleric face.

"Can I help you?" the driver asked in an extremely friendly way.

Although Dupin was standing in front of him, the man was looking at Claire alone. He didn't even seem to have noticed Dupin.

Claire too was perplexed. "We wanted to take a look at the island, with the wonderful castle."

"I'm the owner of both. Jérôme Chastagner. Unfortunately, madame, this is a private island. It's not open to visitors." He still hadn't even glanced at Dupin.

Chastagner, the machine builder. And quarry owner. A completely unexpected meeting. Madame Riou had said, if Dupin remembered rightly, he only came back from Saint-Brieuc late on Thursday evenings.

"In that case, Monsieur Chastagner," Dupin said irritably, "we'll just take a walk around the island. That can't be forbidden."

"As long as you don't enter the castle territory, then that's perfectly okay." He looked at Dupin for the first time, but only just a fleeting glance.

"Enjoy yourselves, and"—he was looking at Claire again—"*au revoir,* madame. I am exceptionally pleased to have made your acquaintance."

He revved up the engine. The window went up again.

Dupin stood to one side.

Chastagner put his foot down and the car shot up the sloping road between the granite blocks, then turned around one particularly large rock and disappeared.

Dupin stood still as a stone. "There was somebody else in the car. Did you see her too?"

"Her? Who?" Claire was irritated.

"A silhouette. A woman. Long hair. In the backseat. I could just see for a fraction of a second through the dark glass, as he was setting off. I'm almost certain."

"I didn't see anybody. And I had a better point of view from the rock."

"She was sitting in the back, on the left. She ducked her head."

"You're seeing ghosts, Georges. Those were probably just reflections."

"Believe me." Dupin's mind was racing. Obviously that would be an explanation. A possibility.

"And even so, why should that interest you? Isn't he allowed to be out and about with his wife or girlfriend?"

"He hasn't got anybody."

"How do you know?"

"Bellet." Dupin was making it up as he went along. "He told me this morning that the castle belonged to a hard-core bachelor, a genuine playboy."

"Then maybe it was one of his lovers."

"So why was she sitting in the back?"

"There was nobody there, Georges."

The best thing to do was to give in for the moment. "I probably did make a mistake, and it was just the headrest."

Claire couldn't know what made the incident so explosive. But what if Madame Durand really was sitting in the backseat? If she was hiding out with Chastagner, her new lover? But was the story plausible? Dupin somehow doubted it. And maybe his senses really were playing a trick on him. The bright sun, the dark reflecting mirrors, the sunglasses . . .

Claire gave him a distrustful look.

"Whatever," Dupin said, and continued walking. "So let's take that walk around the island."

"I don't feel like it anymore, Georges. Should we go somewhere and get something cold to drink?"

Dupin was torn. If they walked around the island they might see something interesting.

"Monsieur Bellet told me about a café, a hotel actually, right on the beach at Ploumanac'h, it must be that over there." Claire had already turned around and set off, without waiting for Dupin's answer.

Dupin understood immediately. Bellet was a sly accomplice. The "café" that he had recommended to Claire was undoubtedly the hotel in which the dead woman had been staying. Which Dupin obviously also wanted to visit. Up until now he hadn't found a reason to do so. Brilliant! And it couldn't be far. Trégastel, Ploumanac'h, and Perros-Guirec ran into one another seamlessly—all three of them on a rugged ledge by the sea—the castle belonging to Trégastel, while the next bit of shoreline, at the eastern end of the bay, was already part of Ploumanac'h.

"I feel like something sweet, a piece of *gâteau Breton*. What do you think?"

"Very much in agreement," Dupin said, walking two steps behind her.

"Oh, and something I forgot." Claire turned back to face him. "Everybody raves about the thalasso center on the main beach, where they're supposed to give wonderful massages. The Forum. I called them and by chance they have a free appointment today at six."

"Excellent, a good idea, it'll be good for you."

He could hardly believe his luck. He had spent the last hour wracking his brain in vain to come up with an excuse he could use later to get some time on his own. He had two important visits to make: the gendarmerie and the deputy's assistant. Now he would be able to make one of them, maybe even both.

"After that," Claire said with a satisfied expression on her face, "we can meet up for an apéritif, in the—"

Dupin's phone interrupted her.

The hairdresser, which probably meant it was important.

The moment couldn't have been more inopportune.

"Yes?"

Monsieur Julien cut straight to the chase. "She was strangled. The dead woman from Bordeaux. With a soft tape or a cloth or something like that. That means she was already dead before she was thrown down the quarry."

The hairdresser paused, clearly waiting for a reply from Dupin. Which took a bit of time. It was, after all, important news, not that he had seriously thought it was an accident. But now there was proof: they were definitely dealing with a murder.

"Thank you, Monsieur Julien, very kind of you to call. How stupid of me. I'll pick up my credit card later. How late are you open?"

It took a while before Monsieur Julien understood. "Ah, you can't speak right now." The hairdresser had wisely lowered his voice. "There's been no missing persons report from Bordeaux for a woman whose description matches the victim. And stranger still . . ." Dupin had used the detour around a shallow pool to drop back at least two meters behind Claire, the phone still clamped to his ear. "She isn't registered under the address she used to make her online reservation. There's no Virginie Inard there. There are just three families living there, and none of them are missing. None of them have ever heard the name."

"No, no, I've enough cash on me, no problem. I'll drop by later, at around seven, before you close . . . No, no, that's no problem for me." It had occurred to him that he could make use of this little hoax to get a bit more time to himself. "See you then, Monsieur Julien. And thanks once again."

Claire looked at him queryingly.

"Idiot that I am, I left my credit card at the hairdresser's."

"I see."

"I need to pick it up before he closes."

For whatever reason or other, Claire didn't pursue the point.

* * *

Even while they were getting closer, Dupin—although he was still occupied with the latest news—suddenly realized that Ploumanac'h and the terrace of the Castel Beau Site were going to make it onto his list of favorite places.

Ploumanac'h was a totally charming little village with stone houses at different angles against the wind and irregular wildflower beds, calm even in the busy season. Even smaller than Trégastel. No long, wild, empty beach like there, but a small and therefore inviting village beach. It was immediately understandable how Ploumanac'h had won the title of "prettiest village in France." And it was here, Dupin recalled, that Deputy Hugues Ellec lived.

Was the murder of this woman from Bordeaux—the question hadn't changed—connected with the attack on Deputy Rabier? There was some very important business going on. Obviously it could be quite possible that there was no connection at all even though the concentration of events was quite a coincidence. That was what had been flitting through Dupin's head ever since the call from the hairdresser.

Claire had read aloud from the little book of local hikes during the quarter-hour walk from the beach to Ploumanac'h. Dupin had little more to say than "very interesting" or "exciting."

He had just gone a few steps ahead, worried that there might be a police car outside the hotel. To his relief, there was none to be seen. Probably they would be relatively discreet in the high season. Just to be careful, though, he had led Claire straight to the terrace, away from the side of the hotel where the main entrance and parking lot were.

The Castel Beau Site was directly on the beach, just slightly above the sand. It couldn't have been prettier. An old, elegant, elongated stone house made of, what else, pink granite, which occasionally changed to gray and brown, giving the building a particular charm. Four stories high, a curved slate roof, narrow balconies outside each room, matte black filigree railings, and the same around the terrace made of weathered wooden planks.

They sat down at one of the low beige tables at the front in dark comfortable armchairs, next to pots of magnificent oleander. A relaxed atmosphere, as if in a lounge.

"This view outdoes everything," Claire said.

She was right. It was gorgeous.

A small sickle-shaped bay amidst the white, just slightly pink-tinted sand, which went out some forty to fifty meters into the damp seabed, a few pink, yellow, and white buoys. Pink piles of rock, scattered effectively in every imaginable size and shape, in water that was pale blue at low tide.

What made the panorama particularly, extraordinarily picturesque was that the bay was framed by wild, jutting outcrops of land that faded away gently on either side, as if someone had tried to enclose it in the most beautiful manner. A few battered pines and firs on the outcrops looked as if perfectly placed. And right in the middle, as if it were another masterpiece of landscape arrangement: the Île de Costaérès. Seagulls circling in a spotless blue sky only added to the effect.

Dupin's gaze wandered from the beach to the hotel and the terrace. It was perfectly equipped, as if designed that way, for guests to admire the scenery from the best perspective possible.

"*Bonjour,*" said a very young man, almost still a boy, who was standing in front of them, in a white shirt and black cotton pants, almost exaggeratedly preppy. "What can I get you?"

"A large water, please." Claire had taken control of the ordering. "Two Breizh colas, and for me a *gâteau Breton,* with caramel." She shot Dupin a questioning glance.

"One for me too, but with raspberry, and a *petit café.*"

"And the Breizh cola as well?"

"The Breizh cola as well, ice cold, if possible."

The young man disappeared.

Everything in the hotel, at least here on the terrace, seemed to be business as usual.

"I'll be back in a minute."

They laughed. They had both stood up at the same time and said the same sentence.

"You go first, Georges." Claire sat down again.

It was a curious situation, but he profited from Claire's secret activities, and she from his.

Dupin made his way toward the terrace entrance to the hotel. First of all he came into a bar, with the same magnificent view. From in between an impressive whiskey collection he could see Claire sitting at the table. Her position made it clear: she was on the phone. It was unbelievable. She had only waited a few seconds.

Dupin left the bar for the reception, which was by the main entrance, to the side of the building. He greeted the two hotel employees extremely politely, and so naturally that it never occurred to them to ask him any questions.

Every bit as naturally, he walked the few meters more to the staircase. He mounted the staircase energetically, but not quickly, left the stairwell on the second floor, and looked down the long corridor.

Nobody to be seen.

He took the stairs to the next floor. At the left end of the corridor was a cart with fresh towels and cleaning supplies. That was what he was looking for. He had to be quick. He didn't have much time.

"Hello?" He walked up to a room with the door open.

The chambermaid came up to him: small, midtwenties maybe, black hair piled high, a welcoming smile. "Can I help you?"

"I . . ."

It was so natural for him just to turn up anywhere during an investigation and ask questions of anyone, that he hadn't thought how he should proceed here.

"I'm investigating the Virginie Inard case." That was going to be the most successful approach, albeit also the riskiest. But he had no other choice if he wanted to get any further.

He made a gesture as if to get out his police ID, then continued talking as if he had already shown it to her. "I have a few questions."

"There are a lot of police on this case," she replied coquettishly. "They've been everywhere in the building, and they're still in the second building. My colleague's been questioned three times!"

"How about you?"

"I've only just got here. I'm doing the evening shift today. But I was called at home by one of your colleagues, but only briefly."

"I know," Dupin faked, hoping he would get away with it. "Could you give me your impression of Madame Inard?"

Chambermaids were always amongst the best sources of information.

"You don't look very much like a policeman."

Dupin had heard the sentence often, even when he was on official duty. "That's a relief. So, what can you tell me about Madame Inard?"

"A very calm person, not unfriendly, but she didn't say much, barely a greeting. She would just be there."

"What does that mean?"

"No idea, just like I said. Your colleague asked me the same question."

"Did you ever see her with anyone else?" Dupin had pulled out his notebook.

"No, never. She was always on her own. It didn't really look like she was on vacation, but she didn't act like a businesswoman either."

"What makes you think that she wasn't on vacation here?"

"I don't know. Just like that. A feeling." She rolled her eyes.

"When did she check in?"

"She arrived on Tuesday evening last week. She was mostly in her room for the first few days, lying on the balcony. I was on the morning shift last week. That's when I saw her most. The same went for my colleague in the afternoon."

"What did she do in her room?"

"No idea."

"Did you notice anything curious about her?"

"There are odd things about everybody, aren't there?"

That was Dupin's own conviction. But he made no reply. The chambermaid continued: "She didn't seem frightened or anything if that's what you mean. Not worked up. More indifferent. Not as if there was anything in particular on her mind. Or," she grimaced, "to make you think she might be killed, or that she was in danger. She had very smart clothes."

"What sort of room did she have?"

"A suite."

"How expensive is that?"

"Two hundred and eighty euros a night."

Money didn't seem to have been a problem for Virginie Inard.

"She booked for a week. So she would have had to leave on Tuesday?"

"You'd have to check that with reception."

"But by Monday night or Tuesday morning, she still hadn't packed?"

"No, nothing at all."

"Were all of Madame Inard's things still in her room on Wednesday morning? Was there anything missing? Had the room been changed in any way?" Dupin hadn't much time left; he increased his normally fast talking speed.

"Everything was there. Just like the day before. You really do all ask the same questions. You haven't conferred very well with your colleagues!" She grinned.

"We question people independently, unselfconsciously. Each one begins from the beginning." He'd given out the preposterous explanation with professional certainty. "Did Madame Inard have any unusual things with her?" he asked.

"No, just the usual."

"Do you know at what time she left the hotel on Tuesday evening?"

"Around ten o'clock, according to reception."

"Fine, and definitely nobody saw her after that?"

"No. Yesterday morning we noticed that the bed was just as it had been early Tuesday evening. The receptionist said that. And when she still hadn't turned up by midday, they told the hotel owner. Everybody had heard that a dead body had been found in the quarry."

Dupin wrote all of this down. It seemed that Virginie Inard had met her murderer shortly after leaving the hotel.

"Was she in her room on Tuesday, when you had made it up for the night?" Dupin was hurrying so much to get his question in that he had to be careful not to muddle things up.

"No."

"Did you speak to her in the few days before?"

"Just a few words. We said hello to each other. And talked about the weather. Nothing more."

"Did she have an accent, from the southwest. Bordeaux?"

"No idea. More like Paris."

"Paris?"

"Yes. But I wouldn't swear to it. Not particularly elegant at any rate. We only interchanged a few meaningless words."

"Thank you, Mademoiselle . . ." Dupin smiled at the chambermaid.

"Mademoiselle Fleur."

"Thank you, Mademoiselle Fleur. That was very thorough information. You were a great help to me."

He turned to leave.

"Would you like me to tell you something else?"

Dupin turned back around.

"I think there were a few nights she didn't spend here."

"What makes you think that?"

"On Sunday morning I made her bed. And it looked like a bed that was supposed to give the impression somebody had slept in it, when in reality they hadn't."

"Can you say that with certainty?"

She gave Dupin an indignant look.

"You said several nights?" he said.

"Saturday to Monday."

"Two nights?"

"Yes."

"But she didn't mention it to reception?"

"I have no idea."

That was the truth.

Dupin had noted all the details.

"Did you mention your suppositions to the policeman who called you?"

"No." It was clearly something she didn't want to say. "I would have done, but I had to be certain first. I've been through all my memories once again."

"Well, now the police know, you don't need to worry about it. So, many thanks once again, Mademoiselle Fleur."

If Dupin was lucky—and he didn't want to think of the other possibility—they wouldn't question the chambermaid again. And never hear anything about her conversation with him.

A minute later he came out of the bar onto the terrace. He had quickly rung Bellet from the stairwell, to ask him to warn Rabier's assistant of his visit. He wanted to ask Bellet why he hadn't told him of his conversation with Madame Durand, but would do so in person.

He got a shock at reception because he found two police cars parked outside and two men, one in uniform, one in plainclothes, coming hurriedly toward the hotel. The one in plainclothes—tall, dark, slightly reddish curly hair, a narrow face with a notable scar on the left cheek—might well be the commissaire from Lannion. Not least because one of the two cars outside was a large Renault Talisman.

Dupin fled hurriedly into the bar. The still guileless women from reception were now looking at him with wrinkled foreheads. Dupin gave them a particularly friendly greeting.

He had already seen through the bar window that Claire was no longer on the phone. She had pushed her chair back and was making herself comfortable. She seemed totally relaxed, or pretending to be so, her view fixed to the horizon. It looked as if she'd been sitting like that forever.

"A remarkable place, isn't it?" Dupin had chosen a casual tone of voice. "I took a bit of a look around." That would sound believable enough; it was a habit of his. "This could be a hotel for us."

He sat down.

Claire had already drunk her water and her Breizh cola and was just sticking her fork in the last piece of *gâteau Breton*. Dupin reached for his *petit café*, which was lukewarm by now.

"I was thinking the same thing. There's a lot of style to the place. Maybe we ought to go and see the monument to Saint Guirec. It seems that in the sixth century he landed here after crossing from the British Isles." Claire seemed really lively again. "There are a couple of amusing customs recorded in the book. Local girls looking to get married down the centuries would stick a needle in the statue's nose; some still do today. The other tradition is that young mothers would kiss the statue's feet, to get their children walking earlier."

"I'm afraid we need to go," Dupin said, looking at his watch. "It's five. Your massage appointment is in an hour and I assume you want to go back to the hotel first."

"Yes, definitely."

Dupin put a big piece of cake in his mouth, washed it down with a gulp of cola, and took out his wallet.

"I've paid already," Claire said, and got to her feet.

"Didn't you need to—?" Dupin stopped speaking.

The man in uniform and the one in plainclothes came toward them from the right.

It was too late to make a run and leave the terrace. He would have to improvise.

"I . . ." He stumbled a bit, then continued decisively. There was nothing to do but attract Claire's full attention until the air was clear. "I wanted to ask you something. Sit down again."

Claire frowned.

"I thought we were just about to go? We can talk on the way."

"It's something best talked about sitting down." What was he saying?

"Can't we do this over dinner?"

"This is the right moment."

His words were getting more and more ridiculous. Claire's expressions showed irritation, and concern.

"Okay then."

She sat down. Dupin changed seats so that he was now sitting opposite her. He leaned toward her, his back to the terrace. That way the police wouldn't in any way be able to recognize him.

"Paul"—the owner of the Amiral and an old friend—"told me about a house in Concarneau, on the corniche, right on the Plage Mine, that nice little beach. To the right coming from my apartment, then maybe four hundred meters. Boulevard Katerine Wylie. One of those dream houses. Ten meters from the sea." He realized how incomprehensible he sounded. "One of those houses you like so much. With the bright blue of those hydrangea bushes in front of it."

Dupin fell silent and turned his head to the side, as inconspicuously as possible. The two men had stopped five meters from them on the terrace.

". . . must have happened somewhere . . ." Dupin heard. The tall man with the scar was speaking but he couldn't say for certain if it was the voice of the commissaire from Lannion he had heard on the phone. It was just a few words, and voices on the phone often sounded different. ". . . have researched . . . nothing . . ."

"Do you want to move?" Claire asked, astonished.

"Do you know which house I mean?"

"I think so."

"It's a big house."

They had both admired it on many walks together.

"What are you getting at?" Claire's puzzlement was combined with curiosity and gentle impatience.

"I like my apartment, but it occurred to me that if you're going to live by the sea, do it properly. There you can get up in the morning and go swimming straightaway. Don't you think that would be wonderful?"

Dupin had lived in the same apartment opposite the aquarium in Concarneau for six years. Claire had moved from Paris to Quimper the year before last, a big step for both of them.

"Of course. Is it up for rent? In which case do it, I think it's a great idea."

"I've already done it."

"What?"

"I've sorted out a few details in the last few days, and finally come to an agreement."

"That's fantastic!" Claire beamed, genuine happiness on her face, if a bit of confusion at the same time. "Great! Congratulations."

"The house has been totally renovated. Very stylishly. You'll like it."

"You've been inside already?"

"Twice. And the agency sent me a floor plan I can show you. But it's too small to see properly on a phone."

Claire didn't ask anything else.

Dupin picked up the policemen's voices again. It appeared they had come a bit closer. The taller one seemed worked up: "Nothing. Not the slightest, damn it!"

If that was a summary of the state of their investigation, then they were fumbling in the dark. Dupin suppressed the beginning of a smile. He now focused totally on his conversation with Claire.

"I was thinking that it could be our house." This was the point that had been occupying him for a long time.

"Our house?"

"If you want, Claire. It could be for the two of us."

"I—" Claire stopped. Her facial expression and body language were hard to read.

She looked Dupin in the eyes for a while.

Then she smiled, a typical Claire smile. Dupin had the feeling there was more to it. Even if he couldn't quite say what it was.

". . . totally mad. But a big thing . . . Madame Guichard . . ." The two policemen were walking right behind Dupin's back.

"We ought to go now, Georges." Claire had said it kindly and got up at the same time. "We can talk quietly later. Maybe over dinner."

One thing was clear: she wasn't going to say any more about it now.

Dupin couldn't blame her. It hadn't gone particularly well. He hadn't exactly staged it very skillfully. And of course a question like that wasn't one he should just have asked on the fly, and under such complicated circumstances. He had been thinking about the idea for so long. And was even more sure from his own point of view.

"Yes. Let's do that: talk about it quietly later."

Dupin dared to glance to one side, to the right this time. The two men were walking straight toward the entrance to the bar. Then they were inside the hotel, and the danger was gone.

He stood up.

Claire took a few steps, then turned around, came up him, and kissed him.

Maybe it hadn't gone all that badly. And at least this way the moment hadn't slipped into solemnity, which he had been worried about.

* * *

"That's spectacular news, Monsieur le Commissaire. Can you believe it? Strangled! Then thrown into the quarry. Who would do a thing like that?"

They had gotten back to the hotel at ten to six. Claire had set off straightaway to her massage. Dupin had sat himself down on the balcony. "Officially" he was due to be at the hairdresser's just before seven to get his credit card back. He waited five minutes after Claire had left the room. Until he could be sure the coast was clear. Then he had hurried down to reception to find Bellet.

"Monsieur Bellet, you had a conversation with Madame Durand on Monday. On the evening she vanished." Dupin stressed the sentence deliberately and left it hanging there. He was curious to hear what Bellet would say.

"It . . . wasn't a conversation. Just a few minutes . . ." Bellet looked both stunned and rattled. "In the days before that I had seen very little of Madame Durand. And never spoken to her. Just hello and good-bye."

"Around ten minutes, you stated. What was it about? And why didn't you say anything about it to me?"

"I was sitting at the bar that evening. On my own. I'd just drunk a Pastis Marin, as I do every evening around six. She sat down next to me, ordered a vodka martini, and began to talk."

Dupin had taken out his Clairefontaine and begun to take meticulous notes.

"About what?"

Bellet's eyes widened. There was something that made him uncomfortable. "About the weather. That we're having a great summer. The way people talk . . ."

"What else?"

"How pretty it is here."

"What else, Bellet? You're hiding something from me."

Bellet was getting grumpy. Dupin didn't have much time: about an hour and a half. He needed to use his free time as economically as possible.

Bellet hesitated, then said: "She was very . . . forward, if you know what I mean?"

"Very forward?"

"Yes, she was . . ." Bellet dithered. ". . . sort of flirting with me."

"Madame Durand? With you?" It sounded unlikely. "I mean, are you sure, Monsieur Bellet?"

"Well." Bellet was obviously finding this very difficult. "More than once she made eyes at me, while we were talking"—he had looked around carefully before saying this; for his wife, Dupin assumed— "and asked me if I knew a nice bar."

"A bar? Where she and you could go together?"

"She didn't say it quite that explicitly."

"So how did she say it?"

"It was her tone of voice," Bellet said, almost indignantly. "I may not be a youngster anymore but I'm not stupid—I can still handle myself, Monsieur le Commissaire. She meant a bar in which we could continue our chitchat."

"I understand. Did you suggest one?"

"No, I changed the subject."

"Did she ask again?"

"No."

Dupin hadn't the faintest idea what he might make of this information.

"I told her I had to work, made my apologies, and left."

"You and she had never met alone in the days prior to that?"

"No."

It was curious.

"Did she come on to you in any other way that evening?"

Bellet looked a little worried. "No. Just that. I mean, what I just told you."

"Okay. Did you get hold of Madame Rabier's assistant?"

"I did." Bellet seemed pleased Dupin had changed the subject. "He's waiting for you. Rue du Roi Arthur, number forty-seven. Right behind the Grève Blanche. Our most famous beach. The finest white sand, if you want a bit of a rest from pink! I've marked it all out here." He gave Dupin a little street map. Dupin would later copy the marks onto his own map. "And given you the full names and contact details. The gendarmerie is right in the middle, for your conversation afterward." He winked at Dupin. "Place Sainte-Anne, obliquely opposite the chapel, on the other side of the newspaper store, right next to the bar Ty Breizh. A stone's throw. That's the advantage of little villages."

It was strange that Dupin had noticed every building on the square, except for the gendarmerie.

"How do you know that I'm going to the gendar—" Dupin didn't finish the sentence. Obviously news flowed in both directions.

Bellet smiled.

"Can you tell me exactly where this Ellec has his house in Ploumanac'h? The deputy."

"Chemin de la Pointe. The big, modern 'architect's house,' on the right at the end of the dead-end street, spanking new." Bellet made a dismissive gesture with his hand. "Unmissable, right by the water."

Dupin made a note. "Do you know the owners of the Castel Beau Site?"

"Christelle and Pierre? Of course. Christelle is my wife's sister's best friend."

Excellent.

"Could you find out from when until when precisely Virginie Inard had booked her room? Seven days? In which case she should have been gone already on Tuesday? Or did she extend her stay?"

There was a twinkle in Bellet's eye. An assignment! He looked flattered. "But of course! I'll get the information for you straightaway. Anything else?"

"Ask them if they thought there was anything unusual about Madame Inard. If she contacted anybody. And if Deputy Ellec, the lady farmer Maïwenn Guichard, or Jérôme Chastagner were in the hotel at any time over the last few days. In the restaurants, the bar, wherever."

"Consider it done."

"Or Madame Rabier—before the 'incident.'" Dupin had deliberately chosen a neutral word.

"The deputy? Really?"

"And if you don't mention that—"

"I am investigating for you. That goes without saying." Bellet sounded indignant. "You know that . . ."

"And the Durands' suite"—Dupin lowered his voice, even though it was totally unnecessary, it was just the two of them—"did it have two beds? Do you know if they slept separately?"

"Yes." Bellet pulled his eyebrows together. "But I really shouldn't mention things like that. I'm only telling you. By the way, your new haircut is pretty cool."

"See you later, Monsieur Bellet."

It was nine minutes past six.

* * *

Dupin headed down the glorious path to the sea at a sprightly pace; past the thalasso center where Claire was now enjoying her massage, over the wild and rugged headland between the two beaches to the Plage Grève Blanche.

Behind the beach were huge sand dunes covered in glimmering bushy grass that fell steeply down to the beach. Partly washed away. Huge stones that looked as if they'd been carted here to avoid anything worse. At the beginning of the year the front pages of *Ouest-France* and *Le Télégramme* had had spectacular photos of a colossal winter storm accompanied by an unusually high tide that had struck the land, sweeping away vast amounts of sand and even a few boats.

If it weren't for these high dunes, this part of Trégastel would have been defenseless before the raging ocean. It was unimaginable on a gentle high summer's day like today, when the sea lay rippling and calm.

The sand really was a blinding white, and the beach, vastly bigger than the one Dupin and Claire lay on, lived fully up to its name. A gentle curve that turned into a sandy, stony tongue of land and linked up with the Grève Rose coming up from the south. Just to make the picture perfect, there was a bizarre pink granite islet at the farthest tip of the tongue of land. The "White Strand" was properly considered one of the finest beaches in Brittany. On either side of the tip the sea was calm, clear, and in bright Caribbean layers of color: first crystalline clear blue, then emerald green, then turquoise, then gradually into green-blue and finally deep blue. The island, perhaps a hundred meters long and surrounded by small neighboring islands, lay there like a gigantic fish in the water. Bright green grass amid the pink granite made for a crazy contrast.

Even though the colors were the same in the protected bay of Ploumanac'h, the atmosphere was quite different. The beach, the landscape, the whole world here was exposed to the open sea; everything was more wild, more rough. Even the color tones here weren't in the slightest warm or mellow, but clear and sharp, as if they were perpetually whipped by the sea breeze.

Dupin searched the dunes for a way down to the beach, found it, then stopped to take a look at the map.

The Rue du Roi Arthur had to be just around the corner.

Two minutes later he was standing outside number 47. A new building. Angular, three floors, flat roof, plain and simple.

VIVIANE RABIER. ÉLUE CONSEIL RÉGIONAL DE LA BRETAGNE. A discreet sign. Third floor. The highest.

Dupin took the stairs, not the elevator. A young man, thirty at most, came down the hallway to meet him. He had tousled blond hair sticking in all directions, and wore a rumpled bright blue shirt. It looked as if Dupin had just woken him.

"*Bonjour,* Monsieur le Commissaire. I'm Aiméric Janvier." He spoke with a subdued, almost conspiratorial voice and looked nervously around the bare corridor. "Come with me." He went through an open door into the office. "As you know, Madame Rabier told me that—"

Dupin's phone. It hadn't rung for an astonishingly long time.

"Excuse me just a moment." Dupin went back out into the hall.

A concealed number.

"Hello?"

"Now you're going too far, Dupin. Clearly too far!"

Dupin recognized the voice immediately. The commissaire from Lannion was beside himself. And from his tone it seemed he was referring to something concrete.

Dupin remained pointedly calm. "I've just been admiring the Grève Blanche, a completely extraordinary—"

"Don't even start with me!" Desespringalle interrupted curtly. "I—"

"What do you mean by that, my dear colleague?" Dupin had no problem being loud when he wanted to. Or interrupting the other man.

"What do I mean? You let your assistant snuffle around! While you yourself play at being on vacation, and think I'm too stupid not to notice?"

It was getting ever more incomprehensible. "What are you talking about? Whom have I got snuffling around?"

"A certain Nolwenn. Your secretary, don't pretend you don't know what I'm talking about!"

Dupin knew nothing.

"She's asked for follow-up investigation into Hugues Ellec on your behalf. The member of staff in the land registry who spoke with your secretary went to her head of department because she wasn't sure if it was right to give information to the Concarneau commissariat. By chance the department head is a good friend of mine."

Nolwenn investigating? Behind his back? In the case concerning the deputy? Because of the sand dune and the possible "advantageous deals"? For Nolwenn to speak to the relevant employee would be typical for her; as a rule she never spoke to any senior staff.

"Thank you. Very good of you." Dupin hung up.

He couldn't believe it. Claire and Nolwenn had sentenced him to strict "vacation time," to a total abstinence from all work, and forbidden him to take any interest in any events in Trégastel. And now one of them was behaving as if it was almost a normal day at the clinic, while the other was researching industriously behind his back into precisely those events she had insisted had nothing to do with him. He was more than a little tempted to pick up the phone straightaway, except that on the one hand he was expecting an urgent call himself, and on the other it was cleverer to see whether he might not do as Claire had done and take advantage of the situation.

But this wasn't the time. He would deal with it later.

Quickly—and still feeling indignant—he walked through the open door into a spacious office, elegant, set out modernly but not extravagantly: light wooden furniture shelves, sideboards. A wide panoramic window with a low table and four comfortable chairs in front of it. Impressive black-and-white photographs on the wall, of Breton landscapes.

"This is where we receive guests. In the room next door there are two desks, and beyond that a small interview room."

A suitable layout.

Dupin came straight to the point: "Madame Rabier confided in me that you're looking into some shady business."

"I'm not sure that 'shady' is the right word. It sounds dangerous." The young man's voice was shaky. He seemed worried.

"Show me what you have."

Aiméric Janvier reached for a blue folder lying on the sideboard. "These are copies of documents relating to the Ellec family's building permission. And to Chastagner's illegal extension of his quarry."

He handed them to Dupin. Janvier had everything well prepared.

"These are copies of your copies?"

"Yes."

"Do you have the originals?"

The young man looked unsure of himself. "No, Madame Rabier said . . . ," he hemmed and hawed, ". . . that the documents shouldn't leave the room. She asks you to leave them here." His eyes were glued to the floor.

"Do you have documents on any other things connected to Monsieur Ellec?"

"Formally, just these."

"What does that mean?"

"There have been lots of accusations over time. But always only vague. Right now we want to look into a concrete issue formally."

"When are the next elections?"

"Next year. But it's about more than just the elections."

Dupin took the blue folder, went over to one of the armchairs, and sat down. Inside the folder there were two plastic envelopes with stickers on them, one pink, the other green: CHASTAGNER and ELLEC.

Dupin started with Ellec, the deputy, and once again he thought of Nolwenn. Why on earth hadn't she let him know?

Dupin laid the first sheet on the table. Rabier's assistant had sat down beside him. "What's your feeling? About who could have been responsible for the attack on your boss?"

"Ellec," he replied without hesitating.

Dupin's eyes flitted down to the first document. "Have you any evidence?"

"No. But he hates Madame Rabier."

"He would appear not to be alone in that. At the very least he agrees with Chastagner and Maïwenn Guichard," Dupin said casually.

He was looking at the ground plan of a piece of property right by the sea. On the outcrop near Ploumanac'h, just about three hundred meters from the beach, where they had just been. Someone had scribbled at the top of the document: *Terrain B 7102/12—Ellec Family. 5300 square meters,* then dozens of technical details, abbreviations, none of which Dupin understood. But without doubt it was a prime location.

"Who found these documents and copied them?"

"I did."

"Without being noticed."

A hesitation.

"I think so."

"But you aren't certain."

"Yes, I am."

It still couldn't be ruled out that somebody had spotted Janvier and used it to justify action against Rabier.

Dupin flicked through other pages. Maybe fifteen. And then back to the architect's plan.

"The decisive document is the last one."

Dupin leafed through them.

"That's it—the special permission, which the Ellec family claim they've had for twelve years. Given to them by the previous mayor, who's long dead now. Here, you can see," Janvier nodded at the page, "that he wrote: *'special permission issued in agreement with the prefect.'*"

Dupin read through the short text. At first glance it all seemed credible.

"It's been done very astutely. The mayor is dead. The prefect is retired. And claims he can't remember this process, but thinks it's quite possible. I've spoken to him in person. He observed that the community has a lot to thank the family for. It's all very vague. But we know that in those days the mayor pursued a very strict line regarding the protection of the undeveloped coastline. Agreeing to something like this would have been very unlike him."

"So you think this document is a forgery?"

"I'm certain of it."

"The former prefect, the one you spoke to, will be wondering why you're interested in this matter. Especially, of course, because he was very strict on the issue. But even if not, he'll still realize that you're investigating further."

This was the second incident that could have led to someone

finding out about Rabier's research and using it for their own aims. And there would be more to it, as is ever the case, if somebody thought they could find out something secretly.

Aiméric was silent, his head hanging down.

"I assume the original document is in the land registry?"

"Yes, and that's in the town hall. Unfortunately I couldn't take the original with me. And that's precisely what we need." The young man looked seriously worried. "I believe the paper the document is written on is genuine. It looks older. But that's not a problem—in the files there are sometimes empty pages that can be used. If you have an old typewriter it looks wholly convincing. And obviously it's possible to make excellent forgeries that can only be proven by an analysis of the original."

"And the document only turned up this year."

"In March, out of nowhere."

"And what did the current mayor say about it?"

"He was very surprised at first. But he didn't do much about it."

"Did you speak to him yourself?"

"No, that was too risky for me."

Nonetheless.

Dupin looked at his watch. Twenty to seven.

"What about the other research? Into Chastagner?"

"The crucial thing here is not any one document. It's the absence of any document. Specifically, the document permitting the extension of the quarry. Which he undertook piece by piece. On the scale plan you can see the most recent official approval of an extension, in the year 2000. But there is no approval for a further extension, as shown by the current actual borders of the quarry."

"And how did you get to see these documents?"

"They're in the commercial office. Madame Rabier submitted that we were looking into the option of extending the three quarries, and want to find out the current status. She went there in person."

Not too great a camouflage. Of course this could also be how someone found out: the three quarry owners, the mayor, the town council.

"Then in April we used a drone to take photos which showed that Chastagner was building in several places up to a hundred meters farther than was specified back in 2000. He claimed he had approval for everything, but saw no grounds for making the firm's secrets public. We want to make an official submission to the town council soon."

"You had a drone fly over the quarry?"

Dupin had taken the relevant pages out of the envelope, to look for the photos. And there they were.

"It's not a big deal. Today you can get these in reasonable quality for a hundred euros."

"Anyone could have witnessed this. Maybe even Chastagner in person."

"We did it at twilight," Janvier said proudly. "We weren't interested in any details, just the actual extension. And you can see that clearly."

Even twilight wasn't a reliable protection.

"Have you announced anywhere that you're about to make this submission?"

Madame Rabier hadn't mentioned anything about this to Dupin.

"Of course not. If we had done they'd have been able to prepare. It's supposed to be a surprise coup."

"When do you intend to do it?"

"After the summer vacation, the middle or end of September."

It was all a lot more concrete than Dupin had been given to believe.

"Right." Dupin stood up. "I'm taking the folder with me."

He began to move. The young man hurried after him.

"But Madame Rabier expressly said that was not on—"

"I'll explain to her." Dupin was already at the door. He turned around. Janvier looked extremely stressed. "Don't you worry, I'll take full responsibility."

With those words, Dupin opened the door and walked out into the corridor.

He had what he needed.

* * *

The gendarmerie turned out to be an inconspicuous narrow little stone house made of reddish brown granite, set back a bit from the road, squeezed between a bar and a wonderful-looking *boulangerie-pâtisserie*. The matte gray notice on the door reading GENDARMERIE DE TRÉGASTEL was particularly unnoticeable. The glass in the ground-floor windows was darkened to stop anyone seeing in from the street.

On the way there, Dupin had concentrated on what he should do with the information about Nolwenn's "undercover investigation." And finally decided on a calculated response: he would try to make the most of the situation in favor of his own operations.

As he left the house behind the Grève Blanche there was a strange moment. There was a man sitting in a white Peugeot parked obliquely opposite the deputy's office, talking on the phone. Dupin couldn't see him properly, but he had the impression that the man was watching him. Usually Dupin had a good nose for these situations, but nonetheless he wasn't certain. Maybe he had just imagined it.

Dupin pushed the office bell, the same model as the one they had in Concarneau, and raised his head to the sturdy-looking camera above the door. Also the same as in Concarneau.

It took a while and then a loud buzzer sounded.

He pushed against the heavy entrance door. A narrow hallway. Directly opposite a door with a MESDAMES/MESSIEURS sign. He was standing right next to the bathrooms.

An open door to the right led into the office, with the darkened windows to the street. An unmissable orange paper arrow on the wall was a clear pointer for the public.

Dupin walked into the room, as modest as the rest of the building, with furniture that had to be decades old, dating back to the heydays of Formica. The air was stuffy, dusty. Dupin guessed there was also the smell of identical insufferable cleaners they used in his commissariat—he was convinced they were standard in French administrative buildings, although that too might be a fantasy, as nobody in Concarneau apart from him could smell it. He wouldn't be able to stick it out here for more than five minutes.

On both sides of the room were beige desks, each with an office chair behind it and two visitor chairs in front. The right wall was covered with shelving, also in gloomy Formica, laden with folders and sheaves of paper.

To the left was a large pinboard—definitely also from the Formica era—and a long bench that looked anything but inviting.

The policewoman, Inès Marchesi, was sitting at the left desk not far from the pinboard, typing on a computer keyboard. An outsize screen, a mess of cables. Sharing the desk was a defiantly high mountain of paper, the lower pages already going yellow at the edges.

Marchesi didn't make a motion to stand up. When Dupin approached she greeted him with a brief nod and even that, judging by the expression on her face, seemed to be an effort. There was still no obvious sign that she allegedly was well disposed to him.

Dupin sat down on one of the visitor's seats. "Thank you for taking the time to see me."

It was probably a good idea to make a friendly start.

"I wanted to—" Dupin's phone rang.

Yet again a concealed number. And yet again at the wrong moment.

"Excuse me, please, I ought to take this."

Not a good start.

Marchesi shrugged indifferently, and continued to type.

Dupin stood up and walked back to the little hallway next to the bathroom, starting the conversation as he walked. "Yes?"

"I've had a new threat against me," the voice whispered. Dupin recognized it immediately: Madame Rabier. "A letter once again, just half an hour ago. I—"

"What does it say?"

"Just a few words: *We know you've spoken to the police. Don't say another word, or face the consequences.*"

"It could be a bluff." It was possible, even though Dupin didn't believe it.

"Is this what you were expecting, Monsieur le Commissaire?" There was hope in her question. He shouldn't have said anything.

"I'm not expecting anything. We just have to consider all possibilities. Was the letter in the general clinic mailbox?"

Dupin imagined that the commissaire from Lannion would be having the entrance to her house and the mailbox watched; anything less would be pure negligence.

"No. This one came in the mail. Stamped yesterday evening in Trégastel. The police have already taken it away for examination."

"What did the commissaire from Lannion say?"

"I rang Commissaire Desespringalle immediately after receiving the letter. He went silent for a while, which wasn't very reassuring. But then he said they were probably about to make a breakthrough."

"He said they were about to make a 'breakthrough'?"

"Yes."

"Is the commissaire from Lannion about one meter ninety, tall and thin? With a gaunt face and a very conspicuous scar?"

"Yes. Why?"

Then it could have been him. So far his comments hadn't sounded remotely like there was a breakthrough pending. Either he was just making something up for the deputy, or in the last hour or so there had been a surprising development, an extremely improbable turn of events.

"Did he hint at any reason for what happened?"

"No. But I wasn't to be afraid. He was going to reinforce the surveillance of my room and in the hospital. On the street too. And on the field in front of the hospital. My room is on the third floor. He had specifically ordered extra surveillance. He wants to keep me here in the hospital until the situation is cleared up, and there is no more danger."

In theory, not a bad idea. That was the safest place.

"Might I ask where your . . . I mean Madame Guichard's husband is at the moment?"

"He's still in Rennes—the wind farm."

The controversial project.

"Desespringalle is having him watched." It seemed she found it somehow annoying.

"Good." Dupin was serious. Obviously it was right to keep him under surveillance. If only to completely dismiss him as a suspect.

"You don't still think he could have something to do with the stone throwing and the threats?" Madame Rabier asked.

"It's always a good idea to keep everything in consideration. I've just been with your assistant. One thing that's very important to me, Madame Rabier: Apart from the two investigations that I know about going on in your office, are there any others? Into other people? If so, now is the time to tell me."

"No, I swear to you." She sounded convincing.

"Are there other things concerning the two you're looking into?"

"I would tell you if there were. As it is, we need to put Ellec's, how should I put it, 'activities' under the microscope. There's something wrong there. But nobody wants to look into it."

"There is no documentation therefore of other incidents?"

"No." That answer also sounded clear and decisive.

"Don't let anyone into your room except for the police and doctors, Madame Rabier. Nobody." Dupin was well aware that this was hardly encouraging.

"Not even my assistant?"

"Not even him. Turn down all visits. Discuss everything on the phone."

"Do you consider Aiméric suspicious? Commissaire Desespringalle said I should only see people I trusted completely."

"Right now, I suspect nobody in particular. It's purely a precautionary measure."

"I understand." She seemed a bit relieved. "Thank you, Monsieur le Commissaire."

"Keep to my recommendations, Madame Rabier."

"I'll do that."

She hung up.

Dupin turned and went back into the policewoman's office.

Whatever it was that was going on in Trégastel, however many cases there would turn out to be—things were coming to a climax.

Inès Marchesi was still typing, with impressive speed. She seemed hardly to notice Dupin coming back. He sat down again.

Suddenly she picked up a folder, gray cardboard, and handed it to Dupin. "Here. Copies of the investigation documents concerning the dead woman found in the quarry seven years ago. But," she gave him a stern look, "they're staying here."

"Fine," Dupin mumbled.

The policewoman continued typing.

"You don't think I could—"

"No."

He was so reliant on Marchesi that he didn't want to risk a confrontation.

"And you haven't found anything in particular?"

"So far nothing out of the ordinary."

"Maybe I could come back sometime to take a closer look? I'm afraid I don't have much time today." He looked at his watch. He really ought to be back at the hotel just after seven. "Tomorrow morning?"

"Up to you." She was already typing again.

"Do you know Madame Rabier's assistant?"

"A little. Why?"

"How long has he been working with the deputy?"

"I'll have a quick look at what we know about him."

He could hear typing again.

Dupin glanced at the pinboard. Calls for help from the local citizenry in regards to local crimes. A chaotic mess of papers made up of maybe two or three layers, almost an artistic installation. Most of the sheets were old, gone orangey brown from the acid in the paper, some of them dating from the eighties and nineties: a Citroën 2CV had been set on fire in the town center on March 2, 1983, and a barn almost exactly a year later. Nobody seemed to have bothered organizing the stuff on the wall.

Close to the middle there was a notice about the death of the employee in the quarry, the "pink corpse." Dupin stretched his head and read the few sentences. A faded photo of the employee. A faded photo of the quarry. The call for people to report anything that "could in any way be related to the event."

The disappearance of the Saint Anne statue had also made it onto the pinboard, as had the disappearance of Madame Durand and the throwing of the stone at Madame Rabier, clearly the most recent post, for some reason right down at the bottom on the left. The pinboard was a concrete, probably definitive chronicle of the criminal history of Trégastel over the past decades. Dupin liked the idea.

"So," Marchesi said, distracting him from his thoughts. "The young man seems controversial. Born in Perros." She stressed it as if it were in the Arctic. "Went to the École Normale Supérieure in Paris, where he studied political science, did his final thesis, called 'The European Regions in the Process of the Unification of Europe,' then came back here. The job with Madame Rabier is his first. He started three years ago, in January. His parents live in Perros, father works for the town tourist office, his mother is a grade school teacher."

Dupin was impressed. The information wouldn't all be out there in that format. She must have pulled it all together at lightning speed.

"Girlfriend?"

"I've only ever seen him on his own. But that doesn't mean anything." Clearly one of her favorite expressions. But she was quite right.

"Any connections to Chastagner, Ellec, or the lady farmer?"

Someone would probably already have mentioned it, but he asked the question nonetheless. Especially here, where everybody was either connected or related to everybody else.

"Not known. Do you think"—she raised her eyebrows ever so slightly—"that he was the one who attempted to attack the deputy? Who's threatening her? Either himself or on behalf of someone else?"

"You know about the threatening letters?"

Marchesi gave him an almost imperceptible smile.

"From whom?" In which case it would mean even the commissaire from Lannion hadn't managed to keep it a secret.

Yet another smile. She wasn't going to say anything but Dupin had no doubt: she knew about the letters. Inès Marchesi was in the know about everything, however relaxed she might seem. Dupin really couldn't say whether or not she liked him. But one thing was certain: he liked her.

"What do you think?"

"I have no idea, but we need to consider everybody without exception."

"Maybe the two of them set up the scene together and then concealed it?" Even this Marchesi said without any expression on her face, staring continuously at the screen. "And the whole business is just a diversion. For whatever reason. Or she wants to make her opponent Ellec a suspect? Or maybe even her rival? It looks worst for Maïwenn Guichard. Maybe the deputy herself is the villain?"

"What about the serious wound the stone caused?"

"An unintended accident."

Dupin himself had wondered about that a couple of times, even though he hadn't followed it up.

"What did you mean by saying it looks worst for the lady farmer?"

"Because of the traces of soil on the stone."

"What traces? On the stone thrown through the window?"

"I found out only an hour ago. The analysis of the remnants of soil on the stone revealed that the earth had an unusually high organic content, which is characteristic of the earth along the Traouïéro Valley, with its lush vegetation."

"What?" Dupin hadn't even realized at all that they were working on the stone. "Guichard's fields lie along the valley," he said.

"To the eastern end of the valley. Ker Gomar is the name of the hamlet where her farm is. But"—she rocked her head to and fro thoughtfully—"that could also be a deliberate maneuver to turn the suspicion toward her."

"It's possible."

Marchesi was flicking the mouse backward and forward. Dupin had no idea what that meant.

"The quarry is three hundred meters from her farm, as the crow flies."

"That close?"

Dupin had put the map in the back of his notebook. He folded it out. He had marked the whereabouts of various pertinent places, but hadn't taken that into account.

"Absolutely."

He had found both now, the hamlet and Chastagner's quarry. A certain geographical connection was undeniable.

The valley had been on their list of essential excursions, and the project was now all the more urgent. However, the prospects of persuading Claire of it tomorrow were not that good. She would want to go to the beach; the unusual high would last a few days more according to the weather forecast. But it occurred to Dupin that she would need "time to herself" again tomorrow. Maybe there might be some way of working it out.

Dupin's phone rang yet again.

Claire! It was just before seven.

Dupin stood up, glanced briefly at Inès Marchesi, who shrugged, and went out into the little hallway. In theory he was on his way to pick up his credit card.

"Hi, Claire, I'm just—"

"Georges, it's brilliant, the massages are brilliant. A real fountain of youth." An expression she almost never used. "Would you be upset with me if I stayed here a bit longer? I could have the hot stone treatment. The physiotherapist specifically recommended it to me."

"Of course, go ahead, by all means. Me upset? No way." He had to make sure he wasn't overdoing it. "We'll meet up later in the garden. For the pre-apéritif!"

"And you won't get bored?"

"I'm just picking up my credit card. Then I might have a beer on the Place Sainte-Anne."

"Do that, absolutely. I'm already looking forward to dinner. And seeing you."

"Me too." Which was quite true.

"See you soon, Georges."

Sometimes—not often, but sometimes—things just go like clockwork. Fate can be kind. Most of the time it's the other way around. It comes straight out of the blue to arbitrarily ruin carefree moments and create awkward complications. But right now: only happy coincidence.

Dupin went back to the visitor's seat.

"Is there anything new about the dead woman in the quarry? Has she been reported missing anywhere?"

"No. All the reports we have been able to check have turned out to be false."

It remained a mystery. Dupin wanted to talk about it again to his friend Jean in Paris. He mustn't forget that.

"They also turned her hotel room upside down without finding anything even remotely interesting."

"And Chastagner, what about him?"

"About the attack, or the corpse in the quarry?"

"Both."

"Nothing new there either."

"You're actively investigating both these cases, I assume? Independently of the commissaire?" He effectively knew she was.

She looked up briefly from the screen. "Of course. It's all Trégastel, which makes it all mine."

"Do you know anything about the alibis that Chastagner, Guichard, and Ellec have for Tuesday evening? Or for the time when Virginie Inard was murdered?"

"No. Unfortunately I'm not allowed to ask them directly"—the same unsatisfactory situation as Dupin was in—"and my source in the Lannion commissariat can't tell me anything."

She was already typing again.

Dupin was uncertain whether or not he should continue, but then decided it was a good idea to give her a clear sign that he was ready to cooperate, and told her: "I have documents and photos that prove Chastagner has extended his quarry without approval." He laid the folder on the desk. "In there you'll also find a copy of Ellec's special permission to build on his magnificent piece of land by the sea, the one that popped up out of nowhere. There is some doubt about the authenticity of the original, it—"

She turned to face Dupin directly. "I know about this 'special permission.' From what I know of Ellec, it's definitely a forgery but probably hard to prove. I'll make copies of everything."

She had stood up while she was speaking, and walked over to the rear side of the wall, where an old-model photocopier stood. Dupin realized that the peculiar mix of smells in the office was partly down to the machine's poisonous toner. He heard the usual copier sound and then Marchesi was back at her desk. He thought he heard her say "Thanks" as she handed back the folder.

"If the story about the quarry extension is true there will certainly be charges brought. That's a serious business, and the landscape and environmental protection laws are extremely strict."

Dupin reflected. "I'm going to hold back initially. We don't want to scare Chastagner off too soon. He will certainly have more up his sleeve and might change his behavior. We can act when the right time comes." It was always good to have an ace in the hole.

Marchesi gave a brief nod. She seemed to have taken on his strategic "we" without protest.

"I've also tried to get a search warrant for Chastagner's castle. In vain."

"Because you want to see if Madame Durand is there?"

"That too."

Yet again she had the same thought as he had.

"I saw Chastagner in his car, right in front of his castle. I thought I saw the silhouette of someone in the rear seat but I'm not certain."

"Yes, the tinted windows, I know."

"Normally Chastagner only comes back from Saint-Brieuc on Thursday evenings. But he was there this afternoon."

"I know he said he had a meeting here in Trégastel. Private. Nothing we could do."

Sadly, that's the way it was.

"Did the autopsy on the dead woman in the quarry produce no leads that could give us a trail to the killer?" Dupin asked, just to be sure, even though Marchesi would almost certainly have mentioned them. But, as he realized with the soil on the stone, he wasn't told everything, at least not automatically.

"No, and we still don't know where the murder took place." She glanced pensively at the screen.

"Has any connection between the dead woman and Madame Rabier been found? Or to Chastagner, Guichard, or Ellec?"

"So far I can't see any. Nor can Desespringalle and his team. But that means nothing."

"And you know that for a fact? That the commissaire is also in the dark on that point?"

She nodded briefly but decisively.

Dupin had a few more points on his list. "As for Madame Durand's disappearance, she had mentioned a 'best friend' to your uncle."

"I've already spoken to Monsieur Durand about that. And spoke on the phone to the friend yesterday. And also to two other friends Monsieur Durand knew. He gave me their names and numbers. They had all heard already about Alizée Durand's disappearance, and insisted they know nothing. They couldn't even imagine where she might be."

That was something else that neither the hairdresser nor Bellet had mentioned to him—it was no good if the chain of information wasn't functioning properly.

"Monsieur Durand himself had rung the girlfriends on the day she disappeared, they confirmed. They said he sounded very worried." Her face darkened. "Their statements in themselves were of no use at all."

"How come?"

"If Alizée Durand had really been staying with one of them, the friend would in any case have denied it to Monsieur Durand, and possibly to me too. Or Madame would deliberately not have gone anywhere her husband might expect her to be. And maybe Monsieur Durand didn't give me the names of all her friends. Maybe," she suggested quite calmly, "he doesn't want her to be found. Or maybe the situation is totally different."

"Indeed," Dupin said. "What did the best friend say?"

"That she didn't see the need to make a fuss of it. She said the quarrels between Alizée and her husband were quite normal. That they'd always been like that. But she had to admit that they'd been more frequent in the past year. Only in the last week before their vacation had they got fewer, so that she thought Madame Durand might actually have a good vacation."

Dupin listened carefully. "That was how she put it?"

"Just like that."

"Do you think I might have her phone number?"

Inès Marchesi clicked her mouse a couple of times and suddenly the printer next to Durand rattled away.

"Name and phone number. Here!" She handed him a sheet.

"Thanks." He folded it and put it in his pocket.

"I'm sure you spoke to Monsieur Durand about what the pair of them had done on the days between Thursday, when they arrived, and Monday."

She took up a brown notebook Dupin hadn't previously noticed from next to the screen.

"Here you go!" She opened a spread and handed the notebook to him.

It was a sort of hourly planner. The days were at the top, and beneath were the pair's activities, written so small that Dupin found it hard to decipher. Not exactly fine writing, but then nor was it his own illegible scribble.

"You can take notes if you want to."

Dupin wanted to.

According to Durand's statement, they had had breakfast in their room on Thursday and Saturday, and on the terrace on Friday, Sunday, and Monday. On Thursday, because of the bad weather, they left for Morlaix around half past one, to go shopping (two pairs of jeans for Madame Durand), had dinner there, and were back at the hotel by about eleven o'clock. Friday morning they went to Saint-Brieuc, and then when the high-summer weather suddenly set in on Friday afternoon they rented a boat (motorboat, six meters eighty) and took it out for the first time. The next day they went to Plage Grève Blanche for breakfast and then between twelve thirty and two had snacks for lunch at various restaurants. That afternoon they went out in the boat again, fishing, and then were back in their hotel room by seven in the evening. Monsieur Durand had had to work in the days in between, making lengthy phone calls, sending e-mails, one telephone conference (early afternoon Sunday), during which time Madame Durand was out and about on her own. After lunch on Sunday she had had a *café* at Plage du Coz-Pors (where she had met Chastagner). They had dinner around eight at the hotel, except for Thursday and Saturday (picnic on the boat: Champagne and lobster), Marchesi had noted. Thursday morning (11:30) and Saturday morning (10:20) were Alizée Durand's visits to the hairdresser.

"Many thanks." Dupin was finished. He had used a page for each day, and with his writing it was rather cramped. "I—"

A hellish noise erupted. It was so loud that it took Dupin a while to identify it as a ringtone.

It was the phone on Marchesi's desk. A landline telephone; they had one like that too in the Concarneau commissariat. Dupin had the "master module" with several buttons, none of which he had ever used.

Marchesi lifted the phone casually. "Gendarmerie de Trégastel."

A female voice. Loud, but unfortunately not loud enough for Dupin to understand everything.

Marchesi was listening calmly, with no sign of particular interest. "A break-in. I understand."

An answer from the other end.

"Fine, I'll be there."

The woman's voice again.

"I'm on my way."

Marchesi ended the phone call and didn't seem inclined to make any explanation.

Dupin stared at her. "What happened?"

"Amorette Abbott. A break-in. Her mixer's been stolen."

"You're kidding me?"

"It happens every couple of weeks, somebody breaks in and steals something. She's ninety-six years old. Apart from anything else, she lives in the Vallée des Traouïéro, on her own. Her husband died three years ago."

"You mean she misplaces things and thinks someone has stolen them?"

"No. She knows exactly where her things are. And nothing has ever been stolen. And there has never been a break-in."

"Which means?" Dupin was baffled.

"She has nobody left. She's lonely. And when it gets really bad, she rings up and reports a break-in."

"And?"

"I drive out there and we have a chat. She always reports the break-in early in the evening, so that I have the time. Usually we have something to eat together. And I leave when she goes to bed."

Dupin rubbed his temples. It was unbelievable. And wonderful.

One of those curious—very Breton—stories, that made him briefly sentimental. Stories like you find in movies or books.

"She has no children. She talks about the old days, about her husband. Her friends and brothers and sisters, all of whom are now gone."

The policewoman could tell the most deeply moving story dry-eyed, as she did with everything else.

"Sometimes she calls Desespringalle."

"What?" Dupin exclaimed. "He plays the game too? And spends time with her?"

"It's the only thing I know that speaks in his favor. That and maybe . . ." She seemed to be weighing things up. ". . . the hard time he's going through."

"By which you mean?"

"Divorce, an endless War of the Roses with his ex." Marchesi could not have said it with less sympathy.

Dupin would rather not have heard. Either story. When he didn't like someone—and Dupin had the best of reasons not to like the commissaire—it was hard to admit such a person was "human."

"How are things with the disappeared statue?" he asked, to think about something else.

"Do you already know about the van?"

"No."

Yet another piece of information that hadn't reached him.

"I told my uncle. The nurse who had lit a candle for her cousin later remembered that she had seen a white van standing outside. Directly in front of the entrance. We showed her various models. It was probably a Citroën Jumper or a Renault Kangoo."

"Parked directly outside the door."

"Yes."

"Is there any evidence that this might have been the thief's vehicle?"

"No. I think I need to go and deal with the break-in now."

Marchesi typed a few last words on the keyboard. Dupin would have loved to have known what she had been doing during all the time he had been sitting there in front of her. The computer—an older model—made strange sounds, probably the hard drive, and the fan running fast. The policewoman stood up.

"Like I said, the copies of the search warrants stay here."

Dupin had gotten up at the same time as her, and she noticed him glance at the folder.

He thought about trying to persuade her otherwise, then let it go.

Things had gone pretty well for him overall. Whether or not she liked him, they had established a solid working relationship, and he wasn't going to risk that.

"I'll look in tomorrow morning as we agreed."

"As you like," she said, shrugging. "My colleague Alan will be here then too."

* * *

There were still a couple of important calls to make.

Dupin was done with the first in half a minute: a call to Madame Riou, the owner of the *Tabac-Presse*, to say he would be dropping by tomorrow morning. He could wait to see Madame Guichard there. And Dupin had asked about Ellec: his desire to "get to know him" had become most urgent. Ellec came to the newspaper store at nine "punctually every morning." Dupin was pleased. His plan for the following morning was set.

He decided not to take the route back through the village but along the coast with a detour via the Renote peninsula. That meant that from the eastern point he would have a good view of the Île de Costaérès and Chastagner's castle, a tremendous vista and at the same time a perfect overview of the whole region. It would mean that he would get back to the hotel around eight or shortly after. For the pre-apéritif in the garden.

Dupin had left the gendarmerie, crossed the street, and was already up by the Sainte-Anne chapel when something made him turn around and he saw the shabby white Peugeot that had previously been outside Rabier's office. The car was driving along behind Dupin at about twenty or thirty kilometers an hour, with its right indicator blinking as if the driver was looking for a parking spot.

Dupin stopped for a second, as casually as possible. It was unquestionably the same car.

Of course it could be chance. But Dupin didn't think so. And that could only mean he was being followed. The man in the Peugeot was after him.

He considered doing a U-turn on the street and going right up to him. To put the man on the spot.

But if he was wrong, it would be an embarrassing performance, and it would be better just to keep an eye on the man secretly, to find out who he was and what he wanted.

Dupin looked up and down the sidewalk as if he'd lost something, bent down, turned round to face front again, and walked on. He didn't turn again until he had reached the footpath at the edge of the bay. There he stopped again and looked around as if he was admiring the landscape. He looked a long way to the right, in the direction of Ploumanac'h, then far to the left, glancing briefly over his shoulder.

Nothing. The Peugeot was no longer there.

He searched the area thoroughly. For either the car or a man who might have been the driver. In vain.

Maybe Dupin might have gotten it wrong after all. Or the guy had realized Dupin had noticed him, and headed off. Or he had found a better way of concealing himself.

Dupin pulled out his phone.

It was an unusually long time before Nolwenn answered.

"Monsieur le Commissaire! I assume you're just back from the beach, having enjoyed the meditative relaxation lying on your towel."

It was noticeable how innocent she sounded.

Not that the line was very good.

"Absolutely, Nolwenn. Absolutely."

He could hear cars in the background, somebody honking. The growl of an engine. Nolwenn was in a car herself.

"And what are you up to on this summer's evening?" Dupin had struck an unusually jovial tone for him. He was eager to see if she had noticed.

"Don't act as if you don't remember. I've been talking about it for weeks!"

Dupin had no idea what she was talking about.

"The festival!"

He had completely forgotten.

Le Festival des Vieilles Charrues. Nolwenn was on her way to the greatest Breton music festival. Even more important, it was the biggest music festival in France, and one of the biggest in Europe: 300,000 visitors, with an offshoot in New York. It was Woodstock-style in the middle of the Breton wasteland, in Carhaix, in high summer every year since 1995. Bob Dylan, Sting, The Cure, Neil Young, Phoenix, Santana, Bruce Springsteen, Joan Baez, Blues Brothers, Patti Smith, ZZ Top, Bryan Ferry, Deep Purple, they'd all been there—in Brittany! New, young artists too, and the *crème de la crème* of Celtic-Breton music.

"Oh yes, it may not be quite in context, Monsieur le Commissaire. I'm going to see Alan Stivell and The Celtic Social Club."

Two of Nolwenn's favorite bands.

"Come with me next year, Monsieur le Commissaire!" Nolwenn didn't wait for an answer—not that it was really a question—and rapidly changed the subject. "What delicacy is on your dinner menu for this evening?"

She apparently hadn't even dreamed that Dupin could have discovered her concealed research. But at the same time she had to know that she had made a mistake. She shouldn't have given her name to the land registry, but it was probably the only way to get any information at all. She had almost certainly said she was investigating the business a year ago.

Dupin was enjoying the situation. "Nolwenn, have you considered whether we shouldn't look into Hugues Ellec after all? The two of us, together? Give him a bit of a grilling. Maybe his permission to bring down the dune could be challenged."

Dupin had no idea if it was even conceivable.

"You're on vacation. End of story. We have nothing to do with this."

He had to force himself not to burst out with one of the bitingly ironic thoughts going through his head. That was the disadvantage to his strategy.

"I ought to be concentrating on the road here, there's a tractor in front of me, and the traffic in the opposite direction is heavy. But I still need to overtake the monster."

Dupin heard the engine growl. She had changed gear, ready to pull out. She hung up before he could reply.

He smiled.

He called the next number. Jean, his Parisian policeman friend. Hopefully he had found out something in the meantime.

It was a while before Jean answered.

"Georges, I've just got home. There was a bit of a problem in the Métro. We had to—"

"Have you got anything for me yet?"

"Hang on a minute, I'm just taking my shoes off."

A few uninterpretable noises, a sort of satisfied grunt, and a slurp. A creak of floorboards.

By now Dupin had reached the Île Renote, which here, to the southeast, toward the big bay, had a wonderful beach where Claire and he had walked across the seabed. It was called Ti al Lia. The obligatory huge pieces of pink stone, piled up in exotic shapes, hemmed him in on the side and protected the peninsula, which rose one and a half meters above the sea here. Tall, mighty, windblown pine trees stood on the protected side, with lush, unkempt grass all around. Most of the harmoniously rounded granite blocks on the seabed were overgrown with pitch-black seaweed, something Dupin had not noticed before.

"Hello." Jean was back. "I just went to fetch a quick beer. And open the windows. Have you any idea how hot it is in Paris? Anne isn't back yet." His wonderful wife. "Georges, where are you, anyway?"

"I'm taking a walk."

"You're taking a walk?"

Dupin didn't reply.

"Whatever. So. Visions—Agence Immobilière is the name of Durand's firm. Founded 2003. Quite a big business: twenty-four employees. Upmarket apartments, but only a few real luxury type, even so. In the past few years he's been specializing in the new build projects, and set up several new firms to deal also with radical restoration of older property. It's all very complicated stuff, done to be tax efficient.

There are about sixteen of them, half of them currently in his wife's name. Don't ask how I found all this out, I—"

"Most of his companies are legally in his wife's name?"

A delay. Probably for a gulp of beer, Dupin thought.

"It's a legal trick. One of the older, simpler tricks."

"Do they have a prenup?"

"Highly likely, everybody with that sort of money does."

"How long have they been married?"

"No idea."

"Where's his office?"

"In the fifteenth arrondissement, thirty-three rue Frémicourt. The couple give their address at Rue du Théâtre, just around the corner."

All the best addresses.

"I've spoken to another real estate agent in the fifteenth who knows something of Durand. He owed me a favor."

The good old favors system, nothing more reliable in police work.

"Have you heard anything about the state of their marriage?"

"An extremely odd, argumentative couple, the real estate agent said. But nothing more than that."

That was no help.

"And about Madame Durand in particular?"

"Nothing. Not known to the police. A blank sheet. Same for Gilbert Durand. No mention of him in either a private or business position. I've got nothing more for you. And my beer is finished."

"Do you think you could find out if the firms belonged to Madame Durand from the beginning, and how long they've been married?"

"How am I supposed to do that? I've no reason to ask for such information; I'm going way beyond my authority."

Dupin didn't reply. There was a long pause.

Jean sighed. He knew how stubborn Dupin could be. "Then you'll owe me one, Georges. And I know what."

"Whatever you want."

"We have a really weird case. And one lead is out toward you, at the end of the world: the Fôret de Brocéliande. There's a few interrogations to be had out there, and I'm not keen to make an expedition out to the provinces."

"I'm on vacation all of next week."

"There's no rush, Georges, do it afterward!"

"Done deal!"

"Good, I'll see to your points. And will be in touch."

"One more thing. The dead woman found in the quarry here—her name is Virginie Inard and she's allegedly from Bordeaux. But she isn't registered there. I was wondering if she might be on a missing persons list in Paris."

Dupin hadn't forgotten the chambermaid having mentioned a Parisian accent.

"You can find a reconstructed picture of her face on the websites of *Ouest-France* and *Le Télégramme*. Probably mid- to late thirties, height about one meter seventy. Dark, longish hair."

"Any other clues?"

"No." It was pathetic.

"You'll write up the report on the interrogations. And you'll still owe me something."

Dupin sighed. "Understood."

"I'm going to grab another beer. Talk to you later, Georges."

Dupin put his phone back in his pants pocket.

The Ti al Lia pink sandstone he had walked along had gotten narrower and narrower, and now ended.

Dupin had to find his way through the sandstone giants to reach the knoll that was the summit of the island, which was about three or four meters high here. There were more and more stones until they formed a broad wall as far as the copse. The stones looked harmless, but since he had gotten lost in the aquarium that afternoon, Dupin had been warned.

The sun was clearly in the west, still quite a bit above the horizon, but the granite giants were already casting long shadows. The sides facing the sun glittered and sparkled like millions of crystals, a dazzling diamond flash.

Dupin looked for the easiest way. He walked along one of the pink juggernauts. At the end there was only one possibility: to the right. Dupin headed toward a large, shapeless rock. On the one side it formed a sort of roof that connected to the next sharply sloping stone, leaving a low passage through. Dupin hesitated, then moved closer and bent down. It looked like a portal. On the other side the route went on.

He slid through. And found himself in a large stone room with a stone floor, none of which had been visible from the other side. There was no way to go farther.

Dupin stood still. An eerie shudder ran down his spine. All of a sudden this stone labyrinth no longer seemed so harmless. He shook himself. It was completely ridiculous. What sort of theatrics was he imagining? He was in the real world; all he had to do was walk around a couple of granite blocks. They might seem imposing, but at the end of the day, they were just a couple of stones lying on the beach, nothing more.

All of a sudden he spotted a small passageway diagonally opposite—he could have sworn it hadn't been there a minute ago. Without hesitating, he squeezed through and found himself on a solid earth path leading through thick scrub to the top of the knoll. Just ten meters and he would be up there.

Here on the northern part of the island grew big, unkempt scrubwood with whitish leaves, but above all fields of chest-high ferns. In their midst, like secretive green seas, grew bright green grass in which thumb-sized elves might live. Here and there pink stones popped up amidst the grass.

When he reached the top, Dupin looked back at the granite blocks on the beach he had just managed to get through.

He breathed deeply.

The next moment he stopped. He had seen something in between the stone blocks. Movement. Something white that had scurried behind a huge rock. He had also heard something, if only faintly.

Instinctively he reached to his right hip. In vain. He was on vacation. No service pistol.

Dupin stood his ground and stared at the granite block on the beach. Half a minute went by. Then two whole minutes. He was certain. There was somebody hiding there. He hadn't imagined it.

Most likely the man in the Peugeot. He had been wearing something white.

Further minutes passed. If it was a question of who was the more stubborn, Dupin would win. Unless of course, the person, the man, had already gone, had taken a left somehow. In that case Dupin would be standing there like an idiot, motionlessly staring at a rock while his follower might possibly even be approaching him from another side. He might have waded through the water, knee-deep at the most, toward the end of the island, and then be climbing over the rocks somewhere.

Dupin looked away and started scanning the coast meticulously toward the end of the island. It was basically just a mess of rocks. Dupin reckoned one of the formations looked like a giant dragon's head.

He waited a few minutes.

Then he began walking again. Still tense. Still with a queasy feeling. If anyone wanted to harm him, was maybe even armed, then he was caught on his own, with nobody else around. But maybe he was really imagining it all.

Dupin followed the footpath. It looked as if it was going to take a curve around the chaos of stones on the island end and come out on the circular route he had taken to get to the beach.

Dupin was striding manfully ahead. He wasn't going to let any uncertainty show. In any case he was absolutely ready for a fight. He had the weight and was surprisingly fast and fit.

With every step Dupin felt freer. In a minute he'd be sitting with Claire in the garden.

He pulled out his phone and the folded piece of paper with the cell phone number of Madame Durand's girlfriend.

He tried to concentrate on how he would formulate the questions he wanted to ask, while still keeping his eyes on his surroundings.

"Hello?"

"*Bonjour*, madame, you already spoke yesterday with Detective Marchesi, and I've just been talking to her about you down at the station." Dupin introduced himself in a way that would make it clear he was police, but if all went well, he wouldn't actually have to say who he was. "I'd like to know a few more things about the vanished Madame Durand." He was using a tone of voice that sounded a bit blunt, hoping it would put her off following up.

"From me?" She sounded a bit confused. "I've already told the police everything. What else do you want to know?"

Dupin's tactic had worked.

"Just a couple of things. Your friend and her husband, we know, quarreled a lot."

Dupin had stopped and turned around on his heel. There was nothing suspicious to be seen.

"I already talked to your colleague about that. That was part of their relationship from the start. But it didn't mean they didn't love each other."

"You would say Alizée loved her husband?"

"Even though he's an idiot and I can't think why, but yes, she loves him."

"You don't seem to think much of Monsieur Durand?"

"I can't stand him."

"Do you think he loves your friend?"

"No idea. I'm always telling Alizée that he's only interested in himself. But I've accepted him."

"You told my colleague that in past weeks they've had fewer fights. Even though it had actually got worse this year."

"Maybe."

"What do you mean by that?"

"We went out for dinner together recently. Once as a threesome, about six weeks ago. You get a feeling for things."

"And on these evenings there were noticeably fewer arguments?"

"Sort of."

"Did she say anything about it to you?"

"No. Whom am I talking to, actually?"

It hadn't worked.

"With Inès Marchesi's colleague."

"And what's your name?"

Why had she suddenly gotten so suspicious? He quickly pulled out his Clairefontaine and leafed through it.

"Alan Lambert, Gendarmerie Nationale de Trégastel."

Dupin spoke as formally as possible, and as fast as possible, in the hope that at best she mightn't notice the name, and continued on without a pause: "Did Alizée Durand ever betray her husband? Did she have an affair?"

It was a highly risky maneuver. Presenting himself as Marchesi's colleague. He didn't have any other idea.

"I told your colleague that too." She seemed outraged to be asked again, but apparently satisfied with Dupin's response to her question about his identity. "No! She's not that type, even if she sometimes gives a different impression, I mean, from her appearance. The clothes she wears. She was always faithful to him, she is respectable."

"Does she flirt now and then? Just for fun?"

"No."

"You need to be truthful with me, madame." Dupin spoke now with a deeper, more forceful voice. "Could a possible affair, a possible lover, have anything to do with your friend's disappearance?"

"No." There was total conviction in her voice, but she couldn't conceal the fact that there was a little bit of worry in it.

"This is an extremely serious incident. Even murder is possible. You could make yourself an accomplice if you hold back information or tell us something false."

Dupin was aware he was going to extremes. But it was too important. Maybe she only wanted to protect her friend.

By now Dupin had gotten back to the circular route. He would soon see on his right the beach on which Claire and he usually lay.

"Alizée had no other men. And wasn't looking for any, either."

"She was seen with a playboy, in a bar, the night before she disappeared. And she was seriously flirting."

"She had no affairs," she replied decisively.

"Do you know how long they've been married?"

"Five years. It was a head-over-heels affair, they'd only known each other a couple of months. He tore her away from one of his fiercest competitors. A tacky real estate agent from the seventh arrondissement; Alizée had only been with him a few months. Durand considered her a trophy wife."

"Are you aware that a whole series of Gilbert Durand's companies are in his wife's name?"

"I'm not interested in that sort of thing."

"But did you know about it?"

"We never talked about her husband's business. Alizée wasn't interested. And I certainly wasn't."

"She never mentioned it?"

"No." She was sounding annoyed now.

Dupin would be back in the hotel in a few minutes. Tonight there was a flaming orange tint to the granite world around him.

"What about Monsieur Durand, does he have affairs?" He had to think things through the other way around. "Are you aware of other women?"

"Alizée never mentioned any. And believe me, she would have done. If there were any, she wasn't aware of them. She would have killed him."

"Fine," Dupin said. "Has anything occurred to you since your phone call with my colleague Marchesi? Even the seemingly most unimportant details could be useful."

"No."

"Then thank you, madame. Just one last question. Is there any way you might suggest why they might have argued less over the last few weeks? Apart from those two evenings?"

She seemed to be thinking about it. It was a while before she answered.

"It might have been down to him. He tried to take it all less seriously when possible. But I can't be certain. I never really thought about it on those evenings."

"That's very helpful. And as to Alizée Durand's whereabouts, has nothing new occurred to you?"

"No, nothing at all."

"Many thanks once again. *Bonsoir*, madame."

"*Bonsoir.*"

Dupin headed up the gradually rising dunes that separated the two beaches—"theirs" and the next one. The summit of the dunes had now formed a sort of wall of sand that the footpath behind the beaches had been dug through. The bay was covered in white sand and was almost free of pink stones. On the other hand, it was now surrounded by even more imposing formations, the famous "pile of crêpes," for example, which really did look like crêpes piled in layers on top of one another. Claire had counted six.

It was just before eight. Dupin would be on time.

He hastened his pace, not least because he was imagining a wonderful cool glass of Quincy. But primarily because he realized how hungry he was. Claire would be the same.

Dupin was about to leave the little bay with its pretty sandy beach when something struck him. The landscape would be perfect for such an exercise.

He would test out whether his senses had been playing games with him or somebody really had been following him. That way he would have a measure of certainty.

With a mighty jump, he suddenly sprinted off at high speed diagonally across the beach toward the "pile of crêpes."

He was out of breath when he reached it, and hid behind it. This was a perfect place from which to watch the bay. He kept his eyes fixed on the narrow passage through the dune.

And indeed, in just a second he saw him. Maybe seventy meters away: a man in a white T-shirt, a wiry, sinewy figure, very short black hair. Searching the way ahead, along the path, and, when he could see nobody, beginning almost to run. The last of Dupin's doubts vanished; this man was following him.

He didn't wait an instant longer. He stormed out toward the man.

It took the man a minute to notice him, and sprint off himself.

Dupin gave it his all. He had to catch him.

But the distance was too long.

The man was running now toward the Coz-Pors promenade, toward the hotels, bars, restaurants, the thalasso center.

Dupin followed him, out of breath.

Not far from the ticket office, Dupin stopped. He had lost him. The terraces were full of people, as was the promenade. The area was impossible to keep a watch on. There were dozens of hiding places.

Dupin had no chance.

"Damnit!"

With no one to check him, he had sworn aloud. Two distinguished elderly married couples wandering along the promenade, absorbed by the wonderful evening atmosphere, flinched and stared at him, appalled.

He really was being followed, he hadn't imagined it.

Frustrated—and cursing somewhat more softly—Dupin turned around.

He could already see the gate to the hotel garden when two men appeared in front of him, in dark beige Gore-Tex uniforms, ridiculous bright baseball caps, and similar rucksacks, one of them tall, the other stocky, both with large binoculars around their necks.

"Oh, how nice, our fellow ornithologist. That's the way things are in our little world, sharing the same passion: we inevitably end up meeting one another time and again. A tour of the paradise bird lands!"

Sweat was running down Dupin's forehead, and he was still breathing heavily. He had no idea what the little man, who had clearly had too much sun, was talking about, but he had the feeling he had met the two of them before. The man was beside himself with enthusiasm.

"Have you seen the gannets? Unbelievable. Sixteen thousand, seven hundred and forty-five pairs. Everybody wants to see the puffins, but it's the gannets that are the real stars here! A whole island full of them. They are extraordinarily monogamous. And with wing-spans of two meters, they can plummet from dizzy heights into the sea, diving up to fifteen meters deep and grabbing the herrings from below the water. From below! We recommend the *Fanfan,* a little boat, a special one." He winked conspiratorially. "For us crazies, they come in just before sunset and stay as long as you want! But of course, you know all that." He gave a strange, deep laugh.

A multitude of unduly obscure information.

Suddenly Dupin got it. The "Fleur de Sel" case. He had met them during his investigation in the Gulf of Morbihan. Even back then the two ornithologists had gone on at him with references to plovers and murrelets, unceasingly, just like today. That's who they were, no doubt about it.

The shorter one scratched his forehead gleefully. "You were so stricken by the 'little penguins'! That was it, I remember now. So you must long since have been to visit your little darlings on the Sept-Îles."

"If one didn't know"—and here his face turned serious—"that we bird-watchers were gentle, peaceful people, you might have thoughts about the fact that they always turn up just where the greatest crimes have been committed! Highly suspicious!" He broke into a loud laugh, and his companion joined in.

"Now that would be a gripping case: a bird-watcher who takes advantage of his expeditions to commit murders. A perfect disguise!" The man's eyes opened wide as if he had suddenly been frightened by his own ideas.

"Very well then, we must be going." He tried to put the smile back on his lips. "We have a couple of wonderful cormorants on the agenda for today."

The taller man nodded eagerly, but still didn't say a word.

They seemed to be in a hurry now.

"So, see you about."

And in the blink of an eye they were gone.

Dupin shook himself, then he set off slowly, taking deep breaths in and out, pulling himself together.

He passed through the gate at a measured pace and took the curving private path to the hotel.

Ever since the conversations with Nolwenn he had given himself no peace, and the business had come back to him again: Had he let her deceive him? Had he been naïve?

It would only take a minute.

He pulled his phone out and leaned against one of the big granite blocks in the garden.

It rang a few times before Inspector Riwal answered.

"Boss," he said in an apologetic tone of voice, "you know I can't do anything for you."

"Riwal, where's Nolwenn?"

"Nolwenn?"

"Yes, she must have left a while ago. In the car. Where was she going?"

"You know! To the festival, her favorite bands are playing."

"And that's really where she's going? Are you certain?"

"Yes. You don't think she'd miss that? What gives you that idea?" Riwal sounded properly confused.

The inspector had sounded genuine enough. Nonetheless . . .

"I'm . . . I'm telling the truth. That's all I know."

"Aha," Dupin said triumphantly, "so you actually might not know what's really going on!"

"I swear." But there was a genuine echo of doubt in Riwal's tone. "All I know is that she's on her way to Carhaix."

Dupin reflected for a moment. He believed Riwal. Nolwenn was acting on her own. That's how it would be. She was on her way to Trégastel without letting anyone know. To do research. She had a mission, and in those circumstances she was capable of anything. Or, also going through Dupin's head was the possibility that he was exaggerating and this really was something he was making up. But then, he hadn't made up the man following him!

"So, how's the vacation, boss? Have you had time to come to terms with the extraordinary peculiarities of the stones all over the place there? There are amazing stories to be told about them."

A classic change of subject, Dupin mused. Riwal had no idea what he ought to do or say. And therefore he had resorted to his most basic—and most Breton—reflex: to start telling stories.

"Nor does that just apply to the pink granite, oh no, parts of the earth you're walking on there belong to the oldest stones in France. More than two billion years old. The oldest French soil is that of Brittany. It all began with Brittany." Naturally, that was always the punchline. While listening to him Dupin couldn't help being almost overcome by sentimental feelings: he missed his inspector in this complex situation, both his support and—insane as it might seem—his lengthy digressions.

"The five places from where the primeval earth emerged are all in the north. Trébeurden-Trégastel is one of them. But everything else there is ancient. The Massif Armoricain, which reaches from Normandy to well beyond Brittany, and at nine thousand meters was higher than the Himalaya, and six hundred million years old. Perhaps the highest mountain range of all time, and Breton! And the Côte de Granit Rose has its most spectacular phenomena. Already three hundred million years ago, powerful magma cycles forced up three gigantic blocks of a unique pink granite. After the Massif mountains were eroded, they came to the surface. And that's where they lie now. The granite block of Ploumanac'h, which covers eight kilometers, is the most noteworthy."

Riwal paused, as if waiting for Dupin to intervene; his voice had sounded a bit uncertain, his enthusiasm strained.

Dupin had understood little of the explanation. He was still thinking about Nolwenn. Whether or not he was right with his supposition. And what he could do to find out.

"The exceptional color," Riwal babbled on, "is actually because of the high amount—over fifty percent—of intensive pink feldspar crystals, mostly coarse-grained, the rest is bright or dark gray quartz and dark mica, a mafic mineral that magnifies the contrast and the pink effect. Take a close look when you're out on your walks and you'll notice—"

Riwal was interrupted. By himself.

"Nolwenn told me . . ." he said, sounding upset now, "that if you rang again, I was to recount lengthy stories to you so as not to let you put pressure on me." He gave what sounded like a sorry sigh. "But I'm just not in the mood. And in any case, the commissaire from Lannion called Nolwenn and told her you were involved in forbidden investigations, and that he would report it to the prefect."

Dupin's pulse soared. "He complained about me? Not about Nolwenn? Just about me?"

There was no way Riwal could understand what Dupin meant.

"Yes. And if I was to help you, I would get you into even greater difficulty, so she said. In the end we would lose you; it could lead to your suspension."

This was heavy-artillery stuff. It was appalling for Nolwenn to put the inspector under pressure—*her*, not him. But she hadn't been wrong in mentioning the possible consequences.

"It's fine, Riwal, I understand."

He wasn't going to involve the inspector any further in the mess.

"See you soon, then."

"See you, boss—and be careful."

Dupin let go of the stone he'd been leaning on. Fifty percent feldspar, he now knew.

He looked at his watch. It was twenty past eight.

He was late now.

* * *

"How were the hot stones, *chérie*?"

Claire was lying on the yellow lounger. On the little side table next to her stood a long-stemmed cocktail glass and two little bowls with the remains of some chips.

She had her eyes closed and her breathing was audibly deep. She jumped a little when Dupin spoke to her.

"Excellent, the hot stones after the massage was a good recommendation. My neck has never been so supple." She moved her head slowly back and forth to prove it. Dupin could see bright red marks on the left and right. She really had had the stone treatment, although certainly not without phoning the clinic during it.

"What can I get you, monsieur?" One of the friendly waitresses had appeared, to take away the empty cocktail glass and the bowls.

"A bottle of very cold Quincy." He glanced at the little table. "And another two portions of chips, please. And olives."

"Gladly, monsieur."

"And some baguette, please."

"I'll have another Manhattan," Claire added quickly. "Then we'll go straight to dinner." She looked at Dupin and smiled. "I'm starving. Did you pick up your credit card?"

"My . . ." Dupin faltered. "Of course, my credit card, yes, I've got it again."

A dangerous faux pas. How could he have been so stupid?

"And did you have a drink at the bar?"

"Yes, the bar is splendid. I had a *petit café*." He looked Claire directly in the eye. "And a small beer. Then I walked back over Île Renote. An absolute dream."

Interestingly, revealingly, she didn't ask any more.

"While I was waiting for the massage, I read an article in a magazine about how classic drinks were disappearing, and I remembered the Manhattan, which I used to enjoy so much." Claire stretched. "What a wonderful day, don't you think? We did lots. What a fabulous area!"

It sounded as if she was about to say something more. Claire left it hanging in the air for a while, then went on.

"But tomorrow I need another serious day on the beach, otherwise the vacation will turn out to be too strenuous."

Very clever. Claire knew all too well that he could never stick it out for too long lying on the towel, which gave her a lot of time on the beach on her own. And there was great phone reception.

He played the game. "That sounds good," he said.

"Then you make a few more of your little expeditions. Deal with your stuff." She smiled. A conniving smile, Dupin thought.

But then he was somewhat alarmed. What did she really know about the "stuff" he was up to? And had she said all that just to make things clear? For both of them?

"Here you are." The waitress had been quick. She smartly set a tray down with their order.

Claire put out her hand to take the new cocktail with impressive speed. "To us! To our vacation! To relaxation, Georges."

He repeated her toast word for word, completely neutral. "To us! To our vacation! To relaxation."

The glass was ice-cold. He couldn't wait for the first mouthful.

Claire had clearly decided to continue leaving the situation as it was. He was very much in agreement.

The glasses clinked as they gently touched them for the toast. Gently and auspiciously.

Claire leaned back and sipped at her drink.

Dupin did the same, making himself comfortable on the lounger.

The Quincy was a joy. Wonderfully fresh, a hint of mandarin and pistachio. He closed his eyes as he took the next sip.

Claire, the wine, the paradise of a garden—even though things had gotten rather rough, the hunt for the man following him, which he hadn't imagined—right now, all of that seemed far away.

Exactly twelve minutes later—or to be more precise: two bowls of chips, a bowl of olives, a few pieces of baguette, and another glass of Quincy later—Claire and he were sitting at their table on the fantastic terrace.

If the seemingly endless jumble of pink stones had been a dark threat when he was being followed, now, here, with the hotel and garden in their midst, they were a calming protection, a bright fortress. And a spectacular stage. An abrupt change of the effect that Dupin had already experienced—a secretive quality that seemed to dwell within the unique stones.

The menu too presented them with heavenly visions: cauliflower and *foie gras* terrine as starter, *crevettes roses* from the local coast with homemade mayonnaise as second course, followed by grilled wild duck breast. And to crown it all, profiteroles with fresh raspberries.

"Did Nolwenn call you? In the last few days, I mean?"

Perhaps Nolwenn had taken Claire into her confidence, even though he considered it unlikely.

"And voilà!" The waitress had appeared in front of them with the starter.

Dupin immediately stuck his fork into the creamy layers. He couldn't remember ever having been as hungry.

"About the house you found by the sea?" Claire hadn't replied to his question about being called by Nolwenn. "Let's talk, Georges, when the time is right."

Her comment—on an issue that was so important to Dupin—was almost by the by. What it meant was left fully open. It could mean anything. He put the fork down again.

"Yes, let's." Dupin looked her attentively in the eye. "I only wanted to—"

"Monsieur Dupin! Monsieur Dupin!"

Bellet. Trying in vain to appear calm and collected. He was standing half a meter from their table. Déjà vu.

Claire had the first bite of terrine in her mouth, and looked at him like a ghost.

"A call. A telephone call for you." Bellet still had himself under control. "Your mother, from Tahiti."

"My mother? Tahiti? From Jamaica, you mean, I hope?"

Now it was Bellet staring at Dupin in confusion: "Jamaica?"

Dupin had to quickly put an end to this. He jumped up.

"I'm coming. I've got my cell phone turned off, that's why she'll be calling me on the landline."

An extremely weak answer.

Claire didn't look as if Dupin's precautionary explanation was of the slightest interest. "Go! She's calling from Jamaica, that must be costing a fortune."

A few moments later—Dupin's eyes had remained reluctantly glued to the terrine as he left the table—he found himself in the narrow hallway with Bellet, who literally dragged him into the reception room.

"Tahiti, Jamaica, what's the difference! They've arrested Maïwenn Guichard," he burst out. "Half an hour ago."

"Guichard," Dupin muttered.

He wasn't surprised. If the Lannion commissaire's investigation really was where he had heard that afternoon, and had been confirmed by Marchesi, given the increased threat to Rabier it was one of the few options the commissaire had. A primitive step to take, undoubtedly, but it was at least a step. It would give him at least breathing space. Everyone wanted "results." Dupin understood him "moving fast." It was of course also possible that the commissaire was in receipt of new information that had forced him to take a drastic step.

"Where have they taken her to? Lannion?"

"Yes."

Excellent, Dupin was happy with that.

"What do you think, Monsieur le Commissaire?" Bellet's question reflected untrammeled curiosity.

"I don't think anything at all."

And he was not going to abide by every speculation.

"Marchesi didn't say there were any more details?"

"No."

But this was secondhand, which always meant there was a risk of uncertainty.

"Hm. And that was it? That was all there was in the call from my mother?"

"Yes."

Bellet looked disappointed. He had obviously hoped for a different reaction.

"But it's a spectacular development, don't you think? I also talked to our friends at the Castel Beau Site hotel. It wasn't easy even to get them to the phone. The dead woman, Madame Inard, had booked the room for eight days, not for seven. But people still say 'a week.'"

"So everything was normal?"

"Yes. She was supposed to leave on Wednesday. Yesterday. But she didn't." A statement of the obvious. "As regards your other questions about the Castel Beau Site, neither Monsieur Ellec, nor Maïwenn Guichard, nor Jérôme Chastagner, either, came by the hotel in the past few weeks. Neither did Madame Rabier. And none of them were known to Madame Inard, the owners said. Nothing unusual had happened to them either."

"I'm going back to my terrine," Dupin grumbled. He hadn't meant to sound so unfriendly, but hunger was driving him mad.

"It's too bad that you now won't be able to see Madame Guichard tomorrow morning." Bellet seemed seriously worried.

They had already discussed Dupin's visit to the newspaper store. Dupin himself had long ago stopped thinking about it.

Half a minute later he was sitting back at the table.

"What did your mother have to say? Has anything happened?"

"Everything's fine. She's well."

"So why did she call?"

"Just to tell us she is well."

"Didn't she say she wasn't going to be in touch?"

Damn. Another faux pas. Dupin took a large gulp of wine and gave the waitress a sign to bring another bottle.

"Whatever! The main thing is that everything's fine," Claire said, surprisingly.

Dupin leaned back. He had been sitting at the very front of the chair when he had his first bite. His face gradually relaxed. He felt the effect of the wine. Quite clearly.

"A Monsieur Quilcuff was looking for you this evening," Claire suddenly said. "Madame Bellet just told me. He came by deliberately to speak to the 'commissaire.' About the baguettes in the *boulangerie*. Over the years they have been getting smaller, and the price higher. The baker disputes it. That was why he wanted to pass on the cheating. He wants you to take on the case."

She burst out laughing. At the beginning of the sentence she had tried to make it sound serious. "He says he'll be back."

Now even Dupin laughed.

"Monsieur Dupin!" It was Bellet again, this time standing right next to their table. "It's your mother again!"

It was getting ridiculous now.

"Very strange," Dupin commented, and stood up. Claire looked at him in curiosity.

They hadn't even got as far as the reception before Bellet whispered to him excitedly: "They aren't going to hold on to Madame Guichard. Only question her. The news that Marchesi had initially wasn't true. I mean, they haven't actually arrested her, only taken her down to the station for an official interview."

"I understand."

They were at the reception by now.

"Is that all?"

"Important news, don't you think?"

"Absolutely, Monsieur Bellet."

Obviously an official interview was something quite different to being arrested.

"Don't think I'm giving you false information, Monsieur le Commissaire. Marchesi herself had heard she had been arrested and has only just found out that the lady farmer will be released after the interview."

"I see."

"One good thing is that you'll be able to meet Madame Guichard in the morning."

Dupin turned to leave. He needed more wine. "Lock the hotel up well tonight, Monsieur Bellet."

Dupin turned around once more; he wanted to avoid Bellet's face. Back at the table, he sat back down silently and, trying to look as relaxed as possible, reached for his glass.

"You don't want to know," he murmured.

He couldn't think of anything, no good story. Just obscure ones. The wine had gone to his head. He had recently seen a movie about the Jamaican jungle, with cheeky parrots and boisterous monkeys. Now he was imagining them clambering over his mother's shoulders while she chased them away.

Claire held up her wineglass. "To our vacation, Georges. Here's to another relaxing day!" She smiled.

It was hard to believe how Claire was dealing with it. It was as if nothing had happened, nothing at all. He had to admire it.

"By the way, on Sunday evening there's the thirty-seventh *nuit de la saucisse,* in Plestin-les-Grèves, not far from here. A 'sausage night,' they're serving sausage specialties from the north. You can try all of them. And there's music."

That sounded very interesting.

"And another thing, you know the whiskey we drank the day before yesterday? This Breton Armorik. Do you remember? It was so good. The eau-de-vie of the Celts."

"Absolutely."

"The distillery is in Lannion. It's the first whiskey ever to be distilled in Brittany. A couple of years ago it won the prize for Best European Single Malt at the World Whiskies Awards."

Dupin didn't know how much Claire was interested in whiskey. But she hadn't asked about the "second call from his mother." And that was the main thing.

"The distillery is called Warenghem, and I've brought the brochure I picked up at the thalasso center. They take only the purest water from their own well. They also make the Elixir de Bretagne and the traditional Chouchen. You haven't ordered me that yet! You're a bad Breton! It says here it takes honey, water, and lots of time. The drink has been brewed from the same recipe for fifteen hundred years—it's the original Celtic drink, invented by the druids."

Dupin had to admit that he had never tasted Chouchen—a fact Nolwenn considered a flaw. Fermented honey water sounded like an acquired taste. The way Claire described it, though, made it almost sound appealing.

"We'd do best to set off right now and try everything!" Claire was unstoppable.

The evening would end in silliness, which was wonderful. Dupin was totally in agreement. It would do them good. They had both worked hard today.

Friday

It was 6:17 A.M.

    They had tumbled into bed tired and happy at half past midnight. Dupin immediately fell into a deep sleep. By the end they had drunk nearly three bottles of Quincy, more than a couple Fines de Bretagne and Elixirs d'Armorique, only to wake up at three and toss and turn restlessly. Toward five he considered getting up, only to fall asleep again.

Vague noises had woken Dupin up.

He sat up in bed and tried to get his bearings. Dawn was just slowly creeping in.

A cautious knocking on the door. Quite clearly. Dupin thought he could hear a muffled "Hello, hello?"

Once again.

Was he dreaming?

"Commissaire!" Seriously louder.

This was no dream. Dupin recognized Bellet's voice.

He climbed carefully out of bed. Claire moved slightly. He walked through the room on tiptoes.

He just hoped that Bellet had a good reason to disturb them so early in the morning.

He opened the door a crack. The hallway was dark. Bellet had at least been careful enough not to turn the light on.

"What is there that's so urgent?" Dupin grunted quietly.

"Another murder."

"What?"

All of a sudden Dupin was wide awake.

His gruff answer had been far too loud. Instinctively he glanced over at Claire. She hadn't moved.

"A man. A taxi driver."

"A taxi driver?"

"He was lying next to his taxi."

"Where?"

"On a lonely forest track, leading from Ker Gomar, at the end of the Traouïéro Valley. A farmer was on his way on his tractor to one of his fields at the edge of the valley. Just as dawn was breaking. He immediately notified the police."

The Traouïéro Valley yet again.

"How was he killed?"

Bellet stuck discreetly by the wall, looking past Dupin, who wasn't wearing a lot.

"Hit with a stone. It was found near the body."

That was the second time that a stone had played the decisive role. Which was hardly surprising in this area.

"When did it happen?" A question that couldn't be answered yet, Dupin knew; it had just leapt out of him.

"I don't know. I mean the police don't know yet. Inès just rang me two minutes ago. She had just got there, Desespringalle hadn't arrived yet."

"I want to talk to her myself."

"Do that." He sounded a little insulted.

"Thank you for telling me quickly."

"But of course." Bellet sounded reconciled.

"I'll get dressed quickly." Dupin closed the door quietly and pulled on a polo shirt and jeans. Within seconds he was standing in front of Bellet in the hallway.

"You have her mobile number."

"I do." Dupin headed for the stairs with Bellet following.

In next to no time Dupin was on the terrace, then down the steps to the garden. Bellet, showing speedy agility, was right behind him.

Dupin would actually have preferred to make the call alone. But he didn't want to put Bellet too out of joint; he had, after all, come to him, and Bellet clearly saw this as a joint undertaking.

Dupin positioned himself next to the hydrangeas and tapped out the number.

"Yes?" Marchesi sounded tied up.

"Dupin here. I just wanted to know if there was anything new?"

"In the last twelve minutes?"

"How does the corpse look? Recent?"

"No."

"What's your opinion?"

"I've never seen a corpse before. This is my first."

"And?"

"I'd say it's been lying here a while."

"What makes you say that?"

"The skin color. The overall impression. Everything I've learned. One way or another, it hasn't just happened."

"Has the commissaire arrived in the meantime?"

"Yes. And the crime scene team. And the pathologist."

"Has he said anything yet?" It was an idle question. They almost never did, and up here in the north it wouldn't be much different.

"Not a word. He's doing a few tests and wants to get the body into his laboratory at Morlaix as soon as possible."

Once again standard pathologist behavior.

"The commissaire has taken on the case?"

"Of course."

He hadn't expected anything different.

"By the way, I've let him know that I have evidence that documents Chastagner's illegal expansion of the quarry. Desespringalle wants to have the evidence."

Even if Dupin didn't like it, Marchesi had done the right thing.

"Did you know the taxi driver?" One of the more obvious questions.

"Not personally. Pierre Séchard. Single. Early sixties. A bit dotty. Drives his own car. Lived a bit out of town. Toward Guingamp."

"And nobody had reported him missing?"

"Apparently not."

"What do you know about him?"

"Nothing really. He was seen now and again in Trégastel."

"I thought Trégastel had its own taxi firm?"

"Two actually, with one car each."

Bellet was standing half a meter from him, listening attentively. Which meant Dupin wouldn't have to sum it up for him.

"How far is the crime scene from the quarry?"

"About four hundred meters as the crow flies."

"That makes it not far from the Guichard farm."

"No."

That couldn't be a coincidence. The same went for the quarry. He would go and take a look. At the whole area too. Including the new crime scene. He would find a way despite the police presence.

"First and foremost we need to know the time of death."

"I'll call you as soon as I have anything new."

"And when the pathologist gives his first vague estimate, particularly then."

The policewoman had ended the call.

"This is taking on incredible dimensions," Bellet said. "It all began so harmlessly. And now this!"

The macabre aside, Bellet was obviously right. It was frightful.

"Did you know the taxi driver, Monsieur Bellet?"

He shrugged his shoulders. "He's not from around here. What will you do now?"

Dupin looked at his watch. "Go back to bed."

"You can't go to bed now. There's been another murder in Trégastel."

"I have a headache."

He really did have a sore head. He had only just noticed. The wine had gone down easily, but the quantity was a different matter.

"I need to take some pills."

Dupin didn't really intend to go back to bed. But he wanted to be alone. And above anything else, he wanted his *café*.

He went out onto the terrace.

"Okay." Bellet was next to him again. "You have your first meeting at half past eight. But another thing." His voice had changed and his forehead was wrinkled. "Why did you tell me to lock up tightly last night? I mean, I did so, made double sure, but why? Was there something concrete you were afraid of? Are we in danger? I preferred not to mention it to my wife. She wouldn't have slept a wink. *I* didn't sleep a wink."

"You did everything properly. Nothing happened, you see."

They had gotten to the terrace, then the hallway. Dupin climbed the stairs. "See you later, Monsieur Bellet."

"I'll let you know if there's anything new."

"Do that."

Bellet still seemed confused.

Dupin stopped outside the door to their room.

He would use the next two hours to think through this newest brutal development and to go through all his notes. He now wished he had done what he wanted to do yesterday but never got around to: make an exact calendar of events, of everything that had occurred here in Trégastel since the first "incident." But where was he going to get a *café*?

The Ty Breizh! The bar he had told Claire about yesterday. From there it was only a few meters to the newspaper store.

Dupin slipped into the room, took his wallet and his Clairefontaine, and left again. Claire was in a sound, deep sleep.

* * *

"A *café*, a *grand crème*, and two *pains au chocolat*, please." A disheveled man in worn jeans and a black T-shirt was behind the bar. He had given Dupin a rough glance.

He was going to drink the *café* first, fast and before anything else, then dunk the *pains au chocolat* in the milk coffee. Dupin had started to do that when he was a child and still did when nobody was watching. He would dunk the *pain au chocolat* until the two chocolate bars began to melt a little. The mixture of coffee, milk, the soft buttery pastry, and the dark chocolate was heavenly.

Dupin liked the early-morning atmosphere. The air was wonderful, fresh but still mild. It was maybe seventeen degrees centigrade, as low as the temperature had fallen overnight. The early rays of sunshine warmed him gently. All around there were sounds of the day beginning. A dozen people were already standing at the counter indoors or were busy coming and going, people coming for a quick *café* before work and the business of the day. Most of them laid out small change on the bar for the newspapers, which they took from the pile lying on it. Dupin, too, had bought *Ouest-France* and *Le Télégramme*. Two tables outside were occupied—an older lady and a bleary-eyed young couple. The people you saw at this time of day usually didn't hang around long. These were the places that Dupin loved. Places where real life was acted out.

He had taken out his notebook and laid it on the table next to the newspapers. He opened it up. More than half of it was already full with his scribbles. He began to take new notes on the second murder, a development that had beyond doubt put a new face to everything. Whatever was going on here had cost the life of another human being.

The disheveled man behind the bar might not have been chatty, but he was quick, which was more important. Without a word he set down Dupin's order and a small worn bowl with the bill. Then he was off.

The *café* was superb. Dupin set his notebook to one side and opened the paper.

Today's "Are You a Breton?" self-test seemed particularly challenging.

You know you're a Breton if you know the three most important
Breton words: bara=bread, gwin=wine, and bizh=kiss.
You know what a rabbit walk is: the route you take to get home
after the nightly visit to the bar, where there are no police on
watch.
You know the number of Breton villages whose name begins with
"Plou." 179.

Dupin had his first *pain au chocolat* in his hand when his phone rang. Inès Marchesi.

"Yes?"

"At least forty-eight hours." Dupin understood immediately what she was referring to. "He'd been lying next to his taxi for at least forty-eight hours. Of course that's only, and I quote, 'a preliminary, not definitive estimate.' The body is on its way to the laboratory. Desespringalle had a peek at the pathologist's supposition, otherwise he wouldn't have let him go."

The commissaire from Lannion had done the right thing there.

"And maximum time?"

"He didn't say that."

"Did the crime scene squad find anything?"

"They intend to make a thorough analysis of the stone the taxi driver was hit with. The track where the taxi was found is stony and grassy, all dried out. So far they haven't found anything significant. Nothing in the car either. Obviously his phone is missing. Two colleagues are already on their way to his house to take a look around."

"What was the man doing at the end of the valley? Was he taking a customer there? Or was he picking someone up?" Dupin was thinking aloud. "And why in hell's name *that* valley?"

"I don't know, but I'm guessing he's been lying there since Tuesday night."

That had been Dupin's first thought too. Marchesi laid out the scenario.

"Virginie Inard left the hotel at about ten o'clock in the evening. Nobody knows where she was going. She was murdered at about ten thirty and then thrown into the quarry, no more than half a kilometer from where the taxi driver was found. She could have called the taxi and taken it to meet the person who decided her fate."

Marchesi laid out her bold reconstruction completely soberly. It sounded extremely compelling. She continued: "For some reason or other, that person then murdered the taxi driver too. Maybe because the taxi driver saw something. Or the killer came with her in the taxi because he didn't want to be seen in his own car."

"And Virginie Inard?" Dupin asked.

"She didn't have a car, as far as we know. At least nobody at the hotel had seen one. And none of the rental car places in the area are missing a car. I've spoken to all of them. To have come the whole way on foot? Possible in theory, it would take about thirty minutes, but in the dark? There is no lighting on the roads."

Naturally Dupin had thought several times about how Inard had gotten to Trégastel in the first place.

"What if the taxi driver himself was somehow involved in the story?" he said.

At the very least they couldn't exclude it.

"Maybe. We also shouldn't exclude the possibility that it was Virginie Inard who killed the taxi driver."

Dupin had also wondered about that, but he didn't consider it very likely.

"Very well, see you soon then." The policewoman ended the conversation rather brusquely, Dupin thought.

He folded his hands behind his neck. "What a mess."

It was extremely mystifying.

The latest murder had something to do with one of the cases, he was sure of that, but with which, and how? And Dupin was still not fully able to say just how many cases there actually were. Could it all in the end come down to just one? What would it mean if the disappearance of Madame Durand didn't just have something to do with the stone thrown through the deputy's window and the dead woman in the quarry, but with the murdered taxi driver too? That sounded too grotesque. And also suggested several separate incidents.

Whatever: there was indisputably another victim. Two murders, an unknown woman from elsewhere and a local taxi driver; an attack, possibly the attempted murder of a parliamentary deputy, and two anonymous threats against her; a woman disappeared from a vacation hotel; the suspicion of serious document forgery; a tragic affair involving a tragic separation; the theft of a historic statue from a chapel; a man on Dupin's heels since yesterday afternoon—just to go through the most obvious elements.

However, Dupin had not laid eyes on his pursuer this morning. On his way to the bar he had stopped at strategically favorable points along the way to check professionally. Either the man had given up following him, or had become more circumspect since the previous evening. And invisible to Dupin.

Dupin dipped his chocolate croissant in the milky coffee, even though he couldn't pay it sufficient attention. It was still very early; he had time to go by the gendarmerie before his visit to the newspaper store, something he had planned to do later this morning. Alan Lambert would be on duty and Dupin could dig into the "pink corpse" files. That was a good idea and he ought not to forget, later when the time was ripe, to get in contact with Claire. Through the happy chance of the night before, which had granted him for a while the best of circumstances for making inquiries, and his early start this morning, he almost had the feeling of being in a proper investigation. But that was in no way the situation. He couldn't get too cocky, and take things too far. They were on vacation, both of them. And he daren't ever forget that.

Dupin glanced at his watch. He would quickly go through the precise timetable of events that he had taken account of.

Fifteen minutes later he was finished.

He had sketched out the order of events on one double page. Beginning with the arrival of the Durands. All completely independent from any possible connection with the cases, one event after the other in strict chronological order. He had used shorthand, unreadable in his minute script, so only he would know what was written on the paper.

Even though the exercise hadn't led to any results relevant to the investigation, and he was no wiser than before, he felt better.

In the meantime he had ordered a third coffee, which had just arrived.

Dupin leaned back and took a sip.

The traffic had picked up significantly in the last half hour. The Place Sainte-Anne was the hub of the village.

All of a sudden Dupin started.

The car over there, the little blue Citroën C3 with the dent in the fender! He recognized it.

Dupin sprang up. The car was now at the roundabout where the main road led out of the village. Twenty meters away. He couldn't work out who was at the wheel.

Even so, he leapt forward and ran after it. Just at the moment when the car pulled onto the roundabout and immediately turned off.

If it was what Dupin thought it was, it was outrageous.

There was no point in him running any farther, it would be childish. He stopped. The car accelerated. Dupin walked back to the bar, grabbed his phone, and dialed a number.

It took a second.

"*Bonjour,* Mon—"

"Careful, you're coming to the second roundabout. Don't accidentally turn toward Perros-Guirec."

There was silence a while, then: "Okay, so you know. What of it?" It was hard to believe, but she sounded genuinely angry, without the slightest hint of guilt. "Monsieur Bellet said you'd gone back to bed."

"You just drove past me."

"So you were sitting in this bar on the main square and yielding to your addiction." Her little attack was after all perhaps betraying a touch of guilt.

"So, talk to me, Nolwenn." Dupin had a sense of foreboding.

"I'm tracking down a criminal politician who deserves nothing less, and it is high time." Even now it didn't sound so much an apology as an attack.

"It's my duty, he—"

"What have you done?"

"After Alan Stivell's little performance, I drove from Calhaix to Perros-Guirec and slept in Les Costans, a wonderful family-run hotel," she rattled on in a provocatively jovial tone. "Greatly to be recommended. You and Claire ought to—"

"Get on with it, Nolwenn."

"A good friend of Bellet's is the concierge in the town hall. When he was doing his first tour just before seven this morning, I—how should I put it?—nipped into the land registry department. It took next to no time before I had the supposed original document referring to Ellec's special building approval in my handbag. I've got an independent expert in Concarneau to examine it."

On several occasions during this brief summary Dupin had wanted to shout at her, but he hadn't done it: for one thing it was *too* unbelievable, and besides he wanted to hear the story through to the end. Of all the "unconventional" actions Nolwenn had undertaken, and there were a good few—this one took the cake. But then he shouldn't have been surprised, it was Nolwenn after all. And above all: he should have started it all himself. Nonetheless he felt great satisfaction. He had been right. He hadn't got it wrong. Nolwenn *had* bitten, even if it hadn't gone at all like he'd planned. She couldn't not have bitten. The bait had been too attractive.

"Did anyone see you, Nolwenn?"

That was actually the most important thing. If the answer was yes, then all his thoughts about what to do next were irrelevant.

"No one. It all went according to plan," she crowed, in the best of moods.

And Bellet—that was shameful too—Bellet had not only known, he had made it possible. He had been jointly responsible for this totally illegal operation. The concierge too. If they were busted it would have immense consequences for all of them. Dupin daren't even think of it.

"Somebody or other will have seen you."

"I parked my car a long way away, on the beach. I was wearing my long coat, a wig, and sunglasses. I went in and out through the rear door. Nobody noticed me."

Dupin was impressed.

"On top of that I had agreed with the concierge that I had it all planned meticulously, and I had managed to sneak in unnoticed. Just in case."

Dupin wasn't sure that would be much help.

"Everything's good," Nolwenn said in closing. "We have the document, and we'll get Ellec. He may be guilty of more too. Who knows?"

What was he to say? It was still a hugely volatile mission. "Brilliant!"

To be truthful there was no other way they would have gotten their hands on the document. Apart from that, Dupin was the last person to be telling Nolwenn off over investigation in the "gray zone."

"Thank you!" He could hear unashamed pride in her voice.

"But why didn't you let me in on it?"

"You're on vacation!" Nolwenn shouted back indignantly.

It was ridiculous. He needed to get this over with.

"I'll make a deal with you: let's forget about the, how shall we put it, *questionable* circumstances under which you got hold of the document, and let's work on it together from now on. You get all the information I have about Ellec, and whatever else I might find out. And, if you want, about everything else that's going on here."

This hadn't come out quite right. It had sounded as if they were competing private detectives, known for getting in each other's way, who all of a sudden are trying to work together. There was a long pause, unusual for Nolwenn. She seemed to be wrestling with herself.

"Done," she said without emotion. Dupin found it a singular moment.

"But"—here came Nolwenn's conditions—"we keep this to ourselves. You tell nobody about it, not even Riwal and Kadeg, nor Docteur Garreg. And not even Claire! Ever. I vouched for the fact that you would be on vacation, and nothing else."

"I'm on vacation and nothing else," Dupin repeated.

He understood her position.

It would be a farce in many ways, but then it already was.

"Very well. Then tell me, Monsieur le Commissaire, I have my hands-free on, and two hours' time. I think I might get into the office a bit later than usual. But of course I was at the Vieilles Charrues."

So Bellet had only helped her in this one instance and hadn't told Nolwenn anything else.

"I have to be at the newspaper store by eight thirty to catch Madame Guichard, the lady farmer, whose husband has been having a serious affair with the deputy. I want to find some way to talk to her. But I need to drop by the gendarmerie first to have a look at a file. Regarding an accident seven years ago. One of Chastagner's employees fell into the quarry."

"I get it."

That he was also hoping to come across Ellec was better left unsaid. Nolwenn was capable of dropping everything and coming with him.

"Okay, so tell me how things are. Starting with the most important. And above all, everything you know about Ellec."

A smile appeared on Dupin's face. He was happy. Nolwenn was with him. In these circumstances he didn't mind being on vacation a while longer.

* * *

Dupin's abbreviated account—particularly focused on the most important and recent events—took fourteen minutes. Nolwenn had indeed (almost) just listened. There was a lot more they could have talked about, but Dupin needed to be off, and they agreed to talk on the phone again later.

The files on the pink corpse turned out to be boring from beginning to end. There were lots and lots of documents, but Dupin had just flicked through most of them, and really only got into a few. The only interesting thing for Dupin would have been to be able to talk to the victim's husband. And, of course, to Chastagner. Even though there was no evidence that the deceased had had the slightest interest in Chastagner's business, such as his illegal extension of the quarry.

Dupin had set out again in time to reach the newspaper store a few minutes before half past eight. Marchesi had rung again. Gendarmes from Perros had carried out a preliminary search of the taxi driver's house, and gone through his last calls on both cell phone and landline. There had been a call to his official taxi number at half past ten on Tuesday night. From a concealed number. That was the last call he had taken. Which fueled the assumption that everything had happened on Tuesday evening. Both his murder and that of Virginie Inard. At least the reconstruction of the events was progressing. It was still unclear, however, who had called the taxi driver: the victim or the killer. Importantly, there were no calls on either the cell phone or landline from Ellec, Chastagner, Guichard, or Rabier.

Dupin opened the door to the newspaper store. He said hello to Madame Riou, who gave him a conspiratorial look before quickly disappearing into the rear of the store. He chose at random to stand in front of one of the shelves, and took down a magazine: *La Pêche et les Poissons*.

It was exactly 8:30.

8:35.

8:40.

By now he was on his fifth fishing magazine: *Toute la Pêche*. He wouldn't have much time for Guichard if Ellec turned up punctually at nine o'clock.

8:45.

Madame Riou came toward him and made a sign for him to follow her. She opened an extremely narrow door that led into a small
storeroom, with crammed metal shelves and boxes piled on the floor.

"I just called Madame Guichard, and asked her if I should put
her papers aside, if she wanted to come by later. She said she wouldn't
come in at all today. Last night's interrogation perturbed her. My impression. What a shame. But Ellec will definitely come. And Bellet
called to talk to you. Monsieur Durand had told him he was going
back to Paris today. And there's been an incident in the clinic. The
deputy—"

Dupin flinched. "Madame Rabier? What's happened?"

"Inès tried to call her but her phone was permanently busy. Nothing serious. At least probably not, Inès said."

"What's that supposed to mean?"

"Something hit the window of her room."

"What, precisely? Is she hurt?"

"She's fine. They don't know yet what it was. Maybe a stone. But
it also could have been a bird. It happens."

It could have varying implications. Riou continued: "There was a
nurse in the room when it happened, so it's not some hysterical fantasy of Rabier's."

Somebody would have had to be very strong and a good shot to
hit one particular window on the second floor. But it was possible.

"The window wasn't broken?"

"It seems there isn't even a scratch on the window. But the commissaire immediately had the deputy transferred to another room.
The crime scene team are investigating. That's all I know."

Madame Riou seemed at ease. "I need to go back." The next second she disappeared back into the store.

Dupin pulled himself together for a moment, then left the store-room.

He immediately bumped into a man walking quickly from the right.

"Pardon, monsieur, sorry I—"

Dupin stopped short.

Chastagner. The lord of the island, the quarry heir, the machinery factory owner. The companion of Madame Durand the night she vanished. And the one who had illegally extended his land. Who only came into the newspaper store on Saturdays.

"Ahh, yesterday's grumbler. But without his pretty friend. What a shame." Chastagner smiled sardonically. "I know tourists think they can do anything here, but they ought to show a little respect to the locals. You should watch that you—"

Dupin interrupted him abruptly: "'Watch out' is the right expression. *You* ought to watch out"—Dupin's voice was soft but piercing, a serious warning sign—"that you don't soon face charges over the illegal extension of your quarry. The extension is documented, there are photos."

Chastagner's face changed colors between red and white several times. He clenched his teeth, and the veins on his temples bulged, while at the same time he looked confused and uncomprehending that this outsider, a complete stranger, would speak openly about this, and in public.

Dupin continued: "On account of this crime alone you're high on the list of suspects for the attack on Madame Rabier. You knew she was aware of the extensions. You're also a serious suspect for two murders. One murder victim was found in your quarry, just like the woman seven years ago, and the other very close. Apart from that, you were sitting in a bar and flirting heavily with Madame Durand the night she disappeared. Maybe she's still with you?"

"Who the devil are you?"

There were a lot of emotions contained in that question: anger, rage, despair, incomprehension, and—what Dupin wanted to see— fear.

"Are you from the police?" There was no trace of Chastagner's former arrogance.

It was something Dupin did now and then: without any thought or diplomacy, but with an investigator's cold calculation, go straight for the jugular. Seemingly completely tactlessly. But it was normally when he was the official investigating officer in a case that was his and his alone. This was a wholly different situation. Even if the technique sometimes achieved remarkable results, he suddenly wondered if the chess move was wise here. But as he'd started, he could continue, and cause the maximum commotion. If Chastagner really was the figure involved—possibly in many ways—then he would be unsettled. At the best he might panic, make mistakes. And the more explicit and open Dupin was, the less the danger that Chastagner would go to the police to complain about some opprobrious tourist.

"As to what concerns my own person"—Dupin was speaking so softly that he was hardly audible, and required Chastagner to stand still to listen to him—"the more you get interested in me, the more dangerous it'll be for you."

Of the multiple emotions Chastagner had gone through there was just one left: dismay. There were a few more things on the tip of Dupin's tongue, but he restrained himself. His "interventions" had had the desired effect. He turned around brusquely and headed for the exit.

Dupin crossed the street toward the chapel and stood in a house doorway so that Chastagner wouldn't see him when he left the store.

He looked around briefly, keeping the newspaper store in his sight.

9:02.

Unfortunately he hadn't met Madame Guichard. But he had an idea how he might bring that about later. It would fit in with his planned trip to the quarry.

He saw Chastagner come out through the open door and look around. Right, left, right again. He still looked stricken. Good.

Eventually he turned left and headed off at a fast pace.

Dupin dialed Marchesi's number and spoke immediately.

"Dupin here. We activate the documents on Chastagner. Straight-away. Give them to the commissaire."

Dupin wasn't going to mention anything about bumping into the quarry owner. Nor was there any time to do so.

"Fine." As always, Marchesi sounded astonishingly indifferent. "Desespringalle has in any case summoned him to the commissariat for ten o'clock. Even though there is already enough against Chas-tagner, the commissaire will be glad to have the documents. And another thing," she continued, "they didn't find any stone outside Rabier's clinic window. And on closer examination of the window, they didn't find any scratches or other marks. Maybe it really was a false alarm."

"We'll see."

"And one more thing. My contact at *Ouest-France* called. Some-body anonymously leaked the story about Guichard's husband's affair with the deputy. I told him they should keep quiet about it."

Who could that have come from? And why?

"Will they do so?"

"I think so."

"Good."

Dupin was standing with his back to a house wall a bit away from the newspaper store.

"The stone that hit the taxi driver," Marchesi went on, "is in the laboratory along with samples from the scene of the crime. Even though they haven't carried out any precise analysis yet, they assume it most likely came from close by. And also, neither Chastagner nor Rabier nor Ellec have a concrete alibi for Tuesday evening. And nor does Madame Rabier's assistant." The last sentence had no edge to it, just a statement of fact. "I'll have him watched."

Dupin thought it wasn't a bad idea.

He suddenly saw Hugues Ellec walking toward him from the left.

Dupin had recognized him immediately; he had looked him up on the Internet, and he clearly liked being photographed; there were an impressive number of photos of him.

"I have to go, I—" Dupin rubbed his temples. "One more thing, get somebody down at the town hall and check if Ellec is planning to take a look at his documents in the land registry."

"What for?"

"I'll explain later. But do it."

Dupin disconnected.

Just at that moment, the phone rang.

Nolwenn.

Not now. She'd have to wait a few minutes.

He tapped on Decline.

Then he hurried to the newspaper store, pulled himself together, and walked in.

Ellec was standing next to the politics magazines, looking re-laxed, as far as Dupin could tell.

He had already set a small pile on a shelf and was just adding *Le Point*. He seemed to be paying no attention to the people around him. Dupin positioned himself directly opposite, on the other side of the magazine stands, and watched him for a while.

Average height, a bit of a belly but not fat; an elegant dark blue suit and dark brown, noticeably shiny shoes; a white shirt, silver cufflinks, a blue tie, a bit brighter than the suit, with a rather casually tied knot, a slight flaw that didn't infringe on his overall conservative impression; short, well-combed dark hair, light gray sideburns, slightly sticking-out ears. Noticeable wrinkles on his forehead, but otherwise smooth facial features. Dupin had heard so much already, and it all fit together. What he saw was an arrogant spectacle presented by a man conscious of his own power.

Ellec had opened *L'Observateur*.

Dupin moved close to him.

"Your special permission, Monsieur Ellec, is a forgery. We know that. As with many other of your affairs. They are backed by a classic case of manipulation and abuse of privilege," Dupin said almost jovially while lowering his voice.

The method had worked with Chastagner, so why not try it again? He still couldn't hold a proper investigative conversation.

Ellec appeared to continue reading indifferently as Dupin began speaking, and only when he heard the word "forgery" did he seem to wince a little and turn his head toward Dupin. There was no reaction, either in Ellec's eyes or the rest of his face. Then he turned back to the magazine as if nothing had happened. Dupin was impressed. Ellec had to have an enormous measure of self-control.

"Madame Rabier was on your tracks. Which you will have noticed." Dupin was staring at him overtly, concentrating on any sign of emotion.

Still no reaction.

Ellec quite calmly added *L'Observateur* to the pile. Madame Riou was staring much too obviously at them, and seemed to have forgotten the elderly man at the cash register wanting to pay.

"I don't know who you are," Ellec suddenly said, "and I couldn't care less. And in particular I'm not interested in a single word you say. I wish you a good weekend."

He took his pile of magazines and went over to the register.

Ellec was good. Without doubt he was used to tough exchanges of words. But it wasn't just experience. He was ice-cold.

"I wish the same to you." Dupin too played his role to the end.

With a meaningful nod to Ellec, Dupin left the newspaper store with his head held high. Things were coming to a head. Dupin knew this nervous, feverish phase of an investigation.

He needed a system now to his behavior. He had to think *holistically*. Keep everything in view.

Claire was probably still asleep. And it wouldn't be a good idea to wake her. With some excuse he hadn't yet thought of. He had to consider what he was going to tell her. He definitely needed some time to himself. The stupid thing was that his expedition could take until midday. Even if Claire slept until eleven, and that had happened before, it might be enough to say that he had only recently gone out, to fetch newspapers and provisions. But it would be different if she were to ring soon. In that case he would have to improvise on the spot.

Dupin took his bearings. He had walked left, toward the bay.

It was actually pretty simple—in any case he had taken out the map that he had put in the back of his Clairefontaine—he just had to follow the bay toward Ploumanac'h, staying on the road until it turned toward the sea again. Just there, under a bridge, the Traouïéro stream flowed into the Atlantic, creating a little lake on the land side. That was where the legendary valley began.

Dupin would take the path along the eastern side of the valley, which led directly to Maïwenn Guichard's farm.

He set off.

Before anything else, he had to talk to Inès Marchesi again.

He dialed her number.

"Yes?"

"Have you got someone in the town hall? I've just spoken to Ellec."

"Alan's there, inconspicuous. What should he do if he sees Ellec coming?"

"Call you, and then you call me. Then—" Dupin stopped short. In his hurry earlier he hadn't really thought it through. Was it really necessary to bring Marchesi into it? It meant he would have to tell her about Nolwenn's—what was the right word?—"misappropriation" of the document. And Marchesi would not be able to keep it secret from the commissaire from Lannion, who could cause serious difficulties for Nolwenn. He would also obviously want to see the original document as proof. And it was right now in Nolwenn's car, on the way to be examined by an expert in Concarneau.

"I have come into the possession—don't ask how—of the original document. It should be," he glanced at his watch, "any moment now, handed over to an expert in Concarneau who will hopefully then tell us if it really is a forgery. My assistant has arranged it all."

For the first time Marchesi hesitated before replying.

"Okay." It sounded more or less neutral.

"You need to reassure the commissaire that you yourself got hold of the document. Via a particularly clever investigatory maneuver." It was the only solution Dupin could think up, even if it was expecting a lot of Marchesi.

"Your assistant got it via the concierge? Am I right?"

She had seen through it all.

"I would have done the same thing. I—" She stopped. "Alan is calling. I need to answer him."

Dupin was about to reply, "Absolutely," but she was already gone.

He had reached the narrow strip of land at the end of the bay.

He walked across the sand. This was just his sort of investigation, out at the scene, with the people involved, in the midst of nature. The tide was almost at its highest point. The water was pouring in. Great masses of it surging powerfully even though the surface of the sea was smooth. The keels and sterns of the yachts felt it, rocking to and fro turbulently, in stark contrast to the calm of the high summer day. Beyond the beach were the brightly colored dinghies the owners used to get out to their yachts.

It wasn't long before Marchesi called back.

"Ellec has just entered the town hall. Just like you expected." He could just hear the slightest hint of excitement in her voice. "That in itself is a clue. Why would he want to take a look at the original document after your conversation if it was genuine? Maybe he wants to destroy it."

"Either way, it means one thing: Ellec is going to discover it's missing."

"I don't think he's going to report it to the police, or at the town hall. He'll be damned if he draws attention to it. What is there for him to do?" Marchesi's voice was emotionless once again.

She was perfectly right.

"I'm on the way to see Fabien Delroux, a young farmer who called me. He wants to speak to me urgently."

Maybe another lonely heart.

"See you later then."

Dupin loved it when a plan worked. Obviously that was a clue. The document, the special approval, had to be a forgery. Probably a favor for something. Nolwenn would grab on to that like a terrier until she had uncovered everything. Dupin smirked and called his assistant.

"I was just about to call you, Monsieur le Commissaire. The document is already being analyzed. He began five minutes ago. I've already been looking to see what important regional decisions were being made at the time when the special approval suddenly turned up, I—"

"I need to bring you up to date quickly."

Dupin summarized the latest development with Ellec.

"Understood. Now, as to why I had been about to call. An unpleasant fact: the prefect for the Côtes-d'Armor tried to get hold of Locmariaquer. About you. He got as far as Locmariaquer's assistant. And she got in touch with me, unofficially. The prefect has a doctor's appointment this morning."

The commissaire from Lannion had actually done it. All attempts at camaraderie had gotten nowhere.

"Has he spoken to the service supervisory authority?"

Dupin didn't know which would be worse.

"Not so far."

Even still.

Dupin had reached the end of the strip of beach. This was the beginning of the outcrop of land that led into the bay. He took the footpath near the road and followed it.

"After a bit of negotiation, Locmariaquer's assistant agreed to the following: as an exception, she won't call him, just send him an e-mail requesting that he get in touch with his colleague."

That wouldn't help much.

"She thinks the earliest he'll get around to reading his e-mails is between one and two."

Dupin understood now. Nolwenn was an inspired genius. That would give him time. Valuable time, hopefully. It was just great to know Nolwenn was on his side again.

"Excellent. See you later."

Dupin hung up and jumped when his phone immediately rang again. It was Jean.

"What have you got?"

"We know who your dead woman is."

Dupin came to a sudden stop, as if struck by lightning.

"Her real name is Marlène Mitou. Parisian. Thirty-six years old. She was reported missing yesterday. The owner of the bar where she's been working the last four years went to the police when she didn't turn up for work either Wednesday or Thursday and couldn't be contacted. I've just spoken to him and he comes across seriously. I've also spoken to a friend of hers—the bar owner gave me her number. We've compared a photo of her with that of the dead woman. It's her."

Dupin had to think of the chambermaid who'd mentioned the Parisian accent. It really had been a lead.

"What else do you know?"

"She trained as an actress, but dropped out. She kept her head above water doing various jobs. Now and then she got an audition, but none successful. She lived in a tiny apartment in Sèvres, in the southwest, and didn't have much money. Her friend said she was Mitou's only close contact she knew about. They saw each other every couple of weeks. But she didn't exclude the possibility that there were people in Mitou's life she knew nothing about. Mitou never said a word about men but there didn't appear to be any regular boyfriend. A colleague of mine is on his way to the bar, Aux Folies, and two others are on their way to her apartment. And before you ask; I'm going to take a look in person too."

The first thought that came to Dupin was that none of that suggested she could afford a week in a suite in the Castel Beau Site. Or her expensive clothes.

"Did you ask the bar owner and her friend whether Mitou had any connections in Brittany, Trégastel in particular?"

"Nothing. Neither knew of any connection, nor had she ever said anything about Brittany. She went down south from time to time, in the Béziers neighborhood. That's where her family are from, but her parents are already dead. The friend knew of a sister who lived somewhere in Cevennen, but she had no contact to her."

Damn it all! Here was a seriously important discovery, but one that threw no light into the darkness and, if anything, made it more of a puzzle. What did it all mean?

"I'll ask the friend and the bar owner specifically about the people you're interested in. Maybe one of the names will register with them. There are no connections to Bordeaux either."

"Does her friend know yet that she's dead?"

"Not yet."

Dupin had begun walking again.

"When did she last see her?"

"Four weeks ago."

"Had Mitou told the bar owner or her friend that she was planning a journey?"

"No. She had taken a week off work. Her friend had sent her a text telling her she needed to chill out a bit."

"I see."

"I'll also get in touch with the commissaire in Lannion. I can't fail to mention this. It is his case, after all."

Little as Dupin liked the thought, there was nothing he could do about it.

"Who do you think might be involved, Georges? Who should I ask about?"

Dupin gave him the names he thought were relevant.

The possible chain of contact could, of course, be very complicated; it usually was. But there had to be some way in which Marlène Mitou had gotten involved in this deadly game. Through somebody or other.

"Okay. Got it. And just quickly, the information about the Durands: civil marriage five years ago. Just six weeks after the wedding, the first two firms were transferred to Alizée Durand's name. Then in the following years, six other property companies. The last was put in her name two years ago. No more after that."

"Is there a prenup?"

"That I don't know. I haven't heard anything about one. So, Georges, I've given you all the information. That's my part of the deal done."

Dupin knew where this was going.

"Now I have to ring the commissaire from Lannion. I'll be in touch as soon as I have anything new about Mitou. With you first, of course."

"Thanks, Jean."

Dupin put his phone away. He had more calls to make. But he needed to take a breath first.

They knew who the dead woman was. But there was no rationale behind it. He couldn't dream up any scenario that interconnected the characters he had been dealing with, which might bring a solution closer.

Dupin had reached the bridge over the Traouïéro. To the left of the picturesque bay there was a view of Ploumanac'h and the pleasant harbor; to the right of the bridge was the little lake that the water ran into at high tide.

The road he had to take would turn to the right here, and then run parallel to the valley until he came to Guichard's farm. Two kilometers, Dupin reckoned.

Behind the lake a thick jungle of greenery obscured the view. That was where the valley began.

At first there were a couple of houses on the road, but then the landscape became more deserted and ever wilder. The road, to the right of the cursed valley, led alternately through little copses and bleak pink granite landscapes full of ferns, scorched grass, thorny bushes, and patches of lilac heathland from which large foxgloves grew. Landscapes that had nothing to do with the nearby sea.

It was just ten o'clock, but the summer sun was already shining mercilessly. The temperatures were trying hard to climb to new record highs; there was not even the smallest breeze to give a bit of relief.

The air changed the farther Dupin went inland. It smelled of cracked earth, dry forest, of the dust that lay over everything in these hot days. Every now and then when the snaking road came very close to the valley, a burst of valley air—heavy, damp, rotting, a unique mix—came swelling up.

Before long, sweat was running down Dupin's forehead. He could have done with his cap and sunglasses.

He didn't take in much of the landscape. But then the whole idea of the walk was that he should be reflecting intensively.

A failed actress and waitress from Paris, whose real name was Marlène Mitou, was apparently a key figure, who had to be involved in one or several of the events. But then was the taxi driver also involved in one of the stories, or was he just an innocent accidental victim? In the wrong place at the wrong time?

An endless multitude of thoughts was constantly leaping this way and that, making Dupin dizzy. One moment he would seize on amazing ideas and connections, become euphoric, and then it all fell apart. The worst of it was that at some stage in the morning, he stupidly couldn't say when or in what connection he had had a strange feeling that, without realizing it, he had a sinister idea. The outlines of a plot that turned everything around. But for a moment only. It was driving him mad. He decided not to concentrate on it anymore, but let his thoughts drift toward the main aspects. But what if the solution was right in front of him? If it was clearly visible? One idea that brought everything else together?

Time and time again during his walk Dupin would suddenly turn around and look about, to see if his tail had returned. The mysterious man in the white T-shirt. That in itself was something he should have been thinking more about. Who could it be? What was the most likely hypothesis? And then his thoughts switched to the next point. Dupin felt as he had done in the maze in the aquarium. Lost. And wherever he started again, he got lost again.

To the right and left of the road were fields now. He would soon be there. The farm had to be on his left.

He pulled out his Clairefontaine while walking. He had previously noted down a few local agricultural specialties—over the past few days he had eaten all of them at least once—he had to be prepared for what turned up.

Suddenly he heard a car coming up fast from behind a barn that he could now see on the curve some hundred meters away.

A police car, a Peugeot.

Dupin stopped by the side of the road.

The car braked shortly before reaching him. It was Inès Marchesi behind the wheel.

She jumped out lithely.

"A little stroll around the Guichard farm?" she asked.

Before Dupin could reply she continued: "I've just come from Fabien Delroux, the farmer who called me. His farm is just up there." She made a vague gesture with her head. "He admitted that it was he who threw the stone. He hadn't intended to hurt Rabier. He hadn't seen her sitting behind the window. He's very worried, and hopes that everything will be all right and Rabier will get well soon. He decided to own up when he heard last night that Maïwenn Guichard had been arrested."

"What?" That news caught Dupin by surprise.

"Do you think it's possible he's covering for somebody?"

"I know Delroux. I think it's unlikely. It's not impossible though."

"Was he able to talk you through it?"

"Very realistically. It fits in with everything we know. And also with the analysis of the soil remnants left on the stone. His fields are also in the valley, just a bit higher up." Once again she nodded her head in the direction from which she had come. "He also named exactly the spot where he had picked up the stones for the tractor protest."

"Why . . . didn't he admit it earlier?" Dupin rubbed his hand over the back of his neck.

"He knew there would be serious consequences if he owned up. If it's true, he acted totally stupidly. But so do most people. Almost always."

"In which case it's no more than a tragic accident."

"And the threatening letters?" Marchesi asked. "Because they certainly didn't come from Fabien Leroux. In which case they had nothing to do with the unfortunate stone throwing. Somebody could have taken advantage of the situation in order to put pressure on Rabier. Maybe because somebody knew about her research. Or just wanted to confuse things."

It was getting all the more complicated. Or, depending on your point of view, simpler. Obviously, that could be true too. Marchesi had a good lead. And, even without the stone-throwing attacks, the possible scenarios were more or less the same. Then somebody might just have been taking advantage of the moment—the stone throwing and the general state of things—to coldbloodedly threaten Rabier. Possibly to prevent further research into Ellec or Chastagner. This scenario would also explain why the threatening letters to Rabier arrived so late after the attack on her with the stone. The threats to Rabier remained serious even if the attack was an accident.

"I have to go."

"One more thing." Dupin was unsure how to formulate it. "I found out from my . . . contacts . . . that the dead woman's real name is now known. She was reported missing in Paris. Her name is Marlène Mitou."

Dupin gave her a brief summary of what Jean had told him. "The Paris police are going to make contact with the commissaire from Lannion."

"The right thing to do."

Marchesi turned on her heel and walked back to the car, then she briefly turned back around.

"Oh, and Desespringalle had Chastagner brought to the police station. They sent a police boat to his castle to fetch him. He had just returned from Trégastel. They also had a search warrant for the castle and for the head offices of his firms."

For a comment that had started off with a laconic "Oh," it was a serious piece of news.

She opened the car door quickly and at the same time added, "Desespringalle considers the illegal quarry extension to be motive enough for the attack, which now might not actually have been one. Whatever. It's certainly not a mistake to tackle Chastagner properly."

A pragmatic way of looking at it.

Dupin found the commissaire's methods less than elegant, a bit premature even. But not mistaken in principle.

"Does the commissaire know about the farmer's confession?"

"No, but he will in a minute."

It would put the commissaire in a greater state of confusion and distress than Dupin himself, especially now that he had brought Chastagner to the station in connection with such a sensational affair.

Marchesi had sat down at the wheel, turned the ignition, and set off with the racing start of a rally driver.

For a split second Dupin had the impression he had seen somebody out of the corner of his eye, between the trees toward the valley. But when he took a closer look he could see nothing suspicious.

He turned around decisively and headed back toward the barn.

To his left he caught sight of a wonderful old stone house, surrounded by fields, bordered by thick forest, heavy bushes, and moss-covered stone walls. That had to be Guichard's house. A simple outline: a long row of bright pink granite, carefully restored and beautifully looked after, with a dark slate roof.

Next to the house was a well-tended vegetable garden, almost a field, certainly twice the area of the house, protected by a waist-high wall, and with two slate-roofed sheds. In front of the house stood three bushy palm trees, typically Breton.

Dupin saw a bent-over figure pulling at something. Long, glistening chestnut brown hair, tied into a ponytail that when she bent over like this almost reached the ground. Dupin opened a little light gray wooden gate and approached her.

The woman still hadn't noticed him.

"Madame Guichard?"

She shot up, a dark purple carrot in her hand.

"You startled me!" The sentence had turned into an amicable, welcoming smile. Even so, there was a certain tension evident.

"Please excuse me, madame."

Everything Dupin had heard was true: Madame Guichard was an exceptionally good-looking woman, the exact opposite of the cliché image of a "lady farmer." She had fine facial features, lightly tanned so that her lively bright green eyes lit up all the more. She was wearing red lipstick, but no other obvious makeup. Dupin's glance fell to her hand, dainty but covered in soil, as she used it to transfer her ponytail from the right shoulder to the left. Her torn jeans, far too big for her, and her deep orange T-shirt and green rubber boots were covered in dirt but at the same time looked like some fashion designer's extravagant arrangement. The contrast was bewitching: this delicate creature—almost like an artist in a studio—in this down-to-earth outfit. And yet somehow or other it all worked together.

Guichard had noticed his look, which he found slightly uncomfortable.

"I hate gloves. I have to feel the soil and my plants."

"I understand. Of course."

A completely meaningless answer. He knew nothing about soil or plants. Dupin was out of his element.

"I'm from L'Île Rose, I mean, I'm a guest at L'Île Rose. I'm on vacation. Monsieur Bellet told me I could buy fruit and vegetables from you, here at the farm, all organic."

This time he had thought up a story to get into conversation; now he just had to make it convincing.

"We're going home tomorrow, and wanted to take something from the region." Dupin faltered, and a little bit quieter than he intended, added: "My wife and I."

"You came on foot to buy vegetables? Without a bag or rucksack?"

A stupid weak point in his story.

"We'll come later with the car. I was just taking a walk in the valley and wanted to take a look and see what you had."

"Take care if you're climbing down the Traouïéro Valley, in particular if you want to get to the water wheel. Lost ar Logoden: the Mouse Tail Lake." Guichard broke into a broad laugh. She had relaxed, took him to be a harmless codger.

"One of the many residences of the devil. Who played evil games on the poor millers. Do you know the story of the flying granite blocks?"

Over the past few days lots of people had told him lots of stories. But not this one. Dupin shook his head.

"A brave lad had heard the hair-raising story of the devil and the mill. He made up his mind to defy the superstition, but on his first night he was woken up around midnight by a hellish noise that made his hair stand on end. Great stones were flying through the air and crashing into one another, as if they were playing leapfrog. They also crashed into the mill, which immediately collapsed. The unlucky character, still in his bed, was blown away onto a neighboring hill. He took to his legs and never set foot in the area again."

Dupin could think of nothing to say other than revert to his original story. "Do you also sell those little purple artichokes, like the ones we ate in L'Île Rose?"

"I plant the artichokes in the fields behind, including the *petits violets*. Here in the garden I just have old-fashioned vegetables that you don't see much anymore, but for which Breton soil has the best conditions: various beets, parsnips, Jerusalem artichokes, rare types of carrot." She held up the carrot in her hand. "This type were planted five thousand years ago. The yellow and purple ones are crammed full of polyphenols, carotenoids, vitamins A and K, and folic acid— the ordinary orange carrot you get everywhere is an industrial breed, mostly water."

"We'll definitely take those." Claire would be delighted. It occurred to Dupin, however, that he would need a good explanation for why he had come here on his own. But he could work on that later.

All of a sudden there was a loud, strange noise. Dupin winced. It came again. The next moment two fine pigs appeared, barely a meter or two away. Pink pigs. Very pink, as if nature here wanted everything to match the granite. Instinctively Dupin moved a step to the side and was immediately embarrassed by it. Guichard had noticed.

"No worries, they won't do you any harm. That's Louis XIV and Marie Antoinette. My domestic pigs."

Dupin had no idea what to say, so said nothing. Pigs in the Breton countryside had had a very special position for centuries, just like horses; some of them were almost treated like family members. Even so, Dupin was uncomfortable in their presence. They were huge. And they stank. He preferred them as sausages, cutlets, or pâté.

One of them looked as if it had read Dupin's mind. It took a remarkably fast few steps toward him and began snuffling the leg of his pants.

"That's enough, Marie, back to your field, hop, hop! You don't belong in the vegetable garden. Off you go!"

The two pigs turned around lazily and trotted toward the gate that Dupin had come in through, still with their noses to the ground, grunting loudly and—to Dupin's mind—angrily.

"I also keep a small breeding farm for pigs. I produce deliciously creamy rillettes: shoulder, breast, and ham cooked for hours in the finest fat. My pâté with seaweed has a light taste of iodine, and Atlantic fish." Maïwenn Guichard laughed again and threw her ponytail to the other side.

"We'll take that too. Both. The pâté and the rillettes." Dupin's mouth was watering.

"What else are you interested in?"

Dupin hesitated.

"I mean, which vegetables, which fruit?"

"Oh, put together some of everything, a little selection." He would only have to call later to set a time to come and collect it. "You have a very attractive farm." Dupin looked around appreciatively.

"Thank you."

"Wonderfully laid out." He watched her carefully as he said the next words: "Right here in this fairy-tale valley, and close to the famous quarry."

Nothing. Not a wince, not a blink; she returned his look, meeting his eyes.

"There was a woman found there yesterday," Dupin added quickly. He wouldn't be able to hold her eyes for long. But once again her facial features showed no reaction.

"In the Carrière Rose, yes, tragic. And particularly mysterious."

"Mysterious?"

"So far nobody knows anything about it. The police are in the dark." Her smile had gone.

"What do you think happened?"

"I don't know." A serious, resigned expression. It was clear she was disturbed by it.

"Several strange things have been happening around here recently. There was an attack on the local deputy."

Yet again Dupin paid attention to Guichard's face.

"A terrible thing." It sounded sincere, but then maybe she was just a good actor.

"Do you know each other personally?"

One more attempt. Pushing things a bit more.

"Yes, of course." For the first time there was suspicion in her voice, and her face had changed. "Fine, monsieur. I'll fill up a basket for you. When do you want to come and pick it up?"

"Being on vacation here, we're a bit unsettled by all the happenings." Dupin had tried to sound clueless, to limit her mistrust. It seemed to work a little.

"I understand that. These are the best days of the year," she smiled, ". . . and then this happens."

Dupin had only half heard her.

It had happened again: something that had just been said, or thought, had touched the shadowy, nebulous thoughts he had had. The possible "dark fancy" that frustratingly just wouldn't materialize. Dupin was familiar with these obscure ideas that got lodged in the back of his mind, more like a strange foreboding, something that had often helped him solve a case. Unfortunately on this occasion he was getting nowhere with the shaky ideas going around in his head.

"I'll get on dealing with my carrots."

"Yes, do, as many as you can," he said, hurrying to add, "for our basket, I mean."

"*Au revoir,* mons—"

A siren interrupted her. A loud siren. The next moment two

police cars appeared and sped toward the farmyard, screeching to a halt just before the entrance.

There was no doubt about it: they wanted to talk to Maïwenn Guichard. And definitely not about buying vegetables.

Dupin knew only one thing: he had to hit the road.

"If you would excuse me." Madame Guichard sounded worried. "Call me tomorrow before you come to pick up your basket." She walked slowly over to the police cars.

Dupin set out quickly on the path that led to one of the barns and then out over a field. "Thank you very much. I'll be in touch," he called over his shoulder.

He took a few large steps toward the barn. Guichard didn't seem to notice his strange behavior. She was too occupied with the police.

What did they want? Were they really going to arrest Madame Guichard? With this exaggerated performance? Even if they must by now have heard that someone had owned up to throwing the stone at Rabier? Did the commissaire from Lannion not know about the farmer's confession, or did he think it unreliable? A bribe? By Guichard? Or had he leads, evidence even, to show Guichard was linked to one or both of the murders? Something Marchesi didn't know about? What was undeniable was that Guichard and Rabier were involved in a dramatic personal feud, full of the deepest emotions and inflicted injuries. Theoretically, that meant anything was possible.

Dupin concealed himself behind the barn so that he could see what was going on, without being seen himself.

Several policemen—four in total—got out of the cars rapidly.

As well as the tall, haggard man with the scar on the left cheek that Dupin had seen in Ploumanac'h yesterday: the commissaire from Lannion.

He marched determinedly toward Guichard. The other police-men had lined up behind him.

It was a comic scene.

The commissaire stood directly in front of Guichard and ad-dressed her, but unfortunately Dupin couldn't hear what he said.

The commissaire and the four policemen turned around and waited for Madame Guichard to walk over to the first of the two cars.

Then she stopped.

A brief exchange of words followed and then the commissaire nodded.

The lady farmer hurried toward her house, followed by the com-missaire and two of the police officers he had waved over.

She was going to get something from the house, her phone maybe, a few things.

It really did look like an arrest, the real thing this time. First Chastagner, now Guichard.

Dupin took out his phone.

"Marchesi?"

"Yes?"

"Maïwenn is being arrested. Do you know of something new that's come to the commissaire's attention?"

"No. Except that he doesn't trust the confession of the young farmer. He considers it 'humbug.' Are you at Guichard's farm?"

"I am. You didn't hear anything about this in advance?"

"No."

"Keep me in the loop."

Dupin was about to hang up, but then added quickly: "I mean we should both keep each other in the loop!" But Marchesi had already ended the conversation.

The next moment, while Dupin still had his phone at his ear, Nolwenn was onto him.

"We've got him!" An expression of total euphoria. "We've got him! It's definitely a forgery. We can nail him with it. The paper is old—okay, around twenty years old—but the printing was only done on a typewriter a year or two ago. The expert wants to use another mode of analysis to confirm this, but he himself reckons it's certain."

"Certain?"

"You know scientists. Of course it's a preliminary finding. Whether or not the prefect knew about this is something we aren't going to find out. But it doesn't matter. The special permit is a forgery. Done and dusted. . . . I won't rest until we have proof to show Ellec that favors were called in for his involvement in the dismantlement of the sand dune. Perhaps in the form of the silent acceptance of this forged document. Or maybe he was given it as a 'gift' and didn't forge it himself."

Ellec had the most merciless opponent imaginable at his throat. He wouldn't escape.

"Nolwenn, can you let Marchesi know about this? The expert must be able to knock out a written version of his preliminary verdict in short form. And you send it to the policewoman. She will forward it to the commissaire." Something else important occurred to Dupin: "And if you could see to it that a Concarneau address doesn't appear. The letterhead should just have the name and title of the expert."

"Will do, but sooner or later the expert's address is going to crop up. At the latest when a thorough evaluation of the document is made. But by then," Nolwenn said happily, "we'll already have the case locked up."

That was Dupin's hope too. He had no illusions. Eventually everything would come out: his "behavior," his investigations, too many people were aware of it all.

"Above all, talk everything through with Marchesi. I have total trust in her. She's helped me a lot. Don't be deceived by her apparent indifference. And now you've got me again."

"Fine, Nolwenn, I need to—"

He felt something on his left leg.

Louis XIV. And now at his right: Marie Antoinette.

"Get out of here! Away with you! Shoo, shoo!" Dupin couldn't say it too loudly, and had gestured instead toward the field with his left arm.

"What?" Nolwenn said irritably.

"Two pigs. At my pants."

They hadn't paid the slightest attention to Dupin's instructions. They kept on snuffling.

"I see . . . two—"

"Talk to you later, Nolwenn." He hung up.

In the meantime, Guichard, the commissaire, and the two policemen were back at the car. The farmer had a bag over her shoulder.

They climbed in and the two police cars drove off. They turned onto the road, but not to the right toward Ploumanac'h and Trégastel, but to the left, toward Lannion.

Dupin waited until they had gone. Only then did he trust himself to come out from behind the barn. With Louis XIV and Marie Antoinette trotting after him.

"Go! Off to your field!"

This time he could be loud. But the two pigs still seemed unimpressed. They were going to come with him.

Dupin was just about to walk out onto the road when he stopped. If he was right, the track he was on led in the opposite direction to the quarry, the Carrière Rose. And it could only be a few hundred meters. The path along the stony wall ended at a wood, and from there he must be able to get to where the taxi driver's body was found.

* * *

Dupin had imagined the quarry otherwise. Somehow more organized.

He had found himself—with the help of the map—at the right spot when he came through the copse, despite scratches on the backs of both hands thanks to two obstructive bracken bushes that had caused him to swear aloud repeatedly. Louis XIV and Marie Antoinette had followed him part of the way, calmly and happily, but then at some stage just wandered off of their own accord.

Suddenly the quarry was there in front of him, no barriers, no fences. Dupin had expected at the very least some signs. But there was just a big, dusty stretch of land with a rusty corrugated iron hut. Bits of rusty steel lay in a large circle around the hut, like leftover pieces of some machine that had exploded years ago. The sun was mercilessly strong. It was strangely quiet. The heat was shimmering, scorching. There was no air, not a single tree, just dust and stones. He wiped the sweat from his brow. The atmosphere was like in some Western. The only sounds were some regular loud, crashing noises some distance away. Work in the quarry was continuing as usual despite the discovery of the body. Only the area where the dead woman had been discovered was closed off. He was probably very close to it.

Dupin walked over to a large basin of water fitted out with turquoise foil. The grass was rough here, dry as dust. All of a sudden, to his right, he came across impressive blocks of granite, two and a half meters long and one meter fifty high. Dozens of them laid out next to one another, each a meter apart. It was impressive.

Dupin walked along past them. Now he knew exactly where he was. The stone repository was marked on the map, one of many, but this one was easily identified because the stones were arranged in a semicircle. He had to take two curves, then continue straight on, and then he was at the spot where Marlène Mitou had been thrown down into the quarry. Totally by chance he had taken the ideal path: he had come from the rear side of the quarry and the chances were good that he had not been seen.

The land here was also dry and dusty. Now and then there was a crane to be seen. The noise of the works had stopped for some reason. Dupin walked by a long hedge with openings here and there. The part of the quarry that mattered had to be behind it.

He let his eyes run along the hedge. A little farther on, he found the bit where the police tape blocked things off. He hurried up to it.

He ducked under the tape. Almost directly in front of him was a hole in the ground. It was an abyss with an extremely steep edge. The ground just fell away sharply, hard to see and with no barrier. Marlène Mitou supposedly had fallen fifty meters. It looked like a lot more than that.

Spectacular. And frightening. A gaping hole in the ground. Shimmering pink.

Dupin went closer, carefully, until he was less than a meter from nothingness. He stopped and looked around.

On the left-hand side of the quarry was the entrance for the workers and trucks: several plateaus and a path that ran downhill in narrow, serpentine turns. The ground was uneven. There were several holes even deeper than the one where Marlène Mitou was attacked. Directly beneath Dupin he could also see the red-and-yellow warning tape. But there was no one guarding the area anymore.

Dupin flinched. The sound of his ringtone in this ghostly silence was extraordinary.

It was Jean.

"Yes?"

"I've just spoken personally with Marlène Mitou's friend. She lives at the Gare de l'Est. The traffic around there was hellish."

"And?" Traffic in Paris was always hellish.

"Well, the vacation business surprised her a lot. She thought Mitou wouldn't have had the money to travel. And even if she had the money, her friend said she would have used it to finance her move. The last time they met, Mitou had told her she had found a new apartment, more central, and was intending to move into it in September."

"What about her connections in Brittany?"

"The names meant nothing to her. Nothing at all. Not one of them."

"Maybe her friend doesn't know everything."

"It's a possibility. They didn't meet or speak every day."

"And Mitou had never mentioned a man?"

"No. Her friend had understood that, now and again let's say, she had brief relationships, but she never got any names or details."

That was all extremely lean. It didn't get Dupin any further.

"As I said," Jean summed up, "her friend couldn't make any sense of it all. The journey was a waste of time."

"Thanks all the same."

It would have been too much to hope for.

"By the way, I also spoke with this Desespringalle. An unpleasant comrade."

"Not quite as bad as he seems when you know more about him."

Dupin had just let the sentence spill out. He was annoyed with himself. Even if the commissaire had a good spot hidden somewhere in his heart and was in a very difficult personal situation, he was doing his best to make things seriously difficult for Dupin.

"Did he tell you anything about his investigations? Whether or not he had any leads as to what role Marlène Mitou might have played?"

"Not a word. He just recorded everything without comment, as if I were one of his inspectors. Two of my colleagues have taken a first look around Mitou's apartment. They found nothing that might be in any way interesting. Nothing relating to her trip or any relation to Brittany. The apartment is in a state of chaos. Tiny, apparently, and very run-down. They found no calendar, diary, or anything similar. Not even a computer."

"Is it unthinkable that somebody else got there before you to get rid of any trace of clues?"

"As far as my colleagues could say, yes. If there had been, then they were very careful."

"Maybe somebody had a key."

"It's possible."

"What about in the bar? Had Mitou said anything interesting to any of the people there?"

"I sent my best man to the bar. He talked to the owner and all of the four other waitstaff, women aged between nineteen and fifty-six. There was only one of them she exchanged words with now and then, smoking a cigarette or drinking a whiskey late in the evening. Nothing relevant. She didn't know anything about her trip either."

Jean was thorough in his job, Dupin knew that.

"At present there is also nothing known about how she made the trip. How she got to Brittany. Alone, with someone else, by train, in a rental car? Desespringalle assumes she took the train from Paris, and the bus from Guingamp. But there was no reservation in her name on the super-fast train on Tuesday of last week, nor on any of the preceding days. Nor anything in the name Virginie Inard."

"She could have used any old name."

"Indeed. There you go, we'll see if we can find anything. I'll be in touch."

"No matter how small."

"I know, I know. Even the tiniest thing."

Jean ended the conversation.

It had brought nothing, absolutely nothing worthwhile.

It was still totally cryptic what Mitou might have been up to in Brittany. And why she might have been in contact with someone here. Maybe everybody, Dupin included, was on the wrong track.

It seemed more and more to Dupin as if he had gotten lost in one of these gigantic stone labyrinths. All of a sudden there was a pathway, then a few meters farther and there was no longer a reference point to go on.

Dupin caught himself staring down into the hole, spellbound and fascinated. He moved a little closer. Centimeter by centimeter, then stopped again. A disturbing sense of vertigo had overtaken him. He needed to pull himself together.

He would leave the quarry and make his way to the scene of the second murder—although it might actually have been the first: assuming that Marlène Mitou had actually got out of the taxi there, she had most probably been strangled between there and here. If it had happened there, the perpetrator might have used a car to bring the corpse here.

Dupin finally dragged himself away from the hole in the ground.

Right at that moment he heard a loud crack.

Someone had trod on a branch. At least that's what it had sounded like. Exactly.

Immediately Dupin was in attack mode. Just like yesterday on the Île Renote, his hand had instinctively shot to his right hip, where his Sig Sauer was—when he was on duty.

He spun around quickly and scanned the area.

There was somebody there, behind the hedge.

He wasn't alone.

And he was in a seriously bad position, just a small step from a fifty-meter plunge into the depths.

Dupin had to act.

He turned back around as if he was going to look back down into the hole. And pulled out his phone. He immediately started a conversation. At easily audible volume: "Nolwenn." It had to sound natural.

A brief pause.

"I'm at the quarry. Everything seems normal so far. I'm just taking a look around. I was wondering if you've got the report from Docteur Garreg, yes?"

It all had to seem authentic. Another pause.

"Very good. That's important. Can you read it out to me? Every word could be decisive. Very good, I'm listening."

He had moved slightly to the left while he was talking.

The next second he sprinted for it. The seconds would count.

Along the hedge. It wasn't far to the next gap. He reached it in a few meters.

Dupin stopped, glanced over the hedge. Over stone blocks, with bushes and a few trees beyond them. He kept watch tensely. Damn, there was nobody there.

He spied along the hedge, back toward the warning tape.

Then he saw him.

His tail from yesterday. Dupin charged him at lightning speed. The man turned around in shock, and took flight in panic.

He rushed toward the hole in the ground, then turned sharply to the left. But Dupin was faster. With a great leap he was on top of him.

The man fell to the ground, Dupin on top of him, a thick cloud of white dust all around them. They rolled across sharp stones, toward the abyss. There were thudding noises. Dupin felt a searing pain at his throat and his right cheek.

The fight was brief.

Dupin had turned the man onto his stomach and twisted his arms behind his back into a police security grip.

The man hadn't defended himself enough. But no matter, Dupin was ready for anything. When you've decided to fight, you have to make your opponent unable to fight back as quickly as possible.

"Stop, stop," the man spluttered. "I'm police."

"Who are you?" Dupin was totally unimpressed.

"Thomas Lemercier." He faltered. "I'm shadowing you . . ." He moaned, Dupin had strengthened his grip. ". . . on the orders of Commissaire Desespringalle. I'm part of his team."

"Desespringalle?" Dupin couldn't pronounce the name without stuttering. "The commissaire is having me followed?"

The policeman's voice was almost shaking. "I'm only following orders."

It was outrageous. The commissaire from Lannion had been driven so far?

"Since when?"

"Since yesterday afternoon."

That was when Dupin had spotted him.

Dupin loosened his grip a little. "Show me your badge." Dupin released his right arm.

The man put his hand into his right pants pocket and pulled something out.

"Set it on the ground in front of you."

The man did as he was told.

It was quite clearly a sweaty official police ID card, with a photo.

Dupin released his other arm and got up, his eyes fixed on the young man.

"Slowly now."

They were still on the edge of the abyss. A false move could have serious consequences.

"Hands behind your head." Dupin stood with his back to the hedge.

The man stood upright now and looked questioningly at Dupin, who let a torturous few moments pass. The man remained motionless.

"All right."

The policeman moved, shook himself, brushed the dust from his T-shirt, which was ripped at the shoulder.

Dupin noticed something warm trickling down his cheek. It was blood. Not too bad, though he would have to think up a good story for Claire.

"So," Dupin said in a harsh but composed tone of voice, "this is what you're going to do: you're going to go to your boss and tell him from me, he's going to immediately withdraw his complaint to both prefectures. And will here and now drop his report to the service supervisory authority. Are you listening to me carefully?"

It was a rhetorical question. The man stood there as if rooted.

"Yes," he said quietly.

"Good. Otherwise I shall escalate this. I shall say that as I was taking a walk through the quarry, your harassment almost caused me to fall down the hole. All in all, this whole shadowing business, the breach of my private space, is extremely serious."

It really was. Above all, it was simply amazing. The Lannion commissaire had made a mistake. He had gone too far. And with one shot, Dupin no longer had any worries.

"Go to your boss straightaway, and if he doesn't do as I said immediately, then I will proceed. And no excuses."

"I'll let him know."

"Then off you go. Out of here."

The young policeman scurried off with hunched shoulders. Dupin almost felt sorry.

Dupin took a deep breath in and out, then walked a few meters away from the abyss.

His phone rang again.

Right now any phone call could be crucial. Dupin fished it out of his pants pocket. The robust Outdoor Model survived almost anything.

It was Claire. It couldn't have been a worse moment. He had to deal with it though.

"Georges?"

"Chérie?"

"Where are you?"

A wholly neutral-sounding question, as far as Dupin could tell.

"At the newspaper store. I've had a *café* at the bar. I woke up early, had breakfast, and sat reading in the garden. I only just left. I'm picking up a couple of magazines and some provisions." It all sounded relatively plausible, Dupin thought, and it gave him a few more flexible options. "I—"

"Don't fuss, Georges. We're on vacation! Take your time. I've had a good night's sleep. I'm just having breakfast. Then I'm going down to the beach. Follow me down there when you're ready."

The beach—the word sounded so out of context right now. How far away that all was: the beach, the towel, the "doing nothing."

Claire's reaction had been astonishingly relaxed. She probably had another operation at long distance to conduct.

"Maybe you should take something to drink. And a croissant, or an apple, just in case."

"Good idea."

"See you later then, Claire."

"See you later, Georges."

It was a bizarre situation. But excellent.

Dupin took a last look at the quarry, and was on his way.

He had seen enough.

* * *

"It's definitive. At twenty-two thirty, according to the pathologist. The taxi driver was killed on Tuesday evening, around twenty-two thirty, the same time as Marlène Mitou, plus or minus an inevitable hour. The pathologist is going to check it over again, but expects it to be confirmed."

It was no surprise, but still important. It was what they had assumed in principle. But it was still good to have confirmation of the scenario. Both murders had taken place on Tuesday evening around half past ten. And most probably around where Dupin was right now.

"Very good."

"Apart from that, nothing new. They still haven't found any trace of the killer."

He had been extremely smart and careful, that had long been clear.

"Your Nolwenn called." Marchesi's tone of voice made it clear she wasn't totally happy about that. "I've got the provisional statement from the expert in Concarneau. With no address on it. I've already forwarded it to the commissaire. He . . ." she hesitated, "asked no questions."

"And what did he say about the matter itself?"

"I don't know whether it will count in the actual investigation itself, but he said it was a 'bombshell.' And added that we need to be extremely careful. And get a second opinion from another expert."

"A second opinion from another expert? That's madness." Dupin was getting furious.

"Nolwenn thought it was right."

"What?"

"In that way, there will be less attention drawn to an expert from Concarneau. I found one in Paimpol. The document is already on its way to him. Nolwenn got a courier."

"And the commissaire didn't think to consider that this 'bombshell' might have something to do with the current case? It would be sufficient motive!"

"He didn't mention that."

"What else is there?"

"Chastagner told the commissaire about the night with Madame Durand."

"And?"

"Nothing happened. Nothing at all. Even though he admitted he had hoped for more. He had suggested to Alizée Durand that they go to the castle. At first, in the bar, she had agreed, but after they had left the bar she didn't want to hear another word about it. And just left in her car. That was that."

"Does the commissaire believe him?"

"I think so."

"Does he have anything else against Chastagner in hand?"

"You mean apart from the illegal extension of the quarry and the intention to keep that secret under all circumstances?"

"Precisely."

"I don't think so."

None of that sounded like major new results of the investigation. But maybe he just hadn't told Marchesi. In the decisive phase of an investigation Dupin himself generally told nobody. In the unusual situation that he did so, it was at most Nolwenn or Riwal.

"And what about against Madame Guichard?"

"You mean if he has something in hand that we don't know about?" As usual, Marchesi had understood straightaway.

"Exactly."

"I don't think so."

"Anything new from the young farmer?"

"No. Why might there be?"

Dupin himself didn't know. If he really had thrown the stone, then he wouldn't suddenly contradict the confession he had forced himself to make. And certainly not if he had been bribed to make it.

"In the meantime we have spoken to all the taxi driver's friends and acquaintances, but there are no indications that he had anything to do with the relevant persons."

"Well done."

"My colleague is trying to investigate who might have sent the anonymous e-mail to *Ouest-France*. Regarding the affair between Monsieur Guichard and Madame Rabier."

"Can he do that?"

"He's a hacker in private. It's a hobby of his. Has been for ages."

"Alan? The policeman?"

"Precisely."

Curious.

"And how is Madame Rabier?"

"Nothing new. She is still in the clinic, which is as well protected as the Élysée Palace at the moment. Probably at the same expense."

"And nothing new as regards—" Dupin suddenly stopped.

Something had occurred to him. It was the word "expense." It wasn't the obscure thing that had been in the back of his mind all along, it was something else, something concrete, from his conversation with Jean.

"I'll call you later, Marchesi." Dupin hung up on the last syllable.

He was standing in the avenue of chestnut trees. Up front, where the road deviated, there had been a barrier—the obligatory red-and-yellow police tape. From there to the taxi it was about a hundred meters. The taxi was guarded by two policemen. Dupin had taken a cautious look around the corner. On no account were they to see him.

Dupin scrolled down his call list, and pressed a number.

"Jean?"

"Yes?"

"One more thing. The move that Mitou's friend mentioned. Did she say any more about it?"

"The move?"

"Yes, Marlène Mitou wanted to move soon."

"What are you looking for?"

"Isn't it strange? The expensive clothes, the hotel suite, and a move like that is also quite expensive. On top of that if the apartment was more central, the rent would be higher. How could she suddenly have more money at her disposition? Where had it come from?"

"You mean . . ." Jean was thinking aloud, "she was being paid for something? Something to do with events in your exciting Breton vacation resort?"

"Exactly."

"I'll call her friend now."

"That would be great."

"Speak to you soon."

Dupin put the phone back in his pants pocket.

Without getting too close to the police, he tried to reconstruct as closely as possible the events of Tuesday evening. All the possible scenarios, and there were several. He wanted to see if he could find anything special relating to them.

Dupin left the path and walked along an overgrown field along the side of the oak copse. It was thick enough for him not to be seen. He would walk in a wide curve around the taxi's position.

Ten minutes later Dupin had gone halfway around, with no result. He couldn't have said what type of clues he had hoped to find, given that the crime scene team had already searched the area systematically. It was probably just to make himself feel better. Not that it had worked. For some reason, since he had left the quarry, the state of his investigation had seemed more awkward. He was never right on the ball. Something he was meaninglessly trying to compensate for. His mood was getting darker, the euphoria of that morning blown away. He felt like a fool. On top of that, he felt he had exhausted every possibility at his disposal. And he hadn't come a single step closer to the core of the story.

In the midst of Dupin's depression, his phone buzzed. He had set it to vibrate when he began to search for tracks.

It was Nolwenn.

"Yes?"

"There's been a miracle!"

She sounded relieved, happy.

"Commissaire Desespringalle's assistant called. The commissaire no longer wants to speak to Locmariaquer. She has just sent our prefect an e-mail that has said it's unnecessary to discuss the subject. And she asked me to pass on the message as soon as possible." She paused for effect and added: "I wonder what can have happened."

It was good news. The thing could have turned into a proper

debacle. Dupin's calculation had gone wonderfully. But even this news wasn't enough to lift his mood.

"Just a little incident, shall we say. I'll tell you about it later."

"You sound very morose."

"How shall I put it? I'm lost in the labyrinth."

"You just need a little distance, Monsieur le Commissaire! Have a *café*. Go swimming. Have something to eat. Have a laugh with Claire! Or go for a long walk. And then think everything through again peacefully."

He had already thought through everything. And had taken several walks. Just now, for example.

"I'll do so, Nolwenn." He sighed.

"You know how things are in Brittany. *Gant pasianted had amzer—e veura ar mesper.* With a little patience and a little time, even the medlar will come to flower."

Nolwenn thought Dupin's state of mind was so grim that she offered a second proverb: "*A van da van—vez graet e vragoù da Yann.* Even Yann's pants will be ready in the end."

"Thanks for your support. I'll treasure it."

Nolwenn loved proverbs. In particular she recited them to cheer people up in critical psychological situations, proverbs that were always somewhat obscure.

"And don't forget your Clairefontaine. Maybe the solution is already in there!"

He hadn't forgotten it. On the contrary, he'd consulted it intensively.

"I have to go, Nolwenn."

"Chin up, Monsieur le Commissaire. Are you a Breton or aren't you? Stubbornness is the greatest of all Breton qualities."

With that, Nolwenn ended the call, as if she wanted to be sure that he would keep going.

Dupin brushed his hands through his hair.

He was standing next to a big oval granite stone that looked as if it had come straight out of the earth vertically, and looked like a menhir. Covered with green and purple lichen. It was as if Nolwenn had made it turn up by magic to warn Dupin: keep upright, persevere, stay stubborn!

Unfortunately that was not remotely how he felt internally.

Maybe he should just go down to the beach. Lie on the towel next to Claire. Swim. Be on vacation. Drink a *café*, something he actually did need. His last had been hours ago, and even that was a matter of necessity. No wonder his brain wasn't working right. He had the feeling that none of him was working. The rough physical confrontation with his pursuer had taken some of his strength.

He would stop the ridiculous search for tracks here and now.

Dupin had checked on the map. The simplest and shortest way back was through the valley. All he had to do was cross straight ahead, then take the path along the bay, the way he had come to Guichard's.

Dupin crossed a field until he reached a copse that was part of the valley offshoot.

Jean had meanwhile got back in touch with Marlène Mitou's friend, but unfortunately she had nothing more to say about her move, except that it was going to be a smarter apartment. More central at all costs. Which only made Dupin's question about the money more acute.

The map showed access to the valley by the copse where he was currently, only just a little farther to the north. To his left was a path through the field. It had to be easy to find the way in.

Indeed it was. It only took Dupin a few minutes to reach the dark, earthy path that disappeared into the valley. Literally. It quickly became pitch dark, and went almost vertically downward. He was stumbling in the dark, as if through a magic gate.

The farther down Dupin went, the more wonderful the world became. Although it had been parched outside, in here it was leaden and damp. The ground, trees, stones, all seemed to surround him. It was quiet too, this other world down here. A soft silence as if every sound had been wrapped in cotton wool, the forest floor, the sea of ferns, even the huge Boston ferns—as Dupin had learned to call them—the moss that looked like mythical archetypes, the beeches, the chestnuts, the alders, the ash trees, all rising together, their fallen branches and the undergrowth, the bright green woody vines, the ivy, the mistletoe up above, the little flowers in rich colors on the ground below. Everything spreading out on top of each other, unbounded.

In the middle of the valley was an extraordinarily bright, clear stream, like something from a fairy tale, weaving its way adventurously between the stones, ferns, and trees, through interwoven grottoes, over fallen trees and their roots, quietly gurgling. In places it looked as if it might vanish forever into a stone. But then it emerged again unexpectedly.

The path ran next to the stream in places, and now and then he had to climb over tree trunks and branches.

Everything here was extraordinary, including the massive granite blocks he already knew well enough and that seemed to represent a peculiar link to the world outside. Here they seemed to lie even more chaotically than on the Île Renote, forming secret caverns. They were the same stones, but they seemed more bizarre here, more mysterious, magical even. Alive, like creatures resting, powerful giants that could awaken at any moment and get to their feet.

He couldn't see the sky. Only indirect, interrupted half-light fell into the valley. In some places the path led under one of the granite giants.

There was a strange smell in the air, a mosaic of many varying green and brown scents: the damp, heavy forest floor, the moss on the stones, the stream.

It was hard to say how warm it was; it was primarily damp. Dupin imagined the Amazon jungle to be like this.

The valley varied in its width: there were places when it narrowed in, others when it widened again, as if breathing out to be ten times as wide as it had been just before.

Dupin was going to ring Marchesi again. Nolwenn was right. They had to keep going no matter how strenuous it was.

He had no reception.

A rotten boardwalk led across the stream; the third time that the path had changed sides. It was seriously narrow. A huge rock lay horizontally on the ground in the shape of a fish, a sea bream maybe, with that head and fat gut, the tail fins. You could have sworn an artist had sculpted it. Dupin was sure Claire would have found it first in her game and scored a point. Yet again a path split off, the first had been to the right, this one to the left, probably the other ways into the valley.

Here there was a cave to the left. He could see a few meters into it, before the darkness swallowed everything. Maybe this was the "bandit cave" that Bellet had whispered about. Or the lepers. Maybe the pirates. Or the sirens. They were all possible. Dozens of caves and dozens of legends surrounding each.

A little farther on Dupin came across a long, meandering pool. He only noticed it when he was standing directly in front of it, because there was no water, just the reflection of the forest: reflections of trunks, branches, leaves, ferns—the whole unique world down here. It was confusing to the senses, and Dupin felt himself as close to fainting as he had been earlier at the abyss in the quarry.

It was only at the end of the pool that it was obvious there was a dam. Piled-up stones, long grown over. This had to be where the old water mill that Guichard had told him about must have stood. That crazy story.

The valley was completely enchanted. Dupin had visited lots of fantastic places in Brittany where it wouldn't have been surprising to see fairies, gnomes, or elves wandering around—but here, in this valley, things were different. The creatures of fantasy were truly missing, because they might have been expected. Anything supernatural would have seemed completely natural here.

The walk had done Dupin good. It felt as if his means and ways of contemplating were changed down here, as if thoughts became natural, as in a dream.

Even time seemed to pass differently. Dupin would have found it difficult to say how long he had been walking. He hadn't looked at his watch when he started downhill. He was sure he was going to reach the ocean soon. He pulled out his map, looking for landmarks to orient himself. The pond, for instance, or the ruins of the mill. But apart from the words Vallée des Traouïéro in curving handwriting, there was nothing marked.

But in fact it was quite simple; Dupin couldn't go wrong.

The valley ended at the bridge by the sea, where he had been earlier.

That meant one of the turnoffs was the right way. Obviously there hadn't been any signs; parallel to the Traouïéro Valley, a little farther to the west, there was another valley, maybe the turn he had taken led him there? Was he going through the wrong valley? It was impossible:

in between them led the road he had taken to Guichard's farm. Or was he going in the wrong direction? But that was nonsense too.

He put the map away and walked on, with fast steps.

Ten minutes later he stopped again, as another path opened up to the right. According to the map, the path through the valley led straight ahead. He couldn't have gotten confused.

But he had been walking too long. Something was wrong. He gave himself a hard shake.

But everything in this valley looked the same. Dupin had the impression that the longer one spent here, the more similar things became. It was like something out of a horror film, something you walked into but could never leave, because it got forever longer.

He gave himself a shake again.

"This can't be happening!" The valley swallowed his words. Nonetheless it had done him good to speak so loud. It brought him back to reality.

"I'm going to go straight ahead now."

Dupin flinched as if he had had an electric shock.

That was it! *Similar. To be similar.*

That was the key. The key to the blurred concept that kept coming back to him but despite everything he tried, never became clear. It had suddenly become a blindingly clear idea.

He had it: the answer to the case.

He was totally sure of it. The other words associated with the obscure concept came to him, like pieces of a jigsaw puzzle fitting together.

If he was right, what was going on here was breathtakingly vicious. The cold-blooded, hard-boiled enactment of a perfectly ingenious plan. It had been a straightforward execution.

Dupin wouldn't have much time. He had to hurry. It might already be too late.

He hurriedly pulled out his phone, but there was still no reception.

He rushed off without thinking.

He could no longer see anything else, he was so preoccupied going through the whole of the last week, everything that had happened now seen in a new light, and every time it came to the same result. It all fitted, everything. He wasn't even surprised when he almost immediately got a clear view of the bridge and the horrible fairy-tale forest suddenly came to an end.

He only stopped when he was on the bridge. He didn't even notice the traffic.

Within a second he had his phone in his hand.

He quickly dialed the number, spoke just a few sentences.

A minute later there was a diabolical smile on his face.

Dupin looked around, checked his whereabouts, then stood in the middle of the road, gesticulating wildly. The next car coming from the right, a Peugeot 105, braked sharply and came to a halt, just centimeters from him. An elderly white-haired woman stared at him, scared to death. He ran to the passenger side, pulled open the door, and before the woman could say a word he had climbed in.

"Police. Emergency. You have to take me with you."

* * *

Dupin came up to Desespringalle. "I can't find any reason why we should meet," the commissaire from Lannion had grumbled when Dupin rang him from the bridge.

Dupin had called again. He wouldn't be too late, it was close but not yet too late. The elderly lady, whose stress—the moment Dupin had climbed into the car—had now turned into a jovial excitement, had taken him to the hotel at breakneck speed and let him out with a

Bon courage. Dupin had sped along the curved path between the granite blocks. Then he caught sight of the hotel entrance and the road up to it between the hydrangea and the sage bush that Bellet looked after so carefully.

He didn't have to wait long before a police car dashed along the little street, the big Renault.

The commissaire from Lannion got out swiftly and came up to Dupin, his head red and his gaunt face distorted with anger.

He immediately began a tirade which reached a high decibel level. "If you think you can lead me astray like this, make a fool—"

"Be quiet and come with me." Dupin wasn't interested in squabbling. There was more important business to be done. He had already set off, while the angry commissaire's face had gone from red to purple. "This way."

Dupin opened the door to the hotel. In the process he almost ran into Monsieur and Madame Bellet, who had hurried out of the reception.

"As fast as the fire brigade," Monsieur Bellet said, and nodded in recognition. "It must really be—"

He broke off when he recognized Desespringalle.

Dupin walked past the Bellets without saying a word, straight along the narrow hallway toward the stairs.

"What do you want, Monsieur le Commissaire?" Bellet said. Desespringalle gave him a look of irritation.

"Not now, Bellet, later." Dupin took the first step.

"Second floor," he told Desespringalle. And took two steps at a time. Without turning around, he called out: "Bellet, watch the fire escape, let us know if there is anyone to see."

Yet again Desespringalle grumbled: "I want to know here and now what the game is here . . ."

"Come along."

A few moments later, Dupin was outside the room. He waited until Desespringalle, breathing heavily, was standing behind him.

"We're going in, I'm going to talk and you're going to listen. That's the game. Here goes."

Dupin knocked loud and strong.

There was noise from inside.

Dupin knocked again, louder. "Open up!"

The next moment the door opened and Dupin barged in.

Monsieur Durand had stood aside, his look more piercing, more lordly than ever. He was just fastening the top button on his dark blue sports jacket.

"What's the meaning of this? What do you want?"

"We're going to have a conversation, Monsieur Durand."

Durand jutted out his chin. "I'm not going to do anything. I'm—"

"This is Commissaire Desespringalle, from Lannion. He is working with Inspector General Odinot from Paris."

Dupin had stressed the word "Paris."

The room was filled with baggage. An extraordinary number of shoe boxes. Jackets, bags, suitcases, rucksacks. Durand had asked Bellet to be ready to take them all to the car. That had been just seven minutes ago, immediately before Dupin had phoned Bellet. It was a bizarre, extremely tense situation. They were still standing half in the doorway.

"Come out onto the balcony," Dupin told him. "We can sit there." Around lunchtime all the other balconies were empty, the guests either eating or on the beach.

Desespringalle looked at him, extremely disgruntled, but it was clear he had pulled himself together.

Dupin strode outside. On the balcony, which was twice the size of Claire's and his, there was a bistro table in Atlantic blue, two suitable chairs, and a pair of sun loungers at the right end.

Dupin leaned against the railing. It was an unusual place for such an important conversation, but then he had already carried out important conversations in even more unusual places.

"I am in no way," Durand began again, "obliged to carry out any instructions."

"No, you aren't, but if you don't, then Commissaire Desespringalle will immediately take you to the commissariat."

"Could you at least tell me in a friendly manner what this conversation is about? I have a meeting in Paris at five, and I was about to set off." Durand sat down. His voice seemed to have changed, he seemed to have changed tactics.

Desespringalle sat down too. Both Durand and the commissaire were sitting in positions that left them looking at Dupin.

"Okay then, let's start at the beginning of the story." Dupin left the railing and walked up and down the balcony a few paces.

"I will try to be brief, Monsieur Durand. Several years ago, you got to know this attractive, temperamental, rather ordinary, but basically likable young woman, and unhitched her from a rival. Maybe you really felt something for her, but that's irrelevant. You soon married her, and began to move companies into her name. A simple way of getting around taxes. So far, so good. One day, when the first flush had faded, the young woman became burdensome to you. You lost all interest. You could have split up, but a woman like that wasn't just going to do it for nothing. It would have turned into a drama, and a very expensive one. It could have ruined you. Your wife was now unfortunately in charge of part of your wealth. A whole row of your firms belonged to her."

There was a dismissive smile on Durand's face. He remained totally in control of himself.

"I have no idea where you're going with this. Your story is already laughable."

"Whatever; divorce wasn't in the cards. So you looked for another plan. You're a pragmatic man, a doer. One day in a bar, I suspect, maybe one called Aux Folies, you by chance met another young woman, a waitress who . . . wait a moment—" Dupin interrupted himself, took his Clairefontaine out of his rear pants pocket and began to flick through it. "I'll have it in a moment."

It took a while.

"Here we go, here it is: the policeman who first came across Marlène Mitou in the quarry"—Dupin slowed his speech, however inappropriate it was; he wanted to enjoy the moment a little—"despite her wounds and her dark hair initially took her for Alizée Durand *because* he had seen her 'missing' photo."

Dupin stayed standing in front of Monsieur Durand, staring him in the eyes.

"Exactly what I wrote down, when I heard the news of the dead woman: 'Policeman thinks he recognized Madame Durand.'"

It was crazy. Dupin had already noted down the solution to the case in his notebook on Wednesday evening when the corpse was found. Just like Nolwenn had said. It had been in his Clairefontaine all this time!

"I'll continue: you noticed a remarkable resemblance between the young woman in the bar to your wife, despite a different hairstyle, color of hair, and makeup. She had similar height and figure. And she was an unsuccessful actress. And that was it, the plan."

"Actress," that was another one of the key words that had unleashed something in Dupin. He had been playing a role on several occasions over the past few days.

Durand's smile had changed to a distorted grimace. "The commissaire, a peddler of fairy tales. Who would have thought it? You are a gifted storyteller, but amusing as it is to listen to you, I'm afraid I have to leave this little spontaneous gathering."

He got to his feet.

Desespringalle quickly got up and blocked Durand's way. There was no more than a hand's breadth between the faces of the two equally sized men. They stared at each other.

Desespringalle didn't say a word. Durand seemed to be thinking what to do.

"I want to call my lawyer."

"You can do that," Dupin said calmly, "but first you have to hear the rest."

Yet again Durand seemed to be contemplating. Then he sat down again. After a moment's hesitation Desespringalle did the same.

"Back to our story," Dupin said, and began walking up and down again. "You found out that the woman in the bar hadn't had much luck in life so far. You found out about her failed dreams and worries about money. Not that that was an issue for you. Fate was playing into your hands. It all seemed perfect. Right in front of your eyes was the possibility of a perfect murder, the solution to all your problems. It would let you keep all your firms, and the money." Dupin wiped the sweat from his brow; the balcony was right in the sun. "Your wife's friend told us that in recent weeks you'd been arguing less than you used to. I suggest that's because you had sight of the solution."

The expression on Durand's face had gotten even emptier. He was staring at a vague point somewhere on the horizon.

"This heaven-sent waitress would play the part of your wife." Yet again Dupin stopped, but this time turned to one side, toward the sea, as if he wanted to take in the panorama. "But after you had murdered your wife."

Durand sat there motionless.

"Other than in the sea, there was nowhere bodies could disappear forever. And yet that was precisely your plan." Now he was getting to the most speculative part, but Dupin spoke as if he had no doubts about it. "I suggest it happened as follows. You and your wife arrived here on Wednesday of last week. Under the pretense of wanting to go fishing, you had planned to rent a boat. Unfortunately there was bad weather for the first two days. But on Friday afternoon the weather changed, to beautiful high summer. You rented the boat and went out to sea for the first time. To check everything out. On Saturday afternoon everything was set. You announced you had planned a romantic picnic on the boat, with Champagne and lobster."

That was how it fitted in Marchesi's timetable. If you looked at it in detail, there was no magic in her reconstruction; it just required putting the pieces together conscientiously.

"You went far out to sea, I suspect. And that's where you threw her overboard, strangled maybe, as Marlène Mitou was later. Nobody saw you. That's when Marlène Mitou began playing the role of your wife. You just had to do a bit of fixing up. It was easy to get a perfect wig made." The wig that Nolwenn had worn in her crazy action at the town hall had come to Dupin's mind. "And you were smart, very smart. You took as many precautions as possible, gave Marlène Mitou comprehensive instructions. You told her she should flirt a bit here and there, create the picture of a flighty wife. Marlène Mitou might have exaggerated a bit there."

Dupin remembered puzzling a few times over the fact that Alizée

Durand's behavior on the Sunday and Monday had been somewhat strange. If only just slightly. But that was the explanation. It wasn't her.

"In the days after you arrived at the hotel with your wife, you deliberately forced arguments. So that everybody heard. And now"— Dupin had come to a stop again in front of Durand—"now we reach the climax. On Monday evening you pulled off a brilliant piece of theater with the new Madame Durand, the highly conspicuous climax of a row over dinner, in front of everyone. Perhaps so that later everybody might think it was about her flirting, going to the bar with Chastagner. It ended with the theatrical storming out of Marlène Mitou in the guise of Madame Durand. Set so that everyone could see that your wife wasn't followed and you remained sitting on the terrace. An abandoned husband, waiting for his wife to come back. Noble, almost."

"Ridiculous, totally ridiculous." Durand's previous comments had been more detailed.

"Oh, and something I forgot: Mitou's motive for getting involved with your plan. I believe you gave her, as payment, an apartment, a nice, comfortable apartment. It was worth it to you. She had mentioned to her friend that she wanted to move. That was the deal. She was to move in after the job was done. In Paris an apartment of your own is like winning the lottery."

That was how Dupin had put it all together on his walk through the valley.

"What I obviously don't know is whether you had planned from the beginning to bring Marlène Mitou with you, or whether something changed in later days to make it necessary? Maybe all of a sudden the apartment was no longer enough, or she was trying to blackmail you. Nor do I know if you even let Madame Mitou into your plan to murder your wife. I suspect you did. Whatever the case, you killed her too."

Dupin stopped. He had walked to the end of the balcony again. For the first time since his walk through the valley he became aware of the world again. From his vantage point he could see the beach, where Claire was already lying. He smiled automatically.

Dupin turned back to Durand.

"But something went seriously wrong. A catastrophe that you couldn't prevent. Marlène Mitou called a taxi to get to the spot you'd agreed on. That wasn't planned. Or the taxi driver saw you. Your car maybe." Dupin pinned Durand with his eyes. "In any case, you had no other choice than to kill him too, with the closest thing to hand."

Nothing. Not even a blink. Not a twitch, not the slightest movement of Durand's face. Nor was there any further contradiction. Dupin waited a while. An unbearable length of time.

Desespringalle finally broke the painful silence.

The commissaire spoke as if Durant weren't present. His voice was now free of all resentment against Dupin, as if he was gripped solely by investigative curiosity. "What about the quarry? Why did he throw Marlène Mitou into the quarry?"

"Here too, chance was kind to Durand." Dupin turned to Desespringalle, as if the two of them were on their own on the balcony. "The morning after the disappearance of his wife he was sitting in Trégastel Gendarmerie. I was sitting there too, opposite Inès Marchesi's desk. His glance, like mine, fell on the pinboard with the report of the dead woman who seven years ago had been found in the quarry. When he realized he had to kill Marlène Mitou, planned from the beginning or not, he had a stroke of genius. An inspired chess move. He would simply throw the corpse into the quarry where the pink corpse had been found."

Desespringalle took up the thread. "Durand knew that someone *had* to see a link. It couldn't be a coincidence. A perfect stroke of confusion.

"The same as the threatening letters to the deputy, I think. Here too it was the luck of the moment. When nobody owned up to the matter he wrote a vaguely threatening letter, the sort that any politician might get. It created an incurable confusion. Obviously several people would come under suspicion, if they had been in conflict with Madame Rabier, or had unfinished business. That's the way it went and we all fell for it! Chastagner, Maïwenn Guichard, and Ellec came into sight, and the greatest of connections was built up, the darkest machinations imagined. He could count on the fact that somebody was probably involved in something wrong. He led everybody by the nose."

All of it—*all*—was one single case. The Durand case. It was crazy. Discovering what Ellec and Chastagner had been up to was pure chance. A side effect. An aside.

"You're both delirious, the two of you!" Durand had suddenly come back to life. "You can never prove any of that." He tried for a sarcastic, superficial laugh.

Durand was right. In the first place it was purely circumstantial—and an extremely complicated hypothesis. But it came together flawlessly, more or less perfectly.

"Don't worry, Monsieur Durand," Dupin said, and smiled. "Now we know what happened, and we know exactly where we have to look. We'll find out something about an apartment that you had set aside for Marlène Mitou, even if you never had any intention of giving it to her."

"We'll take your car apart," Desespringalle said calmly, "the backseat, the trunk. Dead or alive, Marlène Mitou spent time in your car when you drove to the quarry. We'll put the seats and the trunk under the microscope and find something, you can rely on it. You wouldn't believe what's possible these days. And until then, the circumstantial evidence is enough to take you into custody."

"In any case," Dupin agreed, "Commissaire Desespringalle is now going to take you to the commissariat and straightaway issue an arrest order."

Dupin turned away from Durand and demonstratively to the commissaire from Lannion with an open smile: "You've done brilliant work. Thanks to your great persistence you've uncovered the whole dreadful story." And it had been an absolutely dreadful story. Dupin knew people like this, who considered everybody else to be stupid and thought they could get away with anything. Who followed their own interests at any price and considered everything to be justified. Meanwhile, Jérôme Chastagner and Hugues Ellec had been caught out.

Dupin smiled again. "And all of this without upheaval, extremely efficiently, and in impressively short time. That's worthy of promotion, or at least an award."

It would be best, Dupin had decided, *best for everyone*, if he now disappeared, more or less vanished into thin air, like in a magic trick—he would be out of there.

"I take my hat off to you, Commissaire," he added with pleasure.

Desespringalle stood there openmouthed, incomprehension on his face. Durand was still standing there staring absently.

"But I—" Desespringalle began to protest.

"Don't hide your light under a bushel. I observed everything closely. And believe me, I'm a keen observer. That was an extraordinary piece of investigation."

Dupin beamed.

"I have to go down to the beach. Vacation time calls. My wife is waiting. Tasty sandwiches, a chilled rosé. So, if you'll just excuse me, Monsieur le Commissaire, Monsieur Durand."

With those words he headed for the balcony door. The other two sat there as if rooted, even Desespringalle still too puzzled.

Dupin turned back to them.

"It was my pleasure, messieurs."

And then he was gone.

* * *

"So, what happened? Did Durand have anything to do with the murders? What did you talk about?"

Dupin was already on the bottom step when Madame and Monsieur Bellet rushed up to him; it was a miracle that they hadn't been eavesdropping at Durand's door.

He couldn't leave the pair of them without a brief explanation.

"Commissaire Desespringalle has solved the case. He's arresting Monsieur Durand."

It was the briefest summary he could make.

"Monsieur Durand?" Madame Bellet was indignant. "Our guest? Monsieur Durand a criminal? A murderer?" She wrinkled her brow. "Evil under our roof?"

"That's the way it is, Madame Bellet."

"Oh well, he *is* from Paris."

With that decisive piece of information, she seemed to have calmed herself down a bit. To Dupin it rather sounded like "that's the last guest from Paris we'll have staying here."

"What crime is Monsieur Durand accused of?" Monsieur Bellet was going about the situation a bit more professionally. "Did he murder the woman from Paris? Or the poor taxi driver? Did he have anything to do with the attack on the deputy?"

He looked at Dupin expectantly. "His wife even? Did she not just disappear?"

"You'll hear everything soon, Monsieur Bellet."

The good mood he was in made him add: "I think that's how it was. But let's keep it"—he gave Bellet a wink—"strictly between you and me."

The Bellets deserved to know. They had helped him. Supported him. And, above all, covered for him.

"How did Durand—"

There were steps coming down the stairs. Heavy steps.

Bellet stopped intuitively.

"We will have time enough to talk," Dupin said in a lower voice. "I now need to hurry to see my wife. Excuse me, madame, monsieur."

The look on the Bellets' faces showed they had understood. They quickly turned around, still troubled, but no longer dissatisfied.

Dupin headed for the terrace; he was going to take the path through the garden. And there was no danger of running into someone.

He caught himself almost sauntering as he took the wonderful path by the seaside. He had even found himself about to whistle. Shortly he found himself at Rachid's, with his wonderful assortment of delicacies. Dupin decided on the classic *pains bagnats*, four of them. He was hungry, and Claire would be too. Plus cold water and rosé.

As he walked down to the beach, Dupin's good mood got even better.

It was such a beautiful day, here on this—it had to be said once again—extraordinary spot of the world. Dupin looked all around him: in the bay where he had only yesterday been hunting down his shadow, a little sailing school for children was out. This happened all along the coast, and Dupin loved the show of the little motorboat with the teacher followed by a dozen miniature sailing dinghies, looking like model toys all roped together. Like pearls on a necklace. Farther out were the large sailing boats, flying over the water, majestic white and elegant. The Sept-Îles looked razor-sharp and seemed so close that even from the land it would be possible to pick out the little penguins with binoculars. It happened only rarely but there were moments when Dupin really regretted he was so unfit for sailing. He was so close to the little penguins. But he couldn't go and visit them.

Claire had seen him from a distance, and waved—a good sign. Dupin wasn't sure but he thought he had glimpsed a phone at her ear; which she quickly put down.

"At last. I'm starving."

Dupin was still a few meters away. But she soon shifted over to leave half the towel free.

"It's all there." Dupin put down the paper bags and the cooler, on the edge of the towel.

There was no sign that Claire wanted to talk about what she had been up to in the last few hours. But then he hadn't expected her to.

"Come on, sit down." Claire was impatient.

"Just a minute." Dupin got his swimsuit out of the beach bag.

Vacation time at last.

"So, now." Dupin sat down next to Claire, who was already unpacking the sandwiches.

She picked up one of the *pains bagnats,* took a large bite of it, and chewed happily. Then another bite. Dupin tucked in too.

She looked silently at the bay, the famous panorama.

"Isn't it a wonderful day?" Now that completely irresistible typical Claire smile was on her face. Calm. Relaxed.

Happy.

"You've hurt yourself on the cheek. A deep scratch."

Dupin had completely forgotten. His pulse began to race slightly. "Oh yes, those things happen." She couldn't suppress a grin. "This afternoon Pierre will be back in the clinic, by the way. I just found out." She sounded elated, completely carefree.

"And for the next few days I want to do only one thing: relax! Lying on the beach, reading, swimming, sleeping." To his own astonishment, the sentence had come from deep inside Dupin; he really meant it.

It was crazy. After the conversation on the balcony, the whole thing had vanished into the distance. Of course, he would keep on with it. He would exchange information with Desespringalle until they had conclusive proof and Durand was behind bars. The same went for the pursuit of the business with Chastagner and Ellec. However, in his guts it was over. Now he really could let his heart take a vacation.

"But we still have a few expeditions to make. There's so much we still haven't seen. And don't forget"—Claire laughed out loud—"Bellet's brochure. Do you remember? Shark egg collecting, tattoos, the distillery . . ."

"I'm game for anything," Dupin said happily.

"And we need to hunt out more rock formations. I think I'm in the lead."

The bizarre, secretive pink giants surrounded them. All around them. In every direction. Unalterable, invincible, as long as the Earth survived.

Back in Concarneau

It was exactly eight o'clock in the evening when Dupin switched off the engine of his ancient Citroën, which for a few years now had been spluttering noticeably. Dupin had parked directly at the pier, in the first row next to the water, by the old harbor, between the medieval Ville Close on Moros island and the Amiral.

All the piers were extravagantly decorated, and hundreds of blue-and-white flags flew on many of the masts too. On the long piers there were big tents close to one another. Tomorrow was the start of the Transat, the craziest, roughest sailing regatta across the Atlantic. It was legendary. Just two skippers in each of the little sailing boats—ten-meter-long Classe Figaro Bénéteau II—the route went straight from Concarneau to Saint-Barthélemy. Four weeks of unending competition on tossing seas. Unlike other regattas it wasn't a case of the superiority of the equipment—who could invest the most money—but simply a competition between the maritime skills of each and every sailor. *"Être à armes égales"* was the motto: to fight with the same weapons.

The evening before the Transat there was always a very particular atmosphere. It was the last hours before the start, a lively, bright tension in the air. The fifteen competing boats were waiting together at the pier, their skippers going through the last preparations. Locals and tourists were admiring the boats, applauding and drinking a glass from one of the stalls.

Claire and Dupin had set off from Trégastel at a quarter past six and got back easily. They had waved good-bye to Madame and Monsieur Bellet at the exit from the hotel.

After his arrest, Durand had continued to deny everything arrogantly, until what finally broke his neck was the wig. Over the last seven days Desespringalle and Jean had cleverly and systematically sought for indisputable evidence. To carry out his murder plans, Durand had needed an absolutely perfect wig, expertly created to be a perfect match for his wife's hair, perhaps her most conspicuous feature. There weren't that many wig makers, but Durand, obsessive as he was, had found an address abroad, a traditional Spanish wig maker. If no one had specifically asked around—they had made a list covering all of Europe—it would never have come out. Initially there had been no significant clues in Durand's desk, nor on his computer or phone. Durand had carefully erased everything. Just as he had thought through and extremely carefully planned everything else.

The second thing that was disastrous for Durand—and was enough to place charges against him—was the apartment for Marlène Mitou. Apparently Durand hadn't wanted this but Marlène Mitou had insisted: on June 2 he visited a smart apartment in the eighth arrondissement near the Boulevard Haussmann with a "dark-haired woman." Jean and his team, with the help of two co-workers, had gone to see all his firm's empty apartments and checked out all objects of any consequence. Naturally there wasn't a rental or purchase contract in the name of Marlène Mitou on the records. But Jean and his team had inspected every one, on the spot. There were six apartments where they spoke to the concierges, all the other residents, and—insofar as they were available—neighboring shop owners. An elderly, settled married couple had seen Durand and Marlène Mitou leaving the apartment together. Nobody in Durand's office had known they had gone to see it; he himself had mostly looked after the best apartments in the best areas.

Two days earlier, the public prosecutor had confronted Durand with the facts. And after a day to think it over—after the urgent advice of his lawyer—Durand had confessed. Jean reported to Dupin on what the public prosecutor had added to the confession: "matter-of-fact, unfeeling, cold, prepared, and carried out as if it were an expensive property transaction." And, "the accused added to the statement, 'One day I just wanted to be rid of Alizée. But the firms belonged to her.'" Just as Dupin had imagined. Even so he held his breath for a moment. That was the way everyday coldblooded calculating killers were. They weren't psychopaths. But they were still monsters. And there were lots of them.

Durand then went on to confess everything unscrupulously, every detail, almost pedantically. The whole story had gone astonishingly accurately, in large and small details exactly as Dupin had imagined it, the way—boldly, he had to admit—he had put it in his version to Desespringalle and Durand on the balcony. There had been no smart inspiration that struck him out of the blue, just the correct placing together of tiny observations and conclusions, one by one. Plus that vital bit of intuition.

It had indeed been Durand who had written the threatening letters.

The murders too had in principle happened as Dupin had put together. It had been the Saturday when Durand went out for a sea picnic on the boat far to the west of the Sept-Îles. He had then strangled his wife with a towel until she was unconscious, then let her slip overboard in such a way that technically she had "drowned." The current made her impossible to find. He had also strangled Marlène Mitou with a towel, but at the end of the valley. Dupin hadn't been right about that. Durand hadn't shared his plan with Marlène Mitou. She could have worked it out—was bound to—but she had never said anything about it. Not a single word. Durand had nonetheless admitted—a blind spot in Dupin's reconstruction—that from the very beginning he had planned to do away with Mitou as well.

Before Mitou's murder there really had been what Durand called a "complication": the taxi driver, after dropping Marlène Mitou off at their agreed spot, in the dark, turned around. He had probably found the whole thing strange. The taxi driver had seen Durand and threatened to call the police, and Durand had to "deal with the matter."

There hadn't really been too great a risk for Durand; he had come very close to a "perfect murder." He just had bad luck. And Dupin had been on vacation.

What Dupin had not bothered about was the theft of the Saint Anne statue. But even that event was cleared up, in a very Breton fashion. The statue had yesterday morning turned up again exactly where it had stood. Exactly as it had been. Or to be more precise, more exact than it had been. A few months ago the wood of the statue's left shoulder had been scratched and needed to be repaired. A restoration expert from Paimpol, someone who had known the church and chapel in Trégastel for decades, a man in his seventies, had gotten the contract and initially said he could pick up the figure at the beginning of August. All completely in order, in an e-mail to the secretary of the commune. But as she was on vacation, the contract wasn't signed. She had no stand-in, and nobody read the restoration expert's e-mail in which he gave short-term notice that he would be picking up the statue on the Friday afternoon. The restoration expert turned up with a white van—exactly as the witness had said—parked centrally out-side the chapel. Yesterday morning he had brought the figure back.

As absurd as the story was, it was so typical for Brittany. "See, I told you you'd find cases!" Claire had commented, half serious, half in jest, when Marchesi called while they were sitting over their pre-apéritif in the garden. "All made up, a feature of your overheated imagination."

Dupin could have said a lot in reply, but said nothing.

The business with Ellec, the deputy, and his forged special per-mission got a lot of attention. The media were onto it straightaway and were now—along with the police—investigating every major decision Ellec had taken in recent years for an "advantageous deal." Nobody had yet found a direct link to the decision to permit the destruction of the underwater sand dune in Lannion Bay, but Dupin was certain that this dream of Nolwenn's would eventually come true.

Chastagner got away lightly in public, primarily because Durand and Ellec had attracted so much attention. But the lawyer who in the end would have to decide on the illegal extension of the quarry would certainly not consider it a trifle.

All the suspicions against Maïwenn vanished into the air. Im-mediately after Durand's arrest she was brought back home. Claire and Dupin had, after all, picked up the box of organic vegetables. The sneaky attempt to get a story about an affair between Guichard's husband and Rabier into the press was explained as Ellec trying to "shoot back" at Rabier. Marchesi made sure the article never appeared.

Nobody was interested anymore in the attack on Rabier. After the case was solved it seemed that the stone really had been thrown by the angry farmer, who hadn't intended to hurt her or even hit her. It had been an accident. Madame Rabier had been released from the hospital the day before last.

Two days after the decisive "conversation" and Durand's arrest, a postcard for Dupin—of Napoléon's Hat—turned up at the hotel, with just one word written on it: "Thanks," signed Pierrick Desespringalle.

Before they left, Dupin had also thanked Inès Marchesi. "What for?" she replied: a proper Marchesi reply.

In the end—a sad conclusion—it had been a horribly banal case. A sophisticatedly concocted, complicatedly devised, and extremely gruesome case, for sure. But banal.

Claire took a few steps along the edge of the quay, stopped there for a minute. Dupin stood beside her and embraced her. The wind was blowing the music from the tents over to them. Dupin liked the evening before the start. Over the last few years he had become one of the flaneurs.

Claire turned to him. "Let's go, our entrecôtes are waiting."

Dupin laughed.

They had already got in touch with Paul Girard on the drive back.

A minute later they walked into the Amiral. Instinctively Dupin glanced at their regular seats, only to find two men sitting there. His inspectors, Kadeg and Riwal. Both beamed when they saw Dupin and Claire.

"Boss, over here!"

"Don't worry, I recognized you." Dupin was already standing almost next to the table.

"We thought we'd come here to welcome you. I mean, you've been away for two weeks." Unbelievable words coming from Kadeg's mouth. It sounded as if he meant two years, at least.

"You've got seriously short hair." Kadeg's eyes were fixed on Dupin's head. Dupin decided not to go into it. "And a scratch on the cheek," the inspector added. Dupin wasn't going to discuss that either. "And look how tan you are."

Riwal interrupted Kadeg's chain of observations. "Nolwenn will be here too, she just had a couple of calls to answer. In relation to the Ellec business." Riwal didn't seem to think it very important.

He had gotten up and welcomed Claire with the obligatory pecks on the cheek. Kadeg had also got up and—he was really in form tonight—had said an exceptionally friendly *bonsoir*.

Claire sat down.

Dupin had actually been thinking of a meal for two. But nothing could be changed now. Happily they had already had dinner for two fourteen times in a row. And he was glad to see his team.

"There was a lot going on where you were, boss," Riwal said, choosing his words carefully.

Obviously Nolwenn had let both inspectors in on the secret. But Riwal couldn't know what Claire knew about Dupin's part in solving the case. Dupin himself didn't know how much Claire actually knew. In the last seven days they hadn't made the slightest remark that might reveal what and how much she had really gathered about Dupin's investigations. Only when the two of them, like everybody else in Trégastel, had begun to talk about the latest spectacular news— the arrest of Durand, the business with Ellec and Chastagner, and the explanation of the stone thrown through the window. Dupin had tried his best, but with the best will in the world, Claire remained inscrutable. For his part, Dupin hadn't made the slightest reference to Claire's contact with the clinic and the operations she had conducted at a distance. He had been very satisfied with their unspoken arrangement, if that was even what it had been.

"You can say that," Dupin said, and sat down.

"But luckily they had a brilliant local commissaire!" Claire laughed, loudly and cheerfully.

"Indeed," Riwal said in agreement, if a bit confused, "luckily."

"Nolwenn says you had a really good, relaxing time?"

Dupin wasn't sure what Kadeg meant by the statement. But it didn't matter.

"I had an extremely good time."

That was true.

Completely true. The second week had been a "real" vacation week, and was perfectly wonderful. Dupin had almost gotten used to doing nothing. On a few occasions he had almost fallen asleep on the towel. But he couldn't tell anybody that.

"Well, Docteur Garreg will be pleased his therapy has been a total success."

"We're full of new energy." Claire suddenly gave a strange smile. "We'll need it for our move."

She had made the last sentence completely casual, as if she had been talking about the weather. For the whole of the last week she hadn't said a word about the business with the house. And Dupin hadn't challenged her.

"Move?" Riwal shot her an inquisitive look. Alarmed.

"We're moving into the Boulevard Katherine Wylie. Georges and I. Together."

She turned to Dupin, who needed a moment to pull himself together.

"Didn't Georges tell you?" she asked reprovingly. "Soon; I've already ordered the movers' truck."

"That's just great." Riwal's voice sounded genuinely happy. Even Kadeg seemed to agree.

"We have to drink a toast to that."

Dupin and Claire hadn't heard. Dupin had bowed toward her, and kissed her. Dupin whispered something, and she whispered something back.

Paul Girard, the owner of the Amiral, suddenly appeared at the next table. "I've got four entrecôtes reserved for you, three hundred fifty grams each—they're ready now." He had a magnum of Champagne in his hand. "To celebrate the day!"

It was superb, and Paul hadn't a clue *how much* there was to celebrate.

"How was your vacation?"

"Wonderful," Dupin replied, from the depths of his heart, "simply wonderful. *La vie en rose!*"